STORM
OF SILVER
AND ASH

ALSO BY MARION BLACKWOOD

Marion Blackwood has written lots of books across multiple series, and new books are constantly added to her catalogue. To see the most recently updated list of books, please visit: www.marionblackwood.com

CONTENT WARNINGS

The Oncoming Storm series contains quite a lot of violence and morally questionable actions. If you have specific triggers, you can find the full list of content warnings at: www.marionblackwood.com/content-warnings

A STORM OF SILVER AND ASH

THE ONCOMING STORM: BOOK ONE

MARION BLACKWOOD

Copyright © 2019 by Marion Blackwood

All rights reserved. No part of this book may be reproduced in any form or by any electronic or mechanical means, including information storage and retrieval systems, without permission in writing from the publisher, except by reviewers, who may quote brief passages in a review. For more information, contact info@marionblackwood.com

First edition

ISBN: 978-91-985645-6-3 (hardcover)
ISBN 978-91-985645-1-8 (paperback)
ISBN 978-91-986386-0-8 (ebook)

Editing by Julia Gibbs
Book cover design by ebooklaunch.com

This is a work of fiction. Names, characters, places, and incidents either are the product of the author's imagination or are used fictitiously. Any resemblance to actual persons, living or dead, events, or locales is entirely coincidental.

www.marionblackwood.com

For my mom - the strongest, kindest, and wisest person in all the realms

1.

The warm night air carried the sound of pursuit to my ears. I ducked behind cover. Dark clouds blanketed the heavens and blotted out the moon, making my black and gray attire difficult to discern against the soot-stained background. The shadow following me crept closer. Straining my ears, I realized that the soft footfalls were familiar. Very familiar. With my right hand, I slid out one of the hunting knives I had strapped to the small of my back. Then, I waited. My unsuspecting stalker was close now. I didn't need to peek around the corner to know where he was, I could feel him moving closer. The soft wind blew strands of hair over my face as I waited. One more step. My left hand shot out and in one fluid motion, I whipped the not-so-subtle stalker around, slammed him into the bricks and put my hunting knife at his throat. Surprised, dark blue eyes stared into mine.

"Hello, Liam," I said, grinning up at him from the other side of the blade.

"Has anyone ever told you that you're way too heavily armed to be a thief?" Liam sighed, his eyes gliding over the throwing knives lined up behind my shoulders before finally settling on the knife at his throat.

"Has anyone ever told you that you're way too noisy to be a thief?" I replied in kind before removing my hunting knife from his throat and returning it to the small of my back.

"We're on the Thieves Highway, I don't need to be quiet," Liam said with a tone that suggested a three-year-old could've worked that out.

I bit back another snarky reply and instead settled for an eye roll. "Fine. Come on," I said, pulling him away from the brick face of the chimney.

We started out across the rooftops again. Despite being a couple of years younger, Liam is actually taller than me. Not by much, mind you, but enough that his legs have longer reach. That meant I had to put in extra effort to keep up with him and after the long day I'd had, it was even more tiring. But that's just between you and me, I'd never admit that to Liam.

"So... how's the stakeout going, Storm?" Liam asked.

Storm. What an odd name, right? I promise, it gets even odder. Storm is actually short for the Oncoming Storm. What kind of parents would name their child something like that? Well, certainly not mine, I'll tell you. I don't even have any parents. I mean, of course I have parents, somewhere, or at least I did at some point, but you know what I mean. Most members of the Underworld are orphans, which means that the majority of us also don't have given names. Someone just starts calling you something and then it sticks. My guild members apparently started calling me the Oncoming Storm because when I decide to hit a place, I always clean it out thoroughly. Although, I've always suspected that it might also have something to do with my temper, but no one has dared say as much to my face. Yeah, I know, that just kind of adds more proof to it.

"It's going well, I spent the day double-checking the guard rotations," I answered.

"Hmm..." he mused.

I heaved an inwardly sigh. When Liam does something like this, he usually just wants me to ask him how he's been doing. Normally, I'm not the most sociable of people but Liam is the one exception to that rule. Actually, I don't think there's anyone who dislikes Liam. That he decided to be my friend, of all people, still baffles me. So, of course, I humor him.

"How's your day been?"

"I'm glad you asked!" he chirped, eyes sparkling. "I stole this beautiful silver bracelet today, right off this really fancy lady's wrist."

Shaking my head, I smiled to myself. Honestly, I don't even know what I'd do without this sweet and mischievous looking boy. He's like a little brother to me, and the one good and genuine thing I have in my life.

While Liam continued to regale me with his escapades of the day, we drew closer to the Thieves' Guild. "Did you hear King Adrian doubled taxes again?" he said, switching topic, as we jumped the gap between two houses.

"Yeah, but why should we care?" I said, and shrugged one shoulder as we landed on the next roof. "We don't pay taxes."

"No, I know, but I still feel sort of bad for them."

"Don't. The upperworlders have their problems and we have ours. Yeah, alright, so they're trying to figure out how to pay taxes and still put food on the table for their kids. But we're trying not to get hanged. I'd say our troubles are a bit worse."

"He executed half of the Scribes' Guild today."

My mouth fell open as I turned to stare at my only friend while we continued our run. Despite no longer looking at the roof ahead, I avoided the loose tiles on the baker's shop we were now crossing. Having traversed this part of the Thieves' Highway more times than I could count, I could've run across it blindfolded and still not have tripped once.

"But that's an Upperworld guild. Why would he do that?"

"Not paying taxes," Liam said with knit eyebrows. "And something about treason."

"Treason?"

"Yeah, like, working for some lords who are trying to overthrow him, or whatever."

"Do you believe that?"

"Do *you*?"

I shook my head. The scribes are devoted to learning; they don't care about politics. It would seem that the king was growing more unhinged with each passing day. Both of us had fallen silent for this last stretch while we pondered the news, and as we reached the final building, we slowed down as well. Climbing down the side of a building was something both Liam and I could've done in our sleep so we quickly reached the cobbled street below. After descending a short stone staircase, we approached the metal door at the end. I knocked twice. A small hatch slid open and a crossbow bolt appeared between my eyes.

"When the green-clad gentleman laughs..." I said in a calm voice.

"... the whole manor disappears," a man's voice finished from the other side of the door.

The hatch closed and there was a sound of bolts unlocking. Finally, the door was pushed outwards silently.

"Hey, Bones!" Liam said cheerfully.

"Liam. Storm," the heavily muscled man in the doorway replied and nodded to each of us. "You're just in time, the bosses have called a meeting. Better hurry."

I nodded back and started down the stairs with quick steps and Liam close behind. We passed the sleeping quarters on our way to the gathering hall, or the Thieves' Court, as we like to call it. I would've preferred to stop in my room before going there but I decided against it. Normally, I have no problem with pissing people off, in fact I even kind of enjoy it at times, but pissing off the Guild Masters was something even I didn't dare. We reached the Thieves' Court in short order. The whole guild was gathered so the room was packed, but the three high-backed, black chairs on top of the small platform at the far end were still empty. We made it. I surveyed the crowd. I'm not a standing-in-the-back kind of person, at least not in our guild. Don't get me wrong, I'm perfectly content with letting people bicker and argue to their hearts' content without bothering to get involved, but if I have something to say, I make sure that people hear it. I started pushing my way to the front.

"Oi! The bloody hell do you think you're–" a guy I hadn't bothered learning the name of started protesting angrily. "Oh, Storm, sorry, I thought... uhm... never mind," he continued and waved his hands apologetically once he realized who he was addressing.

I gave him a condescending stare and pushed past. The crowd parted before me.

"Shit, that was close," I heard them whisper behind me. "Wouldn't wanna get on her bad side."

Damn straight. I smiled wickedly to myself. Behind me, Liam was muttering apologies. Once I'd reached the first couple of rows, I stopped. No need to stand at the very front, in case the Guild Masters needed to vent their frustration on someone.

"Rude much?" Liam accused once he caught up with me.

"How in the world is that news to you? And here I was thinking you knew that before you befriended me," I replied and arched an eyebrow in his direction.

"Still debating the wisdom of that decision..." Liam teased and leveled his best imitation of an angry stare at me.

A small smile tugged at the corners of my lips. With that mop of curly brown hair and sparkling blue eyes, that boy couldn't look menacing if his life depended on it.

"Storm, I'm glad I caught you!" a girl with short, black hair called as she pushed her way through the crowd.

"What do you want, Cat?" I replied and twisted my head slightly to look at her.

"Information."

Before answering, I cast an impatient glance over my shoulder. The black door behind the Guild Masters' chairs was still closed. "Make it quick."

"Lord Hightwig's mansion."

"You're hitting the Hightwig mansion?" I asked with a dubious expression on my face.

She gave an uncomfortable shrug. "Yeah, that's why I need help."

"You think?" I scoffed. "Alright. Two guards at the front, rotating schedule, one in the back. No dogs. The window to Lady Hightwig's art studio is usually unlocked, if not open, because she likes listening to the blackbirds outside." Furrowing my brows and pursing my lips slightly, I tried to remember if there was anything else. "Oh and there's a hidden safe behind the large painting in Lord Hightwig's study. But I suggest you start with Lady Hightwig's room because most of the valuables in that house are in her jewelry box."

"Thanks," she said with a small smile and tipped five silver coins into my open palm.

As I watched her black bob disappear back into the crowd I could feel Liam glowering at me.

"Five silvers?" he said with a look of disapproval on his face.

"What? It's my standard fee for mansions in the Marble Ring."

"Can't you just help a fellow thief out of the goodness of your heart?" Liam said before he stopped himself short.

He looked at me while pressing his lips together as if trying to keep something from escaping. After a few seconds, he lost the battle and burst out laughing. I gave a half-smile and shook my head.

"Sorry, I forgot who I was taking to," Liam said after one final snort. "But I still think it's weird. Why do you bother breaking into houses without stealing anything?"

"A girl's gotta have a hobby," I said, and spread my arms.

"I'm pretty sure snooping about doesn't qualify as a hobby. It's almost the same as your actual job and–"

A loud bang echoed as the back door was thrust open. Everyone fell silent as three men strode through the doorway and proceeded to seat themselves in each of the high-backed, black chairs. Their appearances were different but the one common denominator was that they all exuded authority. These were men who expected to be obeyed.

As one, we all went down on one knee and with our left fist planted on the floor and our right arm across our leg, bowed our heads.

"Strength and honor to the guild," we said in unison.

"Strength and honor," the Guild Masters replied. "Rise."

There was a rustle of clothing and a clanking of weapons as the room stood back up.

"There are several orders of business today," Guild Master Killian said without preamble. "It has come to our attention that the king is mounting an offensive against the elves."

A murmur broke out and disbelieving voices rose from every corner of the sparsely furnished room.

"The elves? For real?"

"Has he finally lost his mind?"

"That bloody lunatic."

The murmur was allowed to continue for a couple of moments longer before Guild Master Killian silenced the whole room with one wave of his hand. "This means that while all the garrisons will be heavily fortified, everything else in town will be less well-guarded. Use this opportunity wisely."

I grinned. This was perfect. After double-checking the guard rotations one last time, and for sixteen hours straight today, I felt ready to hit it. This piece of news was just the icing on my cake.

"Pipes!" Killian's voice rang out across the high-ceilinged hall and broke my reverie.

"Yes, Guild Master?" a suddenly terrified looking man with mousey blond hair answered from my right.

"You have been working in Assassins' Guild territory," Master Killian continued, his tone making it abundantly clear that this was a statement and not a question. "Their Guild

Master paid us a visit to inform us that if they ever found you working in their territory again, you would be black-marked."

Several sharp intakes of breath could be heard across the room. All Underworld Guild Masters are respected but there's also a hierarchy among our guilds. At the bottom is the Beggars' Guild, followed by the Pleasure Guild. The Bashers' Guild is in the middle of the pack and our guild is the second highest in the Underworld. The most powerful and feared guild, by far, is the Assassins' Guild. All members of that guild are shown respect, even by other Guild Masters. Yeah, I know, that sounds weird. Why would Guild Masters show respect to mere members of another guild? Alright, let me put it like this: if you're going to piss off a guild, don't pick the one that specializes in silently slitting your throat while you're sleeping peacefully in your bed.

"Let me make this clear for you," Guild Master Killian continued with steel in his voice, "you will be found floating face down in the harbor before disgracing our guild with a black mark."

Pipes looked about ready to throw up. Being black-marked was a death sentence all on its own, and a pretty horrible one at that since it meant open season for the entire Assassins' Guild, and now he also had death threats from his own guild. I'd keep a very low profile if I were him.

"Am I making myself clear?"

"Yes, Guild Master," Pipes stammered, doing a poor job of keeping the terror from his voice.

Killian nodded and moved on to the next order of business: guild rates. Paying the guild rates had never been a problem for me as I, more often than not, pulled off very high-profile hits. I only half-listened while everyone was reminded of this sacred obligation. Some people were even called out by name for being behind. One of them had approached me this morning, begging me to lend him some money so that he could pay his dues. I had, of course, turned him down. If you can't pull your own weight, you shouldn't be in the guild.

"...which is why I suspect we have a rogue on our territory," I heard Guild Master Killian say, and realized that he'd switched topic. "We would like to have a chat with this rogue. One of you will be responsible for arranging that meeting."

You could've heard a lockpick drop. Everyone was trying their very best to discreetly look in any other direction than his. Handling these kinds of situations for the Guild Masters was kind of like using a defective gun: it might help you win the day but it might also backfire and melt your face off.

"Storm, do you have some time to spare?" the dark-eyed Guild Master said and turned his raptor gaze on me.

Crap. I wanted to disappear through the floor. No, I most certainly did not have some time to spare, I was getting ready for my big heist, for Nemanan's sake! However, every single person in that room, me included, knew that this wasn't a question. It may have been phrased as one but we all knew that it was an order. And one does not refuse a direct order from the Guild Masters.

"Of course, Guild Master," I answered while carefully keeping the annoyance out of my voice. "It would be an honor."

"Good," Killian nodded, "Guild Master Caleb will see you about the specifics later."

I returned the nod. The rest of the meeting continued in a blur for me because my head just wasn't in it. There was a tornado of irritation mixed with a little panic going on a full rampage in there. I really didn't have time to hunt down some random thief who was trespassing on our territory. Damn. That was what I got for not staying in the back of the crowd. I cursed my sense of self-importance. I really must work on that. And to make matters worse, I hadn't even been paying attention to that part of the meeting. It would be really bad if the Guild Masters found that out.

"Hey, ready to go?" Liam tugged on my sleeve as the crowd started breaking up.

"Yeah."

The two doors on either side of the Thieves' Court were both clogged with exiting guild members. Instead of watching the crowd mill through them, I tipped my head up towards the vaulted ceiling. Well, that meeting went splendidly. I was supposed to hunt down a rogue thief but I had missed the part about where to find said trespasser. Tricking Guild Master Caleb into telling me what I needed to know, without giving my precarious situation away, would be no small feat. I let out something between a sigh and a chuckle. This should be interesting.

2.

Guild Master Caleb found me sitting at the desk in my room cleaning my knives and oiling leather equipment. I quickly stood up when he stepped through the open door to my room.

"Guild Master," I said respectfully.

He waved me back into my chair and proceeded to take a seat on the bed. For a moment, we just sat there and listened to people moving about, chatting, gambling, or cleaning equipment. The sound of the Thieves' Guild. I quite enjoyed that. To me, it was the sound of home.

"You weren't paying attention to that part of the meeting," the brown-haired Guild Master sitting on my bed finally said.

I briefly closed my eyes. How could I possibly have thought that I would get away with that? Guild Master Caleb's observation skills were legendary. And quite uncanny. Well, that was that, no point in trying to be sneaky now.

"No," I answered simply.

He smiled. "You know, for someone who lies as effortlessly as she breathes, you're surprisingly honest."

I returned the smile. "I have my moments."

"So," Caleb continued, straight to business, "we've had reports of a young man pulling off heists in our territory. He's blond, blue-eyed, and a bit on the scrawny side. Apparently, he's hit both the jewelry store and the watchmaker's shop on New Street."

"Successfully?" I asked, a little surprised, because those weren't exactly easy targets.

"Successfully," he confirmed. "Which means that we would very much like to have a chat with him."

"I understand. Any leads on where he can be found?"

"Yes, according to our sources, he's spending a lot of time in the Bowels when he's not working."

I let out a deep mental sigh. The Bowels isn't my favorite part of the city. In fact, I'd almost go as far as saying I hate that part of Keutunan. It's run down, dirty, and filled with all the lowlifes of the Underworld: those who've been banished by their Underworld guild. Most people who live there are therefore, at least partly, skilled in their profession but lack restraint and respect, and have a problem with authority. I really wasn't looking forward to searching through an area full of people whose sole enjoyment in life was messing with everyone they managed to come across. However, this clarified the reason why Guild Master Killian had singled me out for the job. I glanced at the small silver clock on my desk. It was almost five-thirty which meant that the sun would soon be up. Not the best time for a clandestine surprise meeting. And besides, I'd been up for almost twenty-four hours straight. I needed sleep.

"I will arrange it for this evening," I informed Guild Master Caleb. That would give me enough time to get a good day's sleep, make a solid plan, and locate this rogue.

"Good," Master Caleb said and stood up. For a moment he just studied at me with those observant brown eyes. "For someone who is so unremarkable-looking in every way, you really are quite the remarkable person."

To most people, that would probably have sounded like a cleverly concealed insult. I, on the other hand, consider it a compliment in every way. In fact, I pride myself on being thoroughly ordinary-looking because it means I can easily blend in everywhere. It's very hard to be a successful thief when you're beautiful enough to stand out in a crowd. People tend to notice you then, and remember your face, which isn't a very helpful trait when a valuable diamond necklace suddenly goes missing in the same crowd.

"Sleep well, the Oncoming Storm," Caleb said as he turned to leave.

"Thank you, Guild Master," I said to his retreating back before he disappeared through the doorway.

Well, would you look at that? I survived. Guild Master Caleb found out about my inattention at the meeting and I was still in one piece. I sent a quick prayer of thanks to Nemanan, God of Thieves. Now, all that was left was to go into the Bowels, find a meeting place, locate a trespasser with the help of only a generic description while also ducking banished underworlders looking for a fight, plan an ambush, carry out said ambush, and bring the rogue to the meeting place. So, nothing unusual then. Yeah. Piece of cake.

3.

I stalked the rogue thief as he moved around the Bowels throughout the afternoon. I'd sent word to the Guild Masters as soon as I'd found him to let them know that the meeting would take place as planned. Now, all I had to do was wait for the right moment. This evening, the unsuspecting rogue walking the streets below would attend a meeting he'd never forget. Perched on the roof of a butcher's shop, I watched him walk towards the Pig's Head.

"Ah, going for a drink, are you?" I whispered. "Perfect."

That would make it so much easier for me to keep track of him until it was time to bring him to the meeting place. I started silently climbing down from my vantage point so that I could follow the rogue.

I didn't like having to leave the high ground but it was hard to walk into a pub otherwise. Suddenly dropping down from the ceiling inside would unfortunately not be very stealthy. However, this presented a problem. The lowlifes who live in this part of the city don't have a very high opinion of women; they believe that women exist for the sole purpose of being exploited by men. Me being, well, me, you can probably imagine how I feel about that sentiment. Don't get me wrong, I could most likely slit all of their throats before they ever laid a hand on me, but that does, unfortunately, attract a lot of attention. Attention that I couldn't afford. That was the reason I had stuck to the rooftops all day. Now I had to leave them if I wanted to follow him inside.

I silently cursed myself for not wearing a disguise. The thick braid down my back clearly marked me as a woman. Well, that and my figure, I suppose. Wearing big, baggy clothes might be good for a disguise but it's terribly inconvenient when you're scrambling up and down rooftops. For this kind of work, when I don't entirely know who I'm dealing with, nothing beats my usual clothes. They're nondescript, noise-free, and just large enough to fit all of my weapons and tools comfortably. The downside, as I mentioned, is that I do actually look like a woman. Well, it would be fine anyway. Most likely. I reached the street and started walking towards the pub.

"Hey there, pretty lady!" a man with brown unwashed hair and a tooth gap called after me.

Or not. I ignored him and continued walking.

"Hey, wait up!" he called again and ran to catch up with me.

"Just go away, I don't have time for this!" I hissed, though not loudly enough for him to hear. Instead, I picked up the pace. Running was not an option because that would attract too much attention, so I had to settle for a brisk walk. Unfortunately, I didn't get far before a strong hand closed around my wrist and spun me around.

"You have... uhm... a lot of knives," he said, a touch incoherently, while studying my shoulders. His eyes seemed to go in and out of focus but he kept his iron grip on my wrist.

"A lot of knives. Yes, indeed I do. How very perceptive of you. Such terrific observation skills," I replied, my voice practically dripping with sarcasm.

However, he didn't seem to pick up on it, which I guess was another testament to his subpar intelligence. He added further proof to that when he completely disregarded the fact that I was heavily armed and instead started leading me towards the nearest side street. I shook my head and went along while keeping a close eye on the rogue. He was almost at the Pig's Head now. I needed to finish this quickly. Once we were shielded from view by the walls of the side street, he threw me up against the brickwork.

"Now, show me your..."

I feigned a knee kick to his groin. His reflexes kicked in and he brought both hands down to protect it, which is when I used the side of my hand to hit him in the throat. His hands flew back up to his throat as he started gasping for air. To once again leave his groin unprotected was the mistake I'd been counting on, so I used that moment of inattention to land a knee kick that I actually followed through. His eyes widened as my kneecap connected and he dropped to the ground. I stared at him for a few seconds, kneeling there in the alley with one hand on his groin and one on the street to support himself, gasping for air with tears dripping down his face. Pathetic. My hand shot out and gripped his throat. I forced him to look at me as I started to slowly squeeze.

"You picked the wrong woman to mess with," I stated with smoldering fury. "Now, you and I are both gonna walk away from here and for your sake, I'm gonna pretend that this never happened. And if I ever see you again, I'm gonna make you *wish* that I had crushed your windpipe today."

The darkness churned inside my soul, begging to be let out, as my fingers kept their tight grip on his miserable throat. Fear bloomed in his eyes but I kept on squeezing a little while longer anyway, just to make sure he really got the point.

"Am I making myself clear?" I asked.

My eyes might be the color of emeralds but at that moment they were as hard as them too. He nodded desperately while trying to pry my hand from his throat.

"Good," I said and finally released my grip.

He went down on all fours and started to once again gasp for air. Feeling content with putting the fear of women in him, I started out towards the pub. The rogue had most likely already gone inside. I walked along the street at the quickest pace I could without attracting attention but only made it a couple of cross streets before I saw another woman being harassed by two men. I really hated this part of the city. As opposed to me, that woman did not look like someone who carried more than a dozen knives and had been training with them since childhood. Her frightened eyes looked at me pleadingly. I glanced away and continued walking. Yes, yes, I know, I'm such a hypocrite. Whatever happened to girl power, right? If you'd been raised on the streets of Keutunan, you'd understand. To mind my own business was a lesson I learnt long ago. I had enough trouble of my own, I didn't need someone else's as well. Besides, I was in a hurry.

When I opened the door to the pub, I was met with warm air and a packed room. It was dimly lit, noisy, and full of random strangers coming and going. In other words, it was perfect for a stakeout. I picked a small table in the corner where I could see the entire room and also have my back protected by two walls. Or, I guess *picked* is the wrong word. There wasn't exactly a perfect table conveniently free of people. *Took* would probably be a better word since I used my withering glare to scare away the previous occupants. Like I said, the room was packed. Once I had stolen a table, I ordered a mug of ale and then I waited. The ale was horrible, and watered down, but I sipped it anyway. Across and to the left of me, the rogue thief was sitting at a cramped table with three other boys. While waiting, I studied him closely. Guild Master Caleb had called him a young man but he looked to be closer to Liam's age than mine, which meant that he was still a teenager. Laughing and drinking with some other boys in their late teens, he looked like one of those people who'd been on a roll their entire life and thought that life was just one long walk in the sunshine. Boy, was he in for a rude awakening.

After my initial assessment of his character, I checked to see whether he was armed, and in that case, how well. After careful scrutiny, I came to the conclusion that he most likely only had that poorly hidden belt knife that was partly visible under his white shirt. Amateur. This just added more proof to the assessment that he was young, naïve, and that he'd never had to face the cruel and harsh reality of life in the Underworld. Soon, that would all change.

When it was almost time to meet the Guild Masters, I bribed one of the more muscled servers at the pub to kick the rogue out for drunkenness. I followed quietly behind as he was more or less thrown out the door.

"Kicked out for drunkenness? Ha! And here I thought the purpose of a pub was to get drunk..." I heard him mutter to himself.

He stood outside for a while, dusting himself off, before finally deciding to head off. I followed. Once we had reached a somewhat isolated part of the road, I took a couple of quick strides to catch up with him. He hadn't even noticed that I'd come up behind him when I took out my pistol and put it to the small of his back.

"Keep walking," I hissed in his ear. His entire body tensed up but he did as he was told. "I have a gun placed against your lower spinal cord. If I pull the trigger, you'll be paralyzed from the waist down. That is, if you don't die first."

His breath caught and his step faltered a little as this bit of news sank in. Before he could do anything that would draw unwanted attention, I pushed the pistol harder into his spine.

"Now then, are we gonna have a problem?" I asked with enough menace to make a full-grown man tremble in his boots.

"No," he breathed.

"Smart move."

I reached around his waist with my free hand and yanked the knife from his belt. His gangly body jerked a little in surprise but he stayed quiet. In one smooth motion, I threw the knife over the wall to our left. If someone was standing on that side of the wall, they were about to get a nasty surprise. But the sound of metal on stone soon resonated so I assumed it hadn't hit anyone.

"Continue walking straight ahead until I tell you otherwise," I said and watched him nod in reply.

While continuing deeper into the Bowels, we met a few other people who were heading back the way we'd come but none of them bothered us and the young rogue kept his word and made no trouble for us either. The, at least, semi-lamplit streets where all the pubs and other businesses were located soon gave way to the dark and even more poorly built part where all these lowlifes dwelled. Here, we met no one. Most underworlders keep their business hours strictly to the hours

A STORM OF SILVER AND ASH 21

between dusk and dawn and even though these people had been kicked out of their guilds, they still mostly did the same. So, it was hardly a surprise to find the Bowels' residential area completely deserted at this time of night. Apart from my occasional commands to take a right or left, we walked in complete silence.

I glanced down at the gun in my hand. The handle was made of some kind of wood, but I had no idea which kind. Oh don't look at me like that! It's not as if memorizing different kinds of trees is ever going to help me in life. I've lived and worked my whole life in the city. I've never even set foot in the forest, and it's not like I'm the only one. Basically, only those who work in the lumber business do, and even those people only go as far as their walled-in tree farms, as they like to call it. Children in this city are brought up with horror stories about the wicked elves that live in the deep forest to the north and west of the city. There was a great war between elves and men some hundred and fifty years ago. The elves attacked our city and tried to take control of it and turn us all into slaves but after the heroic acts of the royal family's forebears, they were defeated. Or that's what the history books in the royal library claim, at least. Which I know because I may or may not have snuck into the Silver Keep and taken a look for myself. But that's beside the point.

The point is that the royal family claims that they've kept us safe from the elves but the truth is that most people in the city now believe that's a filthy lie. Don't get me wrong, it's an incredibly impressive lie, one that's lasted for more than a hundred and fifty years, but a lie nonetheless. No one has seen an elf since that fateful battle so long ago and if they really do exist, we would've seen one by now, right?

Most people still frighten their children with horror stories about the elves, though. They do that so they won't wander into the forest because the majority of the population do, in fact, believe that there is *something* in the woods. Most likely, vicious animals of one kind or another. So even though no one believes the whole elf story, they stay out of the forest because they're not in any hurry to die from animal attacks either. I don't really care one way or the other. There's nothing to steal in the forest so the hellhounds and dragons, or whatever it is that lives in there, can have it all to themselves.

"Take a left up here," I told the young rogue.

He started crossing the street diagonally. Once we reached the next cross street, he turned left and started following it. It led to a back alley with some broken crates, a couple of trash cans, and rotting straw. Aside from the one low-built house at the back, the alley was completely boxed in by high stone walls. When we reached the middle of the square-shaped area, I told him to stop.

"Turn around," I ordered.

He obeyed and I followed behind him as he turned until he had the low-built house behind him and the small entrance in front. I lifted the gun to the back of his head.

"If you make one threatening move, one wrong move, if you so much as tremble in a way I don't like, I will blow your brains out right across these cobblestones. Clear?"

"Yes," he stammered, terror creeping into his voice.

I retreated a couple of steps while putting the pistol back in its holster. When I reached the far wall, I grabbed a hold of the top and silently swung myself up. With one knee on the stone, I took out two throwing knives. The rogue trembled down there in the alley. I almost let out a short laugh. He really did believe that I'd shoot him in the head if he made a wrong move. I mean, I would, if only I could actually pull off an accurate shot from this distance. In the interest of full disclosure, I don't like guns. At all. They're too noisy and unreliable. You can never really be sure that the shot will go off and when it does, it produces enough noise to make all the Silver Cloaks come running. I'd pick my throwing knives any day of the week over that inconvenient contraption. Unfortunately, people tend to be more scared of a gun than a knife, even though knives are just as deadly, or in my hands, even more so. It was because of that misguided notion that I'd used the gun up until this moment, when the boy could no longer see what I was holding.

Three dark-clad figures glided into the alley.

4.

"You have been trespassing," Guild Master Killian stated.

"Who are you?" the rogue asked, trying to sound brave, but I could see that his knees were about ready to buckle. "And what do you mean *trespassing*?"

"We are the ones who can make your life very difficult, and very short, if you don't own up to your transgressions," Guild Master Eliot rasped in his grating voice.

I couldn't see the expression on the young rogue's face since he had his back to me but the Guild Masters must not have liked what they saw in it. Killian's dark eyes found mine before he flicked them towards the boy's right shoulder. Show time. I threw the knife in my right hand. Steel glinted briefly in the moonlight before the sharpened edge buried itself in the unsuspecting target's shoulder. At the moment of impact, a dull thud drifted to my ears, followed by a sharp cry. The rogue's hand flew up to his shoulder where he tentatively touched the knife protruding from his flesh. He managed a panicked glace in my direction before turning his attention back to the real threat in front of him.

"Okay, look, I'm sorry," he began, "I do know who you are. I just didn't think it would matter if I robbed a shop or two."

The three dark-clad men in front of him looked incredibly unimpressed by that statement.

"But now I know, so I won't be doing that again," he continued lightly.

I wasn't sure if he really was that ignorant, or just stupid. Did he truly believe that he would get off the hook that easily? As if the Guild Masters could read my thoughts, three pairs of eyes looked up pointedly at me. I readied the other throwing knife. They didn't specify a location this time so I assumed it was up to my discretion. Hitting something vital would kind of defeat the purpose so I settled for the other shoulder. Another thud sounded into the night and this time it was followed by a much longer cry. The eyes of the Guild Masters looked at me again. This time, the rogue thief must've seen it because he put up his hands and started frantically waving them. I thought about how much that kind of movement must hurt as I drew back another pair of knives. The wannabe-thief dropped to his knees.

"No, no, please, don't..." he started begging.

Guild Master Caleb glanced in my direction and shook his head slightly. I returned the knives to my shoulder holsters and rolled my eyes. Two knives. Two knives to non-critical parts of the body that would heal quickly and without causing too much damage. That was all it took to break him? Pathetic.

"Please, I'll do whatever you want," he continued down in the gutter. "I'll steal for you."

Killian let out a short laugh and hooked his shoulder-length black hair behind his ear. "We give you permission to steal the Midnight Star for us. If you pull that off, then we can talk about you joining the Thieves' Guild."

"Yes, of course, thank you," the rogue answered, a little bewildered.

"Come find us when it's done," Master Killian said as all three of them turned and glided out of the alley again.

When they'd disappeared from view, the young thief slumped down and exhaled deeply. The Midnight Star – what were they thinking? I dropped down silently from the roof as the boy struggled to his feet. He hadn't heard me so without a word of warning I snuck up behind him and pulled the knife from his right shoulder.

"Ow! What the hell?" he yelled and spun to face me.

I arched an eyebrow at him and he shrank back a little when he remembered who I was.

"I'm gonna need that back," I said matter-of-factly and gestured at the remaining knife sticking out of his shoulder.

His mouth fell open and he was about to protest but then he closed it again, scowled at me, and turned around. Maybe he wasn't that stupid after all. I yanked it out smoothly. He sucked in a sharp breath through his teeth but said nothing. I was almost at the mouth of the alley when he spoke again.

"Wait!" he called. "Please..."

I considered just ignoring him but something in that *please* made me turn around. "What?"

"I... uhm... what is the Midnight Star?"

Just as I thought. Anyone who knew what it was wouldn't have been so eager to commit to stealing it. Even I had never tried it. Poor kid.

"It's a sapphire. A man known as the Admiral owns it. He's pretty savage. And possessive. It's probably the most well-guarded piece of treasure in this entire city." Hope drained from his eyes like water down a drain. "A piece of advice, kid, just cut your losses. Gather whatever money you already have and get the hell out. No good will come of you trying to steal that rock."

"Go? Go where? There is nowhere else to go!" he exclaimed, voice filled with desperation.

He was right. Where would he go? No one knew what was behind that vast sea to the south. There might only be more water. And no one dared venture into the forest to find out what was on the other side. If there even was an end to it. To the east, there were only farms and fishing villages. He really was royally screwed. Oh well. Not really my problem. I shrugged both shoulders and strode out of the alley.

※

WHEN I GOT BACK FROM my little ambush, I went to find Liam. I'd wanted to hit Lord Eberbach's place today, if I'd had a choice, because there were fewer guards today compared to the rest of the week. But now that my plans had been so rudely interrupted, I had to wait another week. Damn. I needed a drink. Probably some food too. Liam being, well, Liam, I knew he'd want to come. That boy is always hungry. Since it was evening and dark outside, the Thieves' Guild was almost empty. Business hours and all. To be honest, I wasn't even sure if Liam would still be there. It was more of a hope than an educated guess. After the day I'd had, I really needed to vent my frustration, and talking to Liam was the best way to do that. Alright, so maybe the alcohol plays a part too.

As I walked through the sleeping quarters towards Liam's room, I looked at all the stuff lying about everywhere. Lockpicks, guns, knives, pieces of leather equipment. Most doors were open, even though no one was inside the room, and through them I could see even more valuable items. Coins lying on desks, fancy jewelry boxes filled with necklaces on shelves, silver candlesticks and cutlery. All of them stolen. I thought about the expensive silver clock sitting on the desk behind the open door to my room. All of it unprotected, there for the taking. And yet, in here, that wasn't a problem. We may be thieves, the whole lot of us, but we'd never steal from each other. Honor among thieves. We take that sentiment very seriously here. Isn't it quite ironic, though? The only place in this entire city where you don't have to worry about getting robbed is a place filled with thieves. I let out a silent chuckle at that thought as I reached Liam's room.

"Hey, come on, let's get some food!" I said to his back, grateful to have found him sitting there at his desk, and rapped my knuckles against his door frame.

"No, I'm okay, I'm not hungry," he replied, a strange note in his voice.

Something was wrong. Like I said, Liam is *always* hungry, and I couldn't shake that odd tone of his voice. He must have sensed my train of thought because he turned his back more squarely towards me.

"Go away, I'm not in the mood."

I was already annoyed, so instead of heeding his wish, I stalked forward and yanked him around to face me. Sometimes I really do have all the social graces of a bull. I recoiled, my frustrations and hunger forgotten, when he turned to face me.

"Liam! What in Nemanan's name happened?" I exclaimed, horrified.

He averted his eyes as I took in the state of his face. Angry, red bruises discolored his cheeks, jaw, and temple, and his lower lip was split. The darkness boiled in my soul.

"It's nothing, I just tripped when I–" he began.

"Don't you dare give me something like that," I growled. "Who did this to you?"

"Storm, please..."

I could tell he was embarrassed about having been beaten up and just wanted the whole subject to be dropped but I didn't care. No one touches Liam. No one.

"A name!" I yelled at him more forcefully than I'd intended, but I was having difficulty keeping my emotions in check.

"I don't know his name!" he snapped back.

Blinking, I retreated a step. What was I even doing? Why was I making Liam angry? That wouldn't accomplish anything and would most certainly not make it better. I really must work on my social skills. I took a deep breath through my nose, closed my eyes, and then exhaled slowly.

"I'm sorry, Liam," I said when I'd calmed down a little, "I didn't mean to yell at you. Just please tell me who did this, and why."

In my head, I couldn't come up with a single logical reason for why someone would want to hurt him. As I've mentioned before, I don't know anyone who knows Liam and dislikes him. He's the kind of person who just gets along with everyone.

"It was a dockworker," Liam said at last. "I was just being polite to a woman that passed. I swear I wasn't even trying to steal anything this time! But I think that it might have been his girlfriend or something because he accused me of trying to sleep with her."

Well, that made sense, I guess. In a twisted sort of way. The curse of being kind and polite.

"Alright, come on," I said.

"Where are we going?"

"To the docks, so you can point him out to me."

I could sense him about to protest so I simply turned around and walked out the door. After a few breaths, I heard him follow.

5.

The night was still young which meant that the taverns along the harbor were far from deserted. Warm light pooled out from the windows. Inside, off-key singing and boisterous laughter rang out. The creaking wooden signs swung gently in the breeze as people moved from tavern to tavern. Because of the closeness to the sea, a thin curtain of mist hung in the air. I could taste the salt on my tongue as we approached our fifth tavern for the night, in search of Liam's assailant. I was beginning to think that he was pretending not to find him when Liam suddenly stopped and stared down a side street.

"Him. That's him," he stated with a hint of surprise mixed with dread.

The man in the alley was leaning with one arm against the wall, taking a piss. He was singing a little tune as if he didn't have a worry in the world. Little did he know that trouble was now waiting for him just a few strides away.

"Are you absolutely sure?" I asked.

"Yes," Liam confirmed. "I'm very good with faces, remember?"

He is. But for what I was about to do, I still had to ask. I glanced at him. He looked like he was about to be sick. Violence, any kind of fight, really, isn't Liam's thing.

"Keep an eye on the street, would you? Make sure that no patrolling Silver Cloaks disturb us."

He relaxed a little and nodded gratefully. I returned the nod. Show time. As I strode towards the blissfully ignorant man leaning against the wall, I pushed back the hood of my dark gray cloak. The cloak was there not so much to keep the weather out but to hide the fact that I was incredibly well-armed. The execution of my plan could definitely have been more sneaky. Pretending to be a damsel in distress in order to get him to drop his guard would certainly have made things easier. Only one problem. I'm not a damsel-in-distress kind of person. Besides, I was angry. I wanted this to be violent and messy.

"You!" I bellowed as I drew close.

"Huh?"

He slowly turned his head towards me while pulling his pants back up. A note of surprise registered on his face when he realized that I was a woman. His eyes narrowed in suspicion.

"Whaddya want? Don't ya know it's dangerous for women to be strollin' about all alone at this hour?" he said mockingly.

He was baiting me but I didn't rise to it. He would get what was coming to him soon enough anyway. Instead, I got straight to the point.

"Today, you beat up a kid by the docks. A kid whose only crime was being kind and polite."

That had been a statement and not a question, but he answered anyway.

"Yeah, what o' it?"

"That was a mistake."

The usual tone of my voice can be described as *annoyed* and now I had purposely increased that to *menacing*. I expected him to be terrified. To my utter surprise, he laughed. My cheeks flushed. He actually laughed. It was a condescending laugh that made me want to rip his throat out and made the darkness in my soul scream for release.

"He sent a girl, a lil' girl, to take care o' it?" he managed to wheeze between bursts of laughter. "I guess I shouldn't be surprised, should I? That brat was the biggest coward I've ever met, yeah. He didn't even try to fight back, just stood there an' let me beat the crap out o' him. He even begged me to stop."

My heart sank. I knew that Liam wasn't a fighter, he was a charmer. Whenever a fight broke out that he couldn't charm his way out of, he always ran in the opposite direction. Running was one thing. Letting someone beat you up and begging was quite another. Bitter shame burned in my stomach on his behalf. The dockworker continued laughing. *Oh, Liam.*

The distinct sound of metal on wood, followed by a scream, rang out in the night. The laughing man was no longer laughing. With disbelief coloring his eyes, he stared at his left hand. It was pinned to the wooden wall behind him by a polished steel knife. His stunned eyes went from his hand to the crumpled dark gray cloak at my feet to the variety of knives strapped to my body. There was a knife missing from the holster on my right shoulder. His pupils dilated in fear as my eyes darkened like an oncoming thunderstorm. Three more knives disappeared from their holsters. One long, piercing scream echoed through the street. The blades above his kneecaps made his legs collapse. The two pinning his hands to the wall left him hanging there. After a while, the screams were broken up by gasps, then by sobs, and finally by pleas.

"Please..." he sobbed pitifully.

"Today, you beat up a kid by the docks. A kid whose only crime was being kind and polite. That was a mistake." I echoed my words from earlier with a voice that sounded frighteningly hollow.

I advanced on him with a terrifying smile on my lips and a hunting knife in my right hand. The long, sharp edge found its mark with deadly accuracy. Blood splattered the stones in front of my feet as his last gasp died on his lips. I watched the dark red stain on his shirt neck spread until it reached his abdomen. Heavy drops fell in the growing pool at my feet. Tilting my head up towards the dark clouds, I felt the cool touch of mist settle on my face. I stayed like that for a few more heartbeats. Except for the muted dripping, the street was silent. Exhaling deeply, I pulled myself out of the trance by forcing the darkness back down into the deep pits of my soul. I stepped around the crimson puddle. Without so much as a second glance, I yanked my throwing knives from the dead body of the previously laughing dockworker and wiped them on his, somewhat, clean sleeve before retreating up the street.

When I reached Liam, I had once again pulled the dark gray cloak tightly around my shoulders.

"I need a drink," Liam surprised me by saying, as I came to a halt next to him.

"You heard?"

"Yeah."

His voice sounded empty. I glanced at him from the corner of my eye. He was staring straight ahead, his face ashen. It was due to the bloodcurdling screams that had cut through the mist a couple of minutes past. Or so I hoped. If his affirmation meant that he'd overheard the whole conversation, and not just the screams, then I didn't know how long it would take for him to bounce back.

"The Mad Archer?" I asked, trying to make my voice light.

He simply nodded and started out. I fell in beside him. We walked east, back through the Harbor District, before turning north towards the Merchants' Quarter. At first, I tried to lighten the mood by commenting on some of the odd, mixed businesses that had sprung up here by the docks. A compass and rum shop. A hat and fishing pole maker. However, as Liam only replied by uttering the occasional noncommittal grunt, I soon abandoned my efforts. We walked in complete silence the rest of the journey. Along the way, we met a few couples and groups of people, in various states of intoxication, heading towards the tavern area we'd just left. None of them bothered us, though. I guess they could tell from our facial expressions that it was best to steer clear of us. Finally, after what felt like a very long walk to the Merchants' Quarter, the tall, dark wooden building that was the Mad Archer rose in front of us.

After the long, heavy silence of our trudge, the Mad Archer felt like stepping into another world. The oil lamps burned brightly, people were laughing, cheering, and playing dice. A fire roared in the fireplace and the smell of food drifted from the kitchen. I inhaled deeply through my nose. Home. A pleasant warmth spread in the pit of my stomach and thawed my soul. The Mad Archer was the unofficial Thieves' Guild tavern. It was run by a husband and wife. The man's name was Nate, but everyone called him Barrel on account of his impressive frame. Since the location of the tavern was so close to the Thieves' Guild it had simply become the most logical place for all our members to eat, drink, gamble, and share stories. Well, the delicious food and the un-watered ale may have had something to do with it too. Barrel and his wife, Hilda, had quickly realized what kind of clientele their tavern catered to but they didn't seem to mind. They still treated us with kindness and served good food and drink. In repayment of that, we'd put out word to the whole Underworld that Barrel and Hilda were strictly off limits.

Not everyone at the Mad Archer was a thief, of course, but as I scanned the room for an empty table, I recognized most of the faces. Some winding, some gentle pushing, and a brief chat with Barrel later, we were finally seated at a table in the back with a plate of hot food and a mug of ale in front of us. I hadn't realized how hungry I was until I started eating; I was famished. Glancing over at Liam, I could tell he felt the same way, so at first we just enjoyed the food in silence. A more comfortable silence this time, though. When our plates were empty and we were halfway through our second mug, Liam spoke for the first time since we left the Harbor District.

"Why did you join the Thieves' Guild?"

I looked up from my mug in surprise. "Where did that come from all of a sudden?" I replied, studying his face.

He looked thoughtful, as if he was genuinely pondering something difficult, while tracing the rim of the mug with his finger. His eyes flicked up to meet mine. They were full of concern. When his eyes looked like that, they made me want to spill all of my secrets. I didn't want to. I couldn't. So instead I brought my sarcasm up as a shield.

"There aren't really that many options for a woman in the Underworld, you know? Could you really picture me in the Pleasure Guild?"

That drew a laugh from him at least. "No, you couldn't even charm a starving dog with an armful of food."

I raised both eyebrows in his direction and stared at him in mock offense. He smiled sheepishly. Then his eyes turned thoughtful again and his voice took on a serious tone.

"Don't take this the wrong way, Storm, but you're very good at killing. And... well, you kill without hesitation... or remorse." His eyes studied my face as if trying to decipher the secrets of an old book. I really wished he wouldn't do that. "So why didn't you join the Assassins' Guild? It's higher status, more well-paid, and there are rumors that they even have ties to the royal family. Anyone who had your skills would've picked it over, well, basically any other guild. But you didn't. You picked the Thieves' Guild. Why? And why is it that you can fight and kill without as much as a second thought?" he finished, breathless.

His expression had gone from concerned to bewildered and a little exasperated as he talked. I leaned back in my chair and rested my head against the wall behind me. *Yes, why can I kill without hesitation or remorse? Oh, Liam. You don't want to know. I wish I didn't know.* Memories came flooding back. Uninvited, painful memories. I closed my eyes to stem the pain bleeding from my heart. As if that would help. *What if...? No. No good would come of that.* I opened my eyes and leaned forward a little again.

"I like stealing. I don't like killing," I said, lifting one shoulder in a shrug.

That was the closest I had ever come to telling Liam, or anyone for that matter, about that night. What I'd told him tonight was technically not a lie, but it wasn't the truth either. It was *a* truth, I guess. I could tell from the look on his face that he knew I was hiding something, but he didn't press the matter. Thank the gods. Instead, Liam's face broke into a sunshine smile and the ache in my heart lessened just a little.

"Well, I'm glad you chose the Thieves' Guild at least! Otherwise, we would never have met," he said happily, his face beaming.

Maybe, just maybe, life would only get better from this point on.

6.

I went over the note several times in my head as I ran. *Need help. Mercer St. Come quick. No visible weapons.* Mercer Street isn't exactly a populated area, which means that there's barely anything worth stealing there, so what was he even doing there in the first place? And what did he need help with? Gods damn it, why couldn't he be more specific?

I'd spent the last couple of days rechecking all the details in preparation for the second attempt at my big heist. Every evening, Liam and I had met at the Mad Archer for breakfast. This time, I'd found a note left at our usual table instead. What in the world had that boy gotten himself into this time?

At the speed I ran, the wide streets of the Merchants' Quarter, and the even wider streets of the Marble Ring soon gave way to the narrow and twisting alleys of Worker's End. The dark wood and stone passages in this part of the city were full of wrong turns and dead ends. Growing up on the streets of Keutunan had always helped me tremendously when it came to navigating it. However, as I mentioned, there's almost nothing worth stealing in this part of Worker's End, and given my proclivity for theft, that meant I hadn't spent much time here. Fortunately, I ended up on Mercer Street sooner rather than later. The street was completely deserted.

"Oh come on, Liam! Where are you?" I muttered.

While casting calculating glances in every direction, I continued sneaking up the road. There was no sound. No one talking, whispering, or making noise of any kind. No creaking from floorboards or windowpanes. Even the wind was quiet. The street made a sharp right turn a couple of strides ahead. I followed it and crept around the corner. A dark gray mass made me draw up short. An empty dead end. I looked at the towering stone walls all around me.

"Well, that's annoying."

They were way too tall and smooth to climb and there was nothing to use as a springboard. The only other thing in the alley, apart from me, was a small stone door that seemed to lead to a cellar of some kind. My irritation flared.

Why couldn't Liam just have written exactly where he was and what he wanted my help with? I'm not a patient person, Liam knows this, and I wasn't going to search every bloody building on this street just because he couldn't be more specific. I rolled my eyes. Of course I was. Because it was Liam, and I would walk through fire for him. I took a deep breath.

"Fine, I'd better get to it then." I sighed. "This night just couldn't get any worse!"

I turned around and was about to take the first step back out when I froze. A dark figure stood in the middle of the alley, blocking the way out of the dead end. Before I could get my feelings under control, panic spread through my chest. How did he get there? I'm a notoriously paranoid and perceptive person. No one sneaks up on me. No one. Normally, I would've heard if someone approached. I would've sensed someone standing behind me watching. But this time, I hadn't. Why was that?

As my feelings were going haywire, the dark figure took a step forward. The light from one of the dirty oil lamps hanging on the wall revealed a man. He was dressed all in black. Even his hair and eyes were black. My intuition put his age around twenty-two, which would make him a little older than me. Or at least, I think so, since I've never been entirely sure how old I am.

"I see you got my note," he said.

That statement took me completely by surprise because it wasn't at all what I had expected a mysterious ambusher to say. Also, there was something about the tone of his voice that I couldn't quite place. Standing there, staring at him with knit brows, I tried to figure out the chaos in my head. Just as he cocked his head slightly to the right, it finally clicked and all the pieces fell into place.

"*You* sent that note?" I asked incredulously, thinking about the short letter in Liam's handwriting that I'd found at the Mad Archer.

His black eyes glittered and he smiled mischievously. Suddenly, I realized what that odd note in his voice had been. He was amused. Now, I was furious. I reached for my throwing knives but my hands met empty shoulders before I remembered that I'd removed them prior to leaving. The words *no visible weapons*, jotted down on a pale scrap of paper, flashed before my eyes. Shit. If it came down to a fight, I only had the two stiletto blades I kept hidden in my sleeves. Maybe I could talk my way out of this instead.

"You must be quite the forger," I said. "I can count the number of people who could manage to fool me like that on one hand."

"Why, thank you." He smiled. "Coming from you, that's some compliment."

"So, do you have a reason for this deception or were you just looking for a fellow forger to compare notes?"

He laughed. It was actually a quite pleasant sound. "I'm looking for some information."

"A lot of people come to me to buy information, no need for an ambush," I replied while breathing a deep inward sigh of relief. Maybe this would turn out well after all.

"Yes, well, there are two problems with that," he said matter-of-factly. "The first one being that I'm not planning on paying for the information. And the second problem is that the information I want is not something you want to give up."

Crap. That was what I got for taking out victory prematurely.

"Then we have a problem," I stated.

"Hence the ambush," he replied with a light shrug of his shoulders.

Before I'd had time to blink, he'd produced two slightly curved short swords from behind either shoulder blade. His lean, muscular body tensed as he crouched into an attack position. As if asking me what my next move would be, he spun the swords once in his hands. The razor-sharp edges gleamed in the moonlight. Well, it turned out that this night could get worse. If I'd known that this was the alternative, I would've happily searched through empty buildings all night. I really must remember to be more thankful for the boring things. Well then, there wasn't much to do about that now.

My stiletto blades shot into my hands. The mysterious ambusher grinned, as if daring me to come try it, but I hung back. Instead, I assessed the situation and started going through battle strategies in my head. My blades looked woefully small compared to his swords and he was almost an entire head taller than me. *Maybe if I cut his head off, then we'd be the same height at least*, I mused grimly before giving myself an internal headshake. That wasn't going to work with two stilettos. From what I could tell by his skintight, black shirt, he was also incredibly fit. I couldn't get close enough to let him grab me because then I'd lose to his superior strength. Shit. He had the reach, both by being taller and having longer weapons, and he had the strength. That didn't leave many options. I was going to have to finish this quickly by slipping past him and escaping into the maze of dark alleyways. My spirits rose. That would work. After concluding that he might have the strength but I had the speed, I finally grinned back at him, daring him to do it.

He took the dare. Quick as a lightning strike, he closed the distance between us and attacked. I barely had time to parry his thrusts, let alone deliver any of my own. His blades were a flurry of silver all around us, as though the great northern storm winds had come calling. Only my highly developed reflexes saved me from being completely outmaneuvered but I could already feel that they wouldn't save me for long. Well, would you look at that? It turned out that I didn't have the speed either. Wasn't this night just full of lessons in humility. Bastard.

The stiletto blade flew from my right hand. I barely had time to register the metallic clanking as it bounced down the alley and stopped along the wall, out of my reach. He was onto me again and now I only had one small blade left to defend against his two lightning storm swords. I pulled short ragged breaths and desperately tried to hold him off as he backed me further into the corner. The towering walls closed in around me. Like a caged animal, I cast quick glances around me for a way out but there was none. These brief moments of inattention ended up costing me dearly as I felt my last remaining stiletto fly from my left hand shortly before he took my legs out from underneath me. My breath was driven from my lungs as I hit the stone street heavily. While sucking in a desperate gasp to refill my lungs, I tried to scramble away but my head hit the wall in the corner. I was trapped. The cool touch of metal appeared in the hollow space at my throat. Lying on my back with my chest propped up on my elbows and my head against the dark stone wall, I swallowed. I was alone and unarmed and a dangerous stranger towered over me with two swords, one of which he held tightly to my throat, the sharp point digging into my skin. This was bad.

"If you go for that knife in your right boot, I will slit your throat," he announced grimly.

I believed him. My chest heaved, but other than that, I stayed completely still. I couldn't even guess how he knew about the knife in my boot but I didn't dare ask. Right now, I was entirely at his mercy.

"Slowly remove the knife and throw it to your right," he ordered.

By raising my knee and dragging my foot closer, I could reach the knife in my boot. I fumbled a little when I tried to pull it free from the strap securing it but finally got it loose. With my right arm extended from my body, I threw the knife towards the side of the alley. For a brief second, the clanking noise of metal on stone filled the night.

"Any other weapons?" he asked, the oil lamp casting flickering shadows over his pale face.

Very carefully, I shook my head.

"I'll know if you're lying," he warned.

"I'm not," I managed to whisper.

He cocked his head a little to the right and I felt as though his black eyes could see into my very soul. I hadn't been lying but I was still nervous when he turned that penetrating gaze on me. Without warning, he took a hold of my shirt, hauled me up, and slammed me into the wall. For the second time that night, my breath was knocked out of me. When I'd finally recovered it, I was once again staring into those intense, black eyes from the pointy end of a sword. His left hand was firmly planted on the wall next to my head and his right arm bent back so he could push the point of the sword through my throat in a heartbeat if I gave him any trouble. Or lied. I noticed that he'd returned his left-hand sword to his shoulder before his eyes pulled me back again.

"Now, I'd like that information, if you don't mind terribly," he said cheerfully.

I almost laughed out loud. Who even was this man who could make me fear for my life in one breath and make me laugh with his next? *If you don't mind terribly* – ha! As a matter of fact, I did mind terribly. However, the sword at my throat dissuaded me from saying so.

"I'm not exactly in any position to refuse," I said instead. "So, what can I help you with?"

"I need information on a house," he replied.

"Any particular house or are you just browsing?"

A soft chuckle escaped his lips. "A very particular house. You know, the big marble one with a light green roof and two stone bears out front, at the end of Plaza Eldren."

"You bastard! I've been casing that house for weeks!" I managed to blurt out before I caught myself. "I mean... uhm... I didn't mean..." I started stammering before ending my sentence very eloquently with, "shit."

I half-expected him to kill me right then but he only laughed his pleasant-sounding laugh. "And now you understand what I meant by *the information I want is not something you want to give up*," he said after he'd stopped laughing.

Yes, I suppose I did now. And he was right, I didn't want to give up that information. I'd spent weeks sneaking around that house to gather intel for my big heist. The man who lived there was one of the king's lords which meant that there were a lot of valuable artifacts to steal. In particular, I had my eye on some very expensive pieces of jewelry that Lord Eberbach kept there for his mistresses. They were perfect: valuable, easy to transport, and quick to fence. If someone else hit that place, my chances of ever stealing them would decrease mightily. Even if this funny but deadly thief didn't steal them for himself, they'd most likely be moved somewhere else, somewhere more secure, after the heist.

Gods damn it. I briefly considered lying about the intel just to get him caught but then I remembered his earlier warning about being able to tell if I was lying. I still wasn't sure if that soul-penetrating gaze really could tell if I was lying or not, I am a highly proficient liar, I'll have you know, but I decided that this probably wasn't the time to test it out. So, I caved and told him everything. I shared my information about the guards, dogs, and other external alarms, and finally about Lord Eberbach's schedule and that of his mistresses.

"Anything else?" the mysterious thief asked casually after I'd finished speaking.

I hesitated for a moment, trying to make up my mind. His intelligent eyes studied me closely. At last, I blew out an exasperated breath and decided that if he was the one who'd get to hit it, he might as well do a thorough job. "There's a hidden safe under the floorboards in the bedroom on the second floor. To the left of the bed between the bedside table and the dresser."

He actually looked genuinely surprised. It was almost worth sharing all my intel just to see that look on his face. Almost.

"Thank you," he nodded. "That was all the information I needed."

Reality came crashing back. Oh, right. Wall. Sword. Throat. Death threats. As much as I'd tried to imagine my situation differently these last couple of minutes, the painful truth was that I was still completely at the mercy of a dangerous man I knew nothing about. Well, apart from the obvious fact that he was also part of the Underworld. The only problem was, I didn't know if he followed our code or not. I mean, we're all thieves, thugs, murderers, beggars, and whores so, naturally, rules aren't really our thing. Even I only half-follow the code, and mostly only when it suits me. Come on, why do you think we became part of the Underworld in the first place?

Anyway, we only really have two rules. The first one is: respect the guilds. That basically means follow the guild rules, don't start guild wars, and show submission to the guild leaders. Though, I wasn't sure how that rule would help improve my current situation. The second rule is that we never treat each other the way that the upperworlders treat us. Very ambiguous, I know. While that might be true within the guilds, because it falls under the first rule to respect the guild, most underworlders still steal, threaten, blackmail, and kill each other across the guilds. Honor, in that sense at least, is very rare among our people. Everyone follows the first rule. Fewer people than I care to admit follow the second. So, my chances of having been ambushed by one of the few people who actually did, were quite slim.

"So, what now?" I asked because I couldn't endure the uncertainty any longer.

"Unfortunately, I can't have you running around." He removed his left hand from the wall and put it in his pocket. The sword stayed at my throat. "You might mess up my plan."

"I won't, I swear," I said, trying to keep from sounding too desperate. "If you let me leave, I'll just go home and pretend that this never happened."

He smiled a lopsided smile. "Sorry, Storm, I can't do that. You put up one hell of a fight, though. Rain would've been proud."

The realization of what he'd said hit me like a brick in the face. As my mouth fell open from the shock of hearing him say that name, he blew a dark purple powder in my face. The sandy substance lodged itself in my throat and brought on a violent coughing fit. Making such a rookie move as breathing in a mysterious powder that someone threw in my face was beyond embarrassing, but after tonight's events it was simply impossible to keep a level head. Rain. I hadn't heard that name in years. How could he possibly have known Rain? Did he know what I'd done? He couldn't. Shouldn't. My thoughts were getting all tangled up. A prickling sensation spread through my hands.

Gods damn it. This was not the time to be worrying about what this murderous thief may or may not know. I could figure that out tomorrow. Well, that is, if there was a tomorrow. Shit. This could end really badly. Black spots appeared in my vision, making it increasingly difficult to see. I sent a quick prayer to Nemanan, God of Thieves. I always left offerings on his altar and never asked for anything in return. Okay, almost never, anyway. Hoping I still had some goodwill left, I vowed to never make such a disgraceful rookie mistake again if he saw me through this. I couldn't feel my hands anymore. Or my arms. Or legs. The last thing I saw before my body gave out was the black, glittering eyes of the man who had outsmarted me.

7.

I awoke with a jolt. Before I even knew what I was doing, I was on my feet with a stiletto blade in each hand. I blinked. Where was I? The room around me was small, cold, and smelled of old vegetables. Light trickled in from underneath a stone door to my left. Where had I seen that stone door before? I stared bewildered at it for a couple of moments before it finally clicked. The stone door. The one in the dead end of Mercer Street. The cobwebs in my mind were swept away as if by a strong morning wind as everything finally made sense. Rage replaced my confusion. He had taken all of my equipment and locked me in the cellar! Bastard. I returned the stiletto blades to my sleeves and stalked to the door.

"Wait... my stiletto blades?" I mumbled.

I quickly got down on one knee and put a hand inside my boot. It was there as well. Striding the last few steps to the stone door, I couldn't for the life of me figure out why he'd returned all three of my knives before locking me in the cellar. I studied the ground in front of my feet. This was just getting more and more confusing. The door was locked, yes, but the key was on the ground in front of the door, as if someone had pushed it in from the outside. The key that could open the door. This made no sense whatsoever. What was this guy up to?

The lock moaned quietly as I turned the key. Before opening the door, I took out my stilettos again. A stone door this old was bound to make a lot of noise, so it was better to be quick about it. I yanked the door open and was met by blinding sunlight. The glare made me blink furiously while my eyes adjusted to the light. Empty. The dead end at Mercer Street was completely empty. My mind reeled. He'd had me at sword point. This night could've ended ridiculously badly. And yet, here I was: alive, unharmed, free, even armed.

I took off at a run as my mind tried to make sense of it all. Alleys, streets, and houses flew by as I tried to figure out if I thoroughly hated him for teaching me a lesson, or three, in humility and making me give up all my hard-earned intel or if I was grateful to him for not doing worse to me. And, whether I was impressed by him for being able to ambush me or terrified of him for the exact same reason. I reached the Thieves' Guild before I could decide whether to thank him or break his jaw if I ever saw him again.

"Hey, congrats on your successful heist, Storm," Bones said as he opened the door after our customary exchange of passwords.

"What?" I answered, perplexed.

"Well, you know, Lord Eberbach's mansion..." he continued, uncertainty creeping into his rumbling voice. "I overheard some Silver Cloaks talking when I was on my lunch break. Unless it wasn't...?"

The thunderous look in my eye stopped him from finishing that sentence. That good-for-nothing, stealing, ambushing forger. He had already hit it. Well, there went my chance at a hasty comeback. I threw a quick glance at Bones. He seemed to have understood the gist of it without any further explanation. One of the best things about our robust gatekeeper is that he doesn't pry. He neither pushed the matter nor looked at me with pity, but instead simply patted my shoulder once and then turned his attention back to the door. As I started down the stairs, I added a mental note to buy him an ale sometime. While winding my way through the passageways of the Thieves' Guild, I thought about my present situation. Everyone in the guild knew I'd been casing that place for weeks since I had specifically told them to steer clear of it. Word was bound to get out sooner rather than later that someone else had beat me to it. This was beyond embarrassing.

"Whoa!"

I'd been so absorbed with trying to come up with a solution that I'd run straight into Jester, who had come around the corner without me realizing it. As his name suggests, he's a jokester, and frankly, I'd always found him annoying, so I didn't even dignify his exclamation with a reply. Instead, I simply pushed him off me and started out again.

"I heard someone else beat you to your grand prize," he said mockingly.

Did I mention that he's also the biggest gossip in the guild? However, I'd had more than enough confrontation for one day so I decided to let his insolence slide. Just this once.

"Oh how the mighty have fallen," he called after me and chuckled.

My body moved before my mind had time to fully process. A loud bang echoed through the halls as I slammed his body into the wall. With one hand around his neck and the other curled around a stiletto, I heard myself spew threats in his face.

"You're very fond of that tongue, aren't you?" I traced the rim of his lips with the glittering point of the blade. "If you ever talk to me like that again, I will have it removed."

Jester licked his lips nervously. I was debating internally whether to follow through on that very threat tonight, and save me some trouble in the future, when I felt a hand on my shoulder.

"I'm sure he's very sorry for his rudeness, please put the knife down," an oddly familiar voice said behind me.

I turned to look and nearly dropped my blade in surprise. "Rogue?"

The rogue thief I'd tracked down for the Masters a week ago smiled self-consciously and scratched the back of his blond head with his hand.

"Yes, I guess that's as good a name as any..." He blushed and laughed softly.

"What are you doing here?" I asked, completely befuddled.

His face broke into a boyish grin. "I pulled it off! I stole the Midnight Star. It actually wasn't all that hard to steal." His face scrunched up in thought. "I think the fact that everyone thought it was ridiculously difficult to steal was actually the main part of the Admiral's security system. Anyway, the Guild Masters let me stay! I'm a real member of the Thieves' Guild now," he beamed.

I blinked at him in stunned silence. This boy. This boy had pulled off a heist that not a thief in the city had dared try before. This inexperienced kid. And I couldn't even manage to rob some mediocre lord's mansion. My confidence hit the floor like a fat man's palanquin. What was I even doing? I opened my mouth and then closed it again. Before I could figure out an appropriate reply to the boy's incredibly unexpected statement, I heard running footsteps approach. Liam rounded the corner and skidded to a halt.

"Storm?" His concerned blue eyes flicked from the knife in my hand to Jester's terrified expression against the wall to Rogue's happy smile before finally settling on me. "Is everything alright?"

"Uhm... yeah," I replied, shot one last murderous look at Jester, who shrank back against the wall, and then slowly returned the stiletto to my sleeve.

Liam raised his eyebrows at me but I just shook my head. After one last look at the odd scene in front of him, he turned to leave. Shaking off the uncomfortable feelings that had gathered in the pit of my stomach, I started out as well.

"Welcome to the Thieves' Guild," I muttered to the blue-eyed former rogue as I pushed past him and followed Liam out of the hall.

8.

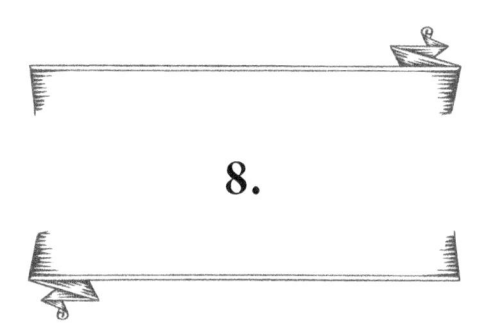

The cool night air caressed my face as I jogged across the rooftops. I had survived the Thieves' Guild's discovery of my miserable failure. Maybe that big gossip's accursed tongue had finally worked in my favor. After our confrontation in the hallway, no one had brought it up, not even the Guild Masters. I was very thankful for that because I didn't want to divulge the exact details of how it had happened. If I did, the Guild Masters would have questions and I was in no mood for tracking down another rogue thief. Especially not him. Also, it was too embarrassing. Only Liam knew and he'd never hold it against me. I, on the other hand, very much held it against me. It had taken me an entire week of grueling physical training and target practice to get my head straight again. After that, I'd spent another couple of weeks pulling off smaller heists. I'd told myself that it was because I needed to stock up on some more coin for my guild rates but the truth is that I did it because I needed to make myself feel better. Pathetic, isn't it? Anyway, now I was hunting for my next target, which is why I found myself on the Thieves' Highway this particular night.

Apart from the soft thudding of my feet against the roof tiles and the whisper of the wind, the night had been quiet so far. All the unsuspecting potential victims were sleeping peacefully in their locked-up houses. Even the patrolling Silver Cloaks were few and far between tonight. Just as I was about to cross into the Artisan District, raised voices broke the night's silent spell.

"Well would ya look at that?" a man's voice roared. "The Admiral's gonna be so happy to see ya."

The Admiral? I'd been about to run past without even bothering to look but that name stopped me in my tracks. Rogue did steal the Midnight Star from him some weeks past and I found it unlikely that he would forgive, or forget, such a grievous offense. What if it was Rogue they'd cornered? That boy was still green enough that he might sell out the guild to save his own skin. Better check it out. I crept towards the edge of the roof to my left as the voices continued.

"Imagine finding you here, alone and unarmed," another man's voice chimed in.

"Must be our lucky night."

"Did the Admiral say if he wanted him dead or alive?"

"Ya know what, Ned? I think he said either way's good."

I finally reached the edge as the men broke into a triumphant laugh. My pupils dilated in shock. The good-for-nothing, stealing, ambushing forger stood there in the middle of the alley. My mind did double time as I tried to make sense of the scene before me. His skin-tight black shirt sported multiple slashes, he was barefoot, and his curved short swords were missing. He looked markedly disheveled. It was such an odd look on someone I knew to be incredibly powerful. However, that wasn't the strangest part of the scene. The black-haired thief was surrounded by four men with raised pistols. How in Nemanan's name had a man so skilled in the art of sneaking and fighting ended up in such a vulnerable position? Ha! Served him right.

That was what he got for acting all high and mighty with me. His luck had finally come back to bite him.

"Well, seeing as it's much, much easier to carry him when he's not alive to fight back, I think the choice is pretty simple," one of the two men with their backs towards me announced.

Wait. I wanted to break his jaw, not watch him get killed. Or did I want to thank him? And what about the secret of Rain? Maybe I did want to kill him?

Four guns were cocked down in the alley.

"Say goodbye."

Four projectiles whistled through the air. No loud bangs were heard, though. Weird. Why had there been no loud noise? There should've been.

The four armed men collapsed, almost simultaneously. A clatter of weapons and armor, mixed with the dull thudding of body parts hitting stone, filled the night. I squinted at the scene as the bodies went down. Had I imagined the short gurgling sounds? As realization hit me, my hands flew up to my shoulder holsters. Four gleaming knives protruded from the now dead men's throats. My knives. Shit. I'd thrown them before I even knew what I was doing. And now I needed them back. Crap. I gave myself a mental slap before quickly scrambling down the side of the building.

As I emerged from the shadows, I realized that the disheveled fighter was still standing there in the middle of the Admiral's fallen men. His confused eyes widened as they found mine.

"You...?" he spluttered.

I deliberately avoided his eyes as I kept striding forward. He bent down, snatched up one of the dead men's pistols, and leveled it at me with a, considering the situation, surprisingly steady hand. I stopped advancing and rolled my eyes at him.

"Oh come on... if I wanted you dead, you would be already," I said and motioned exasperatedly at the four lifeless bodies by his feet.

His eyes narrowed as he seemed to consider this for a moment. Finally, he tilted his head to the side and shrugged one shoulder by way of admitting that I did have a point. He lowered the gun but didn't drop it. I started advancing again anyway.

"Why? Why did you do it?" he asked as I reached the first body.

I yanked the knife from the man's throat and wiped it on his pant leg. Returning it to its holster, I stepped over the body to the next man. "I'm just retrieving my throwing knives. They're very valuable, you know," I said and pulled out the second one.

Casting a glance at him from the corner of my eye, I continued towards the third. His brow was furrowed and he looked thoroughly puzzled.

"Why did you save me?" he persisted.

That was a good question. Why had I saved him? I didn't owe him anything. In fact, if anything, he owed me for stealing my intel. What's more, if I hadn't saved him, the secret of Rain would probably have died with him. So why had I felt so horrified when I realized he was about to die? Well, he hadn't killed me the last time we met. That wasn't much of an answer, though.

I had returned my fourth and final throwing knife to its proper place before I'd formulated a coherent reason. So, instead of speaking my jumbled thoughts out loud, I ignored the question and switched topic. "Exactly two minutes after that clock strikes two-thirty, which should be any minute now, a Silver Cloak passes by this alley."

He answered by giving me a bewildered stare.

"If I were you, I would've made myself scarce by then."

Just as I had finished giving him my unsolicited advice, the clock struck two-thirty. When he, by force of habit, turned to look, I saw my chance. Sprinting silently, I disappeared back into the shadows.

Half a minute later, from atop the roof where this unexpected encounter had begun, I watched him quickly search through the dead men's pockets. Coins jingled as they hit the street. He threw a worried look over his shoulder just as he pulled out a folded piece of paper from the pocket of dead thug number four. Heavy footsteps sounded up the alley. The black-clad ambusher shoved the paper in his own pocket and took off in the other direction. By the time the royal guard in his billowing silver cloak passed by the mouth of the alley, the darkness had swallowed us both.

9.

"...And then I just took off along the Thieves' Highway again," I finished and set my mug down.

A pleasant, warm feeling spread through my stomach. The group to my right roared in laughter and slapped the top of the sturdy wooden table at some unheard joke. At the Mad Archer, my worries always seemed less severe.

"Hmm... I wonder who he is," Liam mused.

"Yeah, me too."

"So do you know why you–" he began.

"Saved him?" I filled in, because I had anticipated his question. "Nope, still haven't figured that part out," I answered honestly and rested the back of my head against the wooden wall.

"Hmm."

We stayed like that, in comfortable silence, listening to the merriment around us. As I studied the room, I realized that everyone here tonight was a guild member. My mouth drew into a half-smile. Who'd have thought thieves could be such a cheerful lot? I continued observing the room, this sanctuary that Barrel provided, with an even warmer feeling in my stomach. After a while, a tall, broad-shouldered man with a shaved head walked through the door. Bones. I still owed him that drink.

"Give me a sec," I told Liam as I slipped into the crowd.

Since the guild members who saw me coming politely stepped out of my way, the Oncoming Storm and all that, you know, I reached the muscled gatekeeper before he'd made it to the bar.

"Bones!" I called before realizing that I had no idea what to do now.

"Oh, hello, Storm," he replied with a surprised look on his face.

Shit. What was I supposed to do now? Of course he was surprised, I'd never done anything like this before. Hell, even I was surprised. This was so out of character for me that I had no frame of reference to go by. I had absolutely no idea how gestures like these were made, so in the end, I decided to just wing it.

"I owe you a drink," I simply informed him because being straight to the point is, on the other hand, very much in character for me.

He raised both eyebrows. I hadn't thought it possible for him to look even more surprised than before. I was wrong.

"Uhm... okay," he replied hesitantly.

I wanted to give myself a high-five. In the face. With a chair. Why was I so incredibly awkward? I had lied and conned my way out of Silver Cloak interrogations at gunpoint, unplanned encounters with lords and ladies of the court, and even out of some trouble with the Masters of the Bashers' Guild. So, why was it so difficult to make a friendly, socially acceptable gesture of gratitude? Ridiculous.

"Join us?" I asked, more self-consciously than I'd wanted, and motioned in the direction of Liam's back.

Bones' gray eyes glanced from me, to Liam, and then back to me. A smile almost as broad as his shoulders spread across his lips.

"I'd love to," he said with sincerity.

Just like that, the awkwardness drained out of me and disappeared down the cracks in floorboards like spilled ale. I caught Barrel's attention and held up three fingers. He nodded in reply as I led Bones back towards our table.

If you thought Bones looked shocked, you should've seen the look on Liam's face when I rejoined our table with Bones and three mugs of ale. I thought his eyes were going to pop out of his head. That boy really needed to work on his poker face.

"Is it Stone Wall's shift now?" Liam asked once he'd gotten over the initial shock and Bones had seated himself in one of the two empty chairs at our table.

"Yeah, Stoney's got the door. I thought I'd grab a drink before I head back to the guild to sleep," the tall man now sitting next to me answered. "But it seems like a drink found *me* this time. To what do I owe this nice surprise?" He turned in his chair to peer at me.

I looked away and laughed uncomfortably. "The failed heist. At Lord Eberbach's mansion," I started and then turned back to meet his eyes. "There weren't a lot of things you could've done to make me feel better and a lot you could've said to make me feel worse, and you picked the one that was just what I needed. So... thanks."

He smiled a genuine smile. You know, one of those that actually reaches the eyes. "Anytime, Storm. Anytime."

I glanced away awkwardly again. What was I supposed to say now? How does one continue the conversation after someone says something like that? I didn't have a clue, and the warm and fuzzy look in his eye made me feel even more awkward. Thankfully, I didn't have to say anything as it was Bones who changed the topic.

"Speaking of, have you heard the news?"

"Not sure, what news?"

"Apparently, King Adrian had Lord Eberbach executed."

"What?" Liam and I exclaimed in unison.

"Wasn't Lord Eberbach one of the king's inner circle? Like, one of those really loyal types that he depended on for support? Why would he have him executed?" I continued, puzzled.

Bones took a big swig of his ale, wiped his mouth on the back of his hand, and leaned back in the chair. "Yeah, that's what everyone thought but apparently he was this huge traitor. The break-in was kind of a blessing for the king because in the investigation, or something afterwards, a ton of stuff was found in a secret safe that showed he'd been secretly working against the king."

"How do you know that?" a now familiar voice said to my right as Rogue proceeded to, uninvited, seat himself in the empty chair next to Liam.

"By all means... come join us, won't you?" I said sarcastically and rolled my eyes.

Rogue's young face went from showing curiosity to uncertainty. Both Liam and Bones gave me a disapproving look. I sighed and then waved my hand dismissively by way of telling him to disregard my previous comment.

"I know because I'm a gatekeeper. I'm like the bridge between our world and theirs. People leaving bring me news of what going on inside the guild and people coming let me know what's happening outside, both in the Underworld and Upperworld," Bones replied and shrugged his broad shoulders. "Simple as that."

"Wow! That's kinda cool. You must know a lot then," Rogue continued, face beaming.

Our steadfast gatekeeper laughed his rumbling laugh. "Only what people tell me."

"I hear things too," Rogue continued in an excited voice. "People say that you're like the best thief in the guild, Storm."

"Well, I won't argue with that," I said nonchalantly. Ha! So that was why he'd been so nice to me since he joined the guild – he was star-struck.

Bones' deep laugh filled the room once more. "You're right, I can think of no one better," he confirmed and then turned to me with one eyebrow raised. "Though her humility needs some work."

All three of my drinking companions chuckled at that and even I smiled a, only half-disgruntled, smile.

"And not only when it comes to stealing, people also say that you're like a really good assassin too, that you could've easily made a name for yourself in the Assassins' Guild," Rogue continued wide-eyed.

I felt Liam casting a sharp glance at me but all I could do was stare at the blond boy in stunned silence. So, people had been talking quite a bit about me, it would seem. Bones didn't seem to notice the odd looks that passed over both our faces. He simply smiled and confirmed the description.

"Yeah, like I said, this girl here is the best of the best." He downed the last of his drink and then stood up. "Gotta head back. Thanks for the drink, Storm," he said and put a hand on my shoulder. "Let's do it again sometime, yeah?"

I shook off the uncomfortable feeling in my stomach and managed a smile and a nod.

"See you, Bones," Liam said and lifted a hand in goodbye as the gatekeeper turned to leave. He raised his hand in acknowledgement while his broad back moved further into the throng.

"So, what now?" Rogue asked enthusiastically once Bones had disappeared through the door.

Liam and I exchanged glances. Rogue only kept looking at us like an excited puppy. Not much social skills on that one. Alright, I'm not really one to talk either, I know. But honestly, didn't he know how to take a hint?

"Maybe we should head back too?" Liam said diplomatically before I could demonstrate the extent of my own social graces.

I finished my drink in a rather unladylike manner and pushed to my feet. "Yeah."

"It was good to see you, Rogue," Liam said and looked at me expectantly, as if hoping I would add to that statement.

I simply stared back at him blankly. What? The boy had butted in on a conversation that was none of his business and joined us at our table uninvited. What's more, his nosy questions had made me feel things I didn't want to feel. So, no, it hadn't been good to see him. When the silence stretched on, Liam gave the boy an awkward smile. I just sighed and I started out.

"Well, uhm, see you around," my much more socially skilled friend called over his shoulder, and followed me out the door.

10.

Sunlight and brisk morning air greeted us as we exited the Mad Archer. Liam started walking towards the Thieves' Guild but I lingered outside the doorway.

"Aren't you coming?" he turned around and called once he realized that I hadn't followed.

"No," I said but stepped a little closer so that we wouldn't have to shout. "I'm gonna take a walk. Need to clear my head."

I was troubled by what Rogue had said inside. I didn't know what I thought about the fact that people were talking, quite freely, about my more murderous side.

"It's daylight," Liam stated.

"I know. I'm not gonna do anything that draws attention, just walk around," I assured him.

"Would you at least come back with me and put on all your knives before you head off?"

"Yeah, because that wouldn't draw attention..." I said, my voice dripping with sarcasm. "I'll be fine. I have my boot knife and like I said, I'm just gonna be strolling about like a normal, law-abiding citizen."

"Hmmph! You don't have a law-abiding bone in your body," I heard Liam mutter as I turned and strode away. "And there's nothing normal about you!" he called after me.

I just smiled and waved at him. He stalked back towards the guild as I continued into the world of normal, law-abiding people doing normal, law-abiding stuff.

As I moved through the Merchants' Quarter, I watched traders go about their morning routine. Shopfronts were unlocked, shutters were pulled from windows, and valuable goods were put back on display. Food vendors rolled their carts into place and secured colorful fabric on top to protect against the sun. People chattering and the smell of food filled the air. I swiped a warm meat pie off one of the carts, savoring it as I walked, and pondered the news I'd received.

Having people be cautious of me did serve me well. No one bothered me with unnecessary crap and when they did need to talk to me, they were always polite. I liked that. If it was common knowledge that I was good at killing, it would most certainly help build upon my reputation as the Oncoming Storm, and I did like that name. It's got a nice ring to it. However, having people be cautious of you was one thing. Having people be outright afraid of you was quite another. I had left the Merchants' Quarter behind and was halfway through the Marble Ring before I'd come to the decision that it was still better to be feared and respected than to be seen as weak. That was not the end of my worries, though. If the Assassins' Guild found out about this, I could end up in a world of trouble.

Killing people, as a member of another guild, isn't prohibited as such. However, if word reaches the assassins that someone outside their guild is skilled in the noble art of assassination, they might interpret that as an attempt at branching out. That, on the other hand, is strictly prohibited and earns the person a black mark. Needless to say, avoiding that is definitely a priority. But the risk of them finding out is slight since friendships are rare across the Underworld guilds in general and with the Assassins' Guild in particular. Fear of being murdered and friendship isn't exactly a winning combination.

Fortunately for me, that meant gossip was unlikely to travel from our guild to theirs. As I crossed into Worker's End, I decided that I really had nothing to worry about. No group of assassins was going to suddenly ambush me and demand answers. With that settled, I decided that I needed to begin heading back before Liam started to worry. Alright, started to worry *too* much. Just as I was about to turn around, two cloaked figures dropped down in front of me.

I went for the knife in my boot while hearing several more people land on the street. When I straightened, knife in hand, and looked around, I realized that I was royally screwed. Fuck. I'd jinxed it. Why did I have to jinx it? This was it, I was done for.

Surrounding me were no fewer than twelve members of the Assassins' Guild. What was worse, it wasn't just any members, they were all wearing their blood red cloaks. These were not assassins that were here of their own volition, they'd been sent on an official mission by their Guild Master and thus wore their cloaks of office. Shit. Very carefully, I dropped the knife and raised my hands.

"I haven't been poaching, or trespassing, I swear," I tried to assure them in as steady a voice as I could manage.

They didn't answer. Instead, they just continued staring at me from under their blood red hoods. My mind spun as I tried to assess the situation. They hadn't killed me on the spot, which was good. Or, wait? Was it? Well, in terms of longevity, yes, but in terms of suffering, maybe not. What if they'd decided to make an example of me? But for what, I hadn't actually done anything. Yet.

My rather inconclusive assessment didn't get any further than that before the assassins in front of me stepped aside to allow a thirteenth figure to pass.

"You?" I exclaimed in utter astonishment and dropped my hands.

It was the forging, ambushing thief. His ruined clothes and confused face from the night before were replaced by new, pristine ones and a look of calm composure. If I'd had trouble putting together a coherent thought before, this almost made my head explode.

"Okay, enough," I said before that actually happened. "I have no idea who you are or why you keep showing up in the most unexpected of situations but you're obviously *someone* if you can secure a contract for twelve assassins from the Master of the Assassins' Guild. So, who are you?" I demanded.

He laughed his pleasant-sounding laugh and cocked his head slightly to the right. "You really don't know who I am, do you?"

"No. I thought that my previous sentence made that abundantly clear. So, how about it? Care to enlighten me?" I answered in an annoyed voice.

With one snap of his fingers, all twelve assassins produced pistols that they proceeded to level at me. Hands raised high again, I swallowed.

"Seeing as I'm the one doing the ambushing, *again*, I'll be the one asking the questions. And I want answers," he said with authority. "Clear?"

I nodded.

"Good. Now correct me if I'm wrong but the first time we met, you were in a similar position. I ambushed you, fought, and beat you, and forced you to give up information that you didn't want to give up. Then, I knocked you out and locked you in a cellar. Did I forget anything?"

"You also threatened to kill me," I muttered sourly.

"Yes, I did do that, didn't I?" He laughed softly before continuing in a more serious voice. "Then, the next time we met, which was yesterday, the situation was completely reversed. I was surrounded and unarmed and about one second away from being executed when my four would-be murderers suddenly dropped dead in front of me. And, lo and behold, out of the shadows, you appear."

I let out a half-chuckle at that.

He continued staring at me with a genuinely puzzled expression in his intelligent eyes. "Now, I want an answer to the question I asked you then: why did you save me? You owed me nothing. So, why did you do it?" he finished and held my gaze.

"I was just retrieving my throwing knives. They're very–"

"Valuable," he finished. "I know, you said. That's not an answer."

I exhaled slowly. There was no point in lying. During my walk, I had actually figured out why I'd saved him. It was a good reason too, but it was also such an awkward thing to say out loud.

"Honor," I blurted out. "I didn't answer you yesterday because I didn't know why at the time. Trust me, back then, I was just as surprised as you were that I'd gotten involved. But I finally figured it out, only a little while ago, actually." I pushed a loose strand of hair out of my face and then crossed my arms in front of my chest. "I saved you because you have honor. Yes, you ambushed me and stole my intel and all that, but that's kind of what we do in the Underworld. What you did do that was rare was to do no more harm than absolutely necessary to accomplish your task. You didn't leave me knocked out in the alley for anyone to take advantage, and you even returned my weapons. Honor, that kind of honor, is rare. I just didn't want it to disappear, that's all," I finished in little more than one breath.

He looked at me with unreadable black eyes. I glanced away and instead occupied myself with trying to dislodge a piece of stone with the toe of my boot.

"I see," he said at last and motioned for the assassins surrounding us to lower their weapons. "You really are an interesting one, aren't you? Alright, I will answer your question as well. You want to know who I am?"

I looked up sharply.

"Shade," he said.

That one word made my entire worldview shatter like a broken mirror. It couldn't be. It couldn't possibly be.

"*The* Shade?" I breathed.

He smiled his lopsided smile and nodded. I immediately dropped to one knee with one arm across and the other on the ground and bowed my head. The Underworld's universal sign of respect. Shit. In my head, I tried to count the number of times that I'd been rude to him during our three encounters. The best I could come up with was: a lot.

"Please forgive my rudeness," I said. "If I'd known I was addressing the Master of the Assassins' Guild, I would never have been so disrespectful. Please accept my sincerest apologies."

I closed my eyes. What had I gotten myself into? My own Guild Masters showed respect to even the lowliest of the

Assassins' Guild and here I was, a mere member of the Thieves' Guild, being disrespectful to the most powerful man in the Underworld, arguably in the whole city.

"Look at me," he said.

I complied. When I met his eyes, they were softer than I'd thought they would be.

"Apology accepted. On account of saving my life and all," he continued and gave me a small smile. "Well then, I'd better get going." He turned around.

"Wait!" I called and got to my feet.

I don't know what gave me the courage to try and tell a Master of the Assassins' Guild what to do, but there was one question that was still burning in my mind.

"How do you know about Rain?" I asked desperately.

He stopped in his tracks and turned towards me again. That unreadable look was back in his eyes. "I was the one sent to investigate."

Shit. How much did the Assassins' Guild know about this? They couldn't know the whole story. I was the only one left who knew the full story. As if reading my mind, the black-clad assassin continued.

"Did you really think that much death, and in such a noteworthy way, wouldn't draw the guild's attention?"

"I guess not." I allowed myself a small mental sigh. That still wasn't enough to land me in deep trouble.

"I found the survivor."

At that, my stomach dropped. A feeling as cold as death spread through my whole body. I stared at him in wide-eyed shock. "What? What survivor?"

"One of the girls. She survived. I found her and she told me everything. Then, I just filled in the blanks," he said in a voice that betrayed no emotion.

My mouth felt like it was filled with dry sand. Blood pounded in my ears. "I see," I said carefully. "Why was I not black-marked?"

"Because of the... unusual circumstances, we decided to let your transgression slide. Be careful though, we won't forgive a second time. Now, go back to Liam before he starts worrying too much."

Rain, my fear, and the whole situation was swept right out of my mind as that last remark summoned a storm in my eyes. What did he mean by that? If that was a threat, I would destroy him. No one threatened Liam. I was about to open my mouth and inform him of that when I saw the expression on his face. He must've seen the storm raging in my eyes because his face had that same come-try-it look as that first night when he'd faced me with his swords. I was promptly reminded of the situation I was in and dropped my eyes.

"I understand," I said instead, furiously trying to bank the roaring thunder inside.

"Goodbye, the Oncoming Storm," he replied.

A soft rustle of clothing was all that marked the Assassins' Guild's withdrawal. When the last blood red cloak had disappeared into the morning, I heaved a deep sigh of relief. I tilted my face up towards the sun beams that had found their way into Keutunan's main residential area. If every day was as nerve-racking as this, my dark brown hair would soon turn gray. I shook off the feeling. It was high time to head home before more trouble decided to come find me.

11.

Deciding not to push my luck any further, I took a detour east through Worker's End instead of heading back via the Marble Ring again. Worker's End is more or less empty at this time of day since it houses the main portion of the city's ordinary, working citizens. The Marble Ring that circles the Silver Keep is, on the other hand, home to the noble and the wealthy who don't need to work and thus can stay at home all day. Running into Silver Cloaks is far more likely there than here.

While I walked, I pondered the events that had unfolded this morning. On the downside, I'd found out that I had, on no less than three separate occasions, been rude to the most powerful and deadly man in the city. That was bad. I'd also been made aware of the fact that the Assassins' Guild could apparently find and ambush me whenever they wanted. That was really bad. Furthermore, I'd been informed that the assassins knew about that night with Rain and the others. That was really super bad.

On a more positive note, however, I'd finally found out who the mysterious, black-haired, thieving forger was. That was good. I'd also realized that I'd saved the life of the Master of the Assassins' Guild. That was really good. If I ever needed help, like, really needed help, I could always cash in that favor. Lastly, I'd come to the conclusion that I was still breathing, even though the Assassins' Guild had known about that night for the last nine years. If that couldn't be classified as really super good, then I don't know what could.

So, all in all, I guess the scales were pretty well-balanced. As I rounded the corner of the last street separating Worker's End from the Merchants' Quarter, I concluded that maybe Cadentia, Goddess of Luck, had my back after all.

Or not. An entire squad of Silver Cloaks waited for me around that corner. I narrowly prevented myself from stopping dead in the street upon realizing that and instead forced myself to continue forward, but in a slower pace. I gave Lady Luck an internal eye roll.

Oh Cadentia, you can be such a bitch. Alright, calm down. Today, you're just a normal, law-abiding citizen doing normal, law-abiding stuff. I adopted a leisurely gait and schooled my features into a carefree expression.

The royal guards were leaning against the walls ahead of me, talking and resting. They didn't seem to be on high alert. However, I was still troubled. Not for my own sake, mind you, I've conned my way out of situations like this more times than I can count.

No, what troubled me was this location. We were alarmingly close to the Thieves' Guild, and the thing that made it even worse was that they were on this particular street. When returning to the guild, both from Worker's End and the Marble Ring, this was the most logical route to take. It might just have been an unfortunate coincidence but I'm too much of a paranoid pessimist to believe in such things.

I was almost on top of them now. They fell silent as I approached. I watched their hands: most of them rested lightly on their swords. I kept the carefree look on my face. Just as I passed between the two rows of armed men lounging against the walls, one of them looked up and met my eyes.

"Morning," he grunted.

"Good morning," I nodded back.

All hell broke loose. The distinct ringing of swords being pulled from scabbards and the clanking of armor filled the morning as the eight Silver Cloaks launched themselves off the walls and swarmed in on me.

During those precious few seconds, a dozen or so thoughts and plans had passed through my head and been discarded. Surprise, irritation, and anger had been the first three. Fighting and running had presented themselves as logical options but were swiftly discarded given the fact that I was already surrounded and only had a boot knife with which to defend myself.

In the end, I settled for lying. I transformed my face into one of a scared, innocent girl and put my hands up.

"Please don't hurt me," I said in a high-pitched voice. I even added a tremor in it for maximum effect.

The men now surrounding me with raised swords faltered a little. *Got you now.* I made my eyes tear up a little.

"I'm sorry if I disturbed you or did something wrong. I didn't know. I was just on my way to the market to buy some food for my mom," I lied in a masterfully weak and frightened voice.

Confused and uncertain looks passed between the guards.

"She's sick and couldn't go herself so she asked me," I continued and let a couple of tears fall down my cheeks. "Am I not allowed to use this street? I'm sorry, I didn't know."

Some of the Silver Cloaks started to lower their swords.

"She's just a little girl."

"Did we make a mistake?"

"You're scaring her."

"This can't be her. She's not the one we're looking for."

This was it. A couple of seconds more and they'd have convinced themselves that I was just a scared, innocent girl. I kept my eyes looking terrified and bewildered. The murmur continued. I counted down the seconds in my head. *And three, two...*

"Don't be fooled, this is her!" the captain of the squad yelled forcefully. All eight swords were raised again.

I blinked in surprised. How in Nemanan's name had that not worked? That always worked.

"Remember, she's a master liar. And we were given a detailed description of what she looks like, even down to the clothes she's wearing today, and that she would be coming by this road. This is her. Don't be fooled," he continued.

A detailed description? So, someone had known both my whereabouts and what I looked like. This was trouble. I dropped my hands, let my face project the irritation I truly felt, and allowed the annoyed note back in my voice.

"So, it would seem I've been betrayed. By who?" I demanded with enough authority that one of the guards actually looked about ready to answer.

"Told you," the captain said to his men with a triumphant smile, ignoring my question.

With one jerk of his head, they all descended on me. Given my exposed position there really wasn't much I could to. I fought back as best as I could but eventually the hilt of a sword connected with the base of my skull. I heard the crack more than I felt it. The world tilted dangerously and as the street rose up to meet my face, the brisk morning was replaced by oppressive darkness.

12.

Cold water hit my face. I coughed furiously and tried to wipe the water from my eyes, only to realize that my arms were restrained behind my back. Filing that discovery under the slightly-annoying-things category in the scheming part of my brain, I decided that I'd deal with that snafu in a minute. I shook my head violently and blinked the remaining water from my eyes. Men snickered around me.

"She looks just like an animal shaking water from its fur."

"Yeah, just like the filthy street rat she truly is."

With the water gone from my eyes, I took in the scene around me. My hands and feet were shackled and I was sitting on the floor of a vast hall with four Silver Cloaks around me. However, their cloaks weren't the only things made of silver in there. The floor and walls were smooth marble but all decorations were made of that gleaming metal. Side tables, candelabras, even the frames of the oil paintings on the wall were silver. I recognized the hallway. This was the Silver Keep. *Crap*. Rough hands grabbed me by the shoulders and hauled me to my feet.

"Get moving!" one of the guards shouted and gave me a hard shove between the shoulder blades.

I tried to take a long step forward to steady myself but the chain between my ankles wasn't long enough. Before I'd realized that, however, I'd tripped over it and fallen hard on the floor. The men laughed again. As they once again dragged me to my feet, I made careful note of their faces. Once this was over, they would all meet the God of Death.

We made slow but steady progress along the marble hall. I had instantly recognized this hallway because I'd been here before. Mostly, I'd stalked in the shadows of this place to steal stuff, but sometimes I came just to snoop. Like that time when I'd snuck in to read the royal historians' books. The more you know about your enemy, the easier it is to outsmart them. However, it would seem as though I was the one who'd been outsmarted this time. Or actually, outsmarted wasn't the right word. Betrayed. I had to find out by whom.

The grand, silver-speckled hall we'd followed ended in a gigantic marble arch. Beyond it was a vast room with a vaulted ceiling, in which hung a huge silver chandelier. On the floor along the walls there were rows of candelabras, all in silver, of course. At the end of the grand chamber, on top of a raised marble dais, was a black obsidian throne. As the guards led me through the marble arch and into the throne room, I saw that there were three people on that dais.

To the left of the throne stood a pale woman in a silver dress. Apart from her light brown hair, she looked to have been carved from the very marble that made up the Keep. Her face betrayed no emotions and her eyes looked straight through me as if neither she nor I were truly there. The figure to the right of the sturdy black seat of power was a boy who looked to be about Liam's age. His face was pale like his mother's, but as opposed to the living statue on the left, it revealed an abundance of emotions. Black eyes full of concern and discomfort flicked from me to the man sitting on the obsidian throne. King Adrian. He welcomed me with a haughty smirk as I was forced down on my knees at the foot of the dais.

I briefly thought about how different his black eyes were from Shade's. They were the same color, and yet not. The black in Shade's eyes were the comforting darkness of a warm, unlit room that hides you from your pursuers. King Adrian's eyes, on the other hand, were the black of a cold, moonless winter night that is slowly trying to freeze you to death. I suppressed a shudder. Yes, that was exactly what his eyes looked like.

"How good of you to join us," he said with a voice that sounded just as arrogant as the expression he wore on his face.

"Didn't have much of a choice, did I?" I retorted sourly.

Eyes that had turned as hard as his obsidian throne flicked towards one of the Silver Cloaks who had taken up position behind my back. For a moment, I felt the cold touch of steel against my cheek before it withdrew again.

"Watch that tongue," was all the king said.

Yeah, alright. This probably wasn't the best time to be a smartmouth, I know, but I just can't help myself sometimes. I really had to play this smarter. This was the king, after all.

"In case you were wondering, this is my wife, Queen Charlotte, and my son, Crown Prince Edward," he said and gave a nonchalant wave by way of introduction.

In case I was wondering? I was very tempted to say something snarky in reply. I mean, come on, I could obviously see that. Crown Prince Edward had the same pale complexion as his mother and the same eye color as his father. Both he and the king also had the same thick, glossy, black hair. And even if I could somehow have missed all of that, they all wore crowns on their heads, though of different sizes and designs. You would have to have been a complete idiot to miss the fact that this was the royal family. I pushed a very rude reply out of my mind.

"Honored to meet you," I said instead, and nodded to the two silent royals beside the throne, because I didn't actually have a score to settle with them. Yet.

Queen Charlotte's gray eyes kept staring straight through me and Edward's facial expression went from concern and discomfort to looking almost apologetic. Such an odd bunch.

"I want you to do a job for me," King Adrian stated now that the somewhat redundant introductions were out of the way.

"I work for no one but myself," I answered automatically.

And there I was again, not playing it smart. Idiot.

The king tilted his head to the right while amusement spread across his face. "I have been told as much. I have also been told that you are the perfect person for this kind of job, so I am going to make you do it anyway."

"I'd like to see you try," I replied with narrowed eyes.

What? I had already charged headfirst down the not-playing-it-smart path and it was too late to turn back now so I might as well see where this idiotic road led.

King Adrian smiled with a vicious sparkle in his eyes. "Oh I intend to." He raised his voice and called over my head. "Ah, there you are, come join us!"

"You summoned me, Your Majesty?" a terrifyingly familiar voice answered somewhere behind me.

I whipped my head around and stared at the black-clad assassin striding towards us. Shade. I could almost smell the smoke billowing out of my brain as I tried to make sense of it. What in Nemanan's name was he doing here? And why was he greeting the king as a loyal subordinate would? Wait. The rumors. There had always been rumors that the Assassins' Guild had ties to the royal family. I'd just never believed that they were actually true. As the deadly Guild Master reached the dais and came to a halt a little to my left, the next lightning bolt struck.

"You son of a bitch!" I yelled as I tried to get to my feet. "You're the one who set me up!" I continued shouting as I fought against the strong hands now clamped on my shoulders.

Of course it had been no coincidence that I'd met him right before being ambushed by the guards who had both a detailed description of my face and my clothes as well as knowledge about which route I would take. That back-stabbing, double-dealing piece of shit!

King Adrian's eyes watched me in amusement but Shade didn't even look at me.

"What do you require, sire?" he asked instead.

"I need you to get to work on this street rat. I need her compliant by tomorrow."

I stopped struggling as the king's words sank in. He wanted to torture me into submission and who better for the task than a Master of the Assassins' Guild. Great. Just great.

"Of course, Your Majesty. However, first I have to attend to the other task you assigned me. I will return at midnight."

"Hmm... yes, yes, I suppose that will still be plenty of time," the king answered while stroking his chin. "I will get some of the guards to soften her up until you arrive."

When the queen continued looking like a statue, and the crown prince started looking even more uncomfortable, and Shade said nothing, the king finally flicked his wrist.

"Dismissed," he said with authority.

Shade bowed low before retreating from the room. I shot venomous glances at him when he passed me but I wasn't sure if he saw them since he kept his eyes fixed on the marble arch.

"You are in for a very long day," King Adrian stated maliciously when Shade had disappeared into the hallway beyond. "You are going to beg for permission to serve me."

"I don't beg. For anything," I replied with a voice as hard as the marble beneath me.

He jerked his head. Armor clanked behind me. "We shall see about that," he promised with a smile as his guards dragged me away.

EVENING FOUND ME TIED to a whipping post. The day had started with some good old-fashioned beatings when the king's guards first had dragged me to this courtyard. However, since I'd grown up a scrawny kid on the streets of Keutunan, beatings were not exactly unfamiliar territory. Fortunately for me, it had taken the Silver Cloaks quite some time to come to the same conclusion. Once they'd realized that, though, they'd gotten a little more creative. Hence, my current predicament. I heard the lash whistle through the air before it made contact with my exposed back. A soft groan was all they'd been able to elicit from me and I intended to keep it that way.

"Beg," King Adrian commanded once more.

He had done so every time his guard's whip had struck and every time I had refused to comply. He was lounging in a chair in front of me with that customary arrogant look on his face. I wanted to slit his throat. Sipping fine ale from a bejeweled cup, he watched me receive each lash.

The whip cracked across my skin again. I simply let the pain flow through me and disappear into the dirt below my feet. The king was getting frustrated now. He threw the cup across the courtyard, pushed to his feet, and stalked towards me. With a firm grip on my throat he resorted to threats once again.

"You will submit," he said through gritted teeth. "When Shade gets back, you will submit."

I gave him an arrogant, blood-soaked smile in return. He backhanded me across the mouth and jerked his head.

"Take her away!" he shouted to his guards and stormed from the courtyard.

A couple of minutes later, I was thrown through a narrow doorway and onto a cold, wet, stone floor. The door to my cell banged metallically as the guards slammed it shut. The hiss of the torch outside the bars to my cell and the slow dripping of water were the only sounds present once the Silver Cloaks had retreated up the stairs. Finally.

I pushed myself into a sitting position and started analyzing the situation. Hands shackled behind my back, feet free, one locked cell door, no guards watching. Also, thanks to Shade's careless comment, I knew the timeline. I had hours before he'd be back. Piece of cake. I rolled onto my back and started the slow and careful task of getting my hands in front of me by threading the rest of my body through my arms. My body screamed in pain at the movement after the beating and the lashes, but I pushed it aside. I didn't have time to think about how much everything hurt right now. Not until I was out. Luckily, the whip appeared to only have actually split my skin in a few places. It would leave some scars, but all things considered, it wasn't too bad. I'd survived far worse. Shoving the pain to the back of my mind again, I concentrated on my task. This was a maneuver that required quite a bit of agility and flexibility. Fortunately for me, I had an abundance of both.

With a satisfied sigh, I unfurled my body again and stood up. Alright, that was one problem solved. On to the next one. I always kept several pairs of lockpicks hidden in my clothes, for emergencies, you know, but as my hands came up empty each time, I concluded that the first guards who searched me had found and removed all of them. A thin, metallic edge pricked my palm. Almost all of them. My practiced fingers found the ones I'd sewn into the side of my belt without much effort. Prying them loose, I got to work on my shackles and the locked door.

Some very satisfying clicks later, I was sneaking my way up the stone stairs that the guards had used. Now came the tricky part. There could be ten Silver Cloaks waiting on the other side of that door. Or there could be none. I just didn't know and there was no way for me to check except by opening the door. Sucking in a deep breath, I very carefully pushed the door outwards until a crack formed.

No alarm sounded. I kept pushing until I could poke my head out. An armed guard was standing only a few strides in front of me, but luckily, he had his back towards me. He had a sword on his left hip and a knife sticking out of his belt on the right. Squeezing myself through the crack in the door, I snuck up behind him on the balls of my feet. I eyed his weapons. *Sword or knife? Knife. Definitely knife.*

In one swift motion, I yanked the knife from his belt and drew it across his throat. A wet gurgling escaped as he brought his hands up to stop the blood. As if that would work. I caught him before he and his heavy, clanking armor hit the floor and alerted the whole castle.

Once I'd stashed the dead Silver Cloak in the stairwell beyond the door, and sent a quick prayer of thanks to both Nemanan and Cadentia, I started out again with the stolen dagger in my hand. Seriously? One pair of manacles, one locked door, and one guard. What was this, amateur hour? I shook my head in disgust as I ducked some patrolling Silver Cloaks and moved into the residential part of the Silver Keep. Suddenly, a voice coming from inside a set of heavy wooden doors stopped me in my tracks.

"–smug, arrogant face! If I didn't need her in full working capacity I would've cut off her every limb!" the king's angry voice spilled out of the small crack in the door.

"Why do you even need to hurt her, Father?" the concerned voice of the crown prince asked. "Why don't you just pay her for the job?"

The sound of a hard slap echoed from the room.

"You dare question me, boy?" the king demanded.

"I'm sorry, Father."

"It's about time you learn. I don't pay her because she's an underworlder. If I gave her money she would just disappear with it. Fear, threats, and pain are the only things these people understand."

Wow. What a complete moron. He really didn't understand a single thing about us. Okay, so let's say your cousin was about to inherit a house because they had the letter of ownership, but you wanted the house too. Yeah? So, you pay someone from the Thieves' Guild to steal it. You pay them and you get your letter. Easy. Then, you decide that you want some of your cousin's pottery too. You remember what a good job that thief did last time so you hire him again. You pay him and get the pottery. And so on. Now, if said thief had just taken the money and not delivered the letter, you would never have hired him a second time. No hire, no money. It's just common business sense. Okay, yeah, so I only steal for myself and never for hire, but that's beside the point.

"In fact, they're no different than those bloody nobles!" the king resumed yelling. "They smile and nod in my face and then drag their feet when I'm not looking. They've slowed down the war effort with their ridiculous excuses and they're doing it on purpose. I will execute every one of them!"

"Please, Father, you need the nobles. You can't kill them all. Just wait until Shade comes back with proof of which nobles are actually working against you and then you can execute them and leave the ones who do obey you."

"Fine," the king admitted. "Now get out!"

I quickly moved behind one of the heavy, wooden doors in case the prince would be coming through this one but when I heard another door open and then close inside the room I returned to my eavesdropping spot. There was a minute or so of the king grunting and muttering incoherently while the sound of furniture being turned over made its way out the door.

"Bloody boy and his bloody logic. *You need the nobles,*" he mimicked in the prince's voice. "All the nobles ever do is lie and scheme and stall and all the commoners ever do is bloody complain! *We don't have enough food, the taxes are too high, you killed my wife's brother's second cousin's inbred niece,*" he mimicked again before raising his voice to shout. "Guess what? That's what happens when you bloody break the law!"

I blinked in surprise. Okay, that was unexpected. Leaning forward, I risked a quick peek into the room. By the desk, King Adrian raked his fingers through his hair with a deflated look on his face. It was as if all the fight had gone out of him. He looked weary. Almost... human. How odd. I pulled back again.

"They think running a city is easy?" he spat. "Why can't they just do as they're told? Pompous fools. They've all grown complacent because of the peace, but I'll show them. I will execute the traitors that Shade uncovers, and then, once I bring them the Queen's head, the rest will never dare disobey me again."

I stared at the door, perplexed. How would killing his wife solve anything? The sound of books hitting the wall echoed into the hall.

"Oh shut up, Father!" the king yelled. "You never had this problem because the nobles were still grateful that Great-grandfather had killed the elves. I already told you that I'm going to war! How am I supposed to rule with you constantly yammering in my ear?"

That didn't make any sense; King Adrian's father had been dead for years. I dared risk another peek through the crack in the door. Apart from the book-throwing king, there was no one else in the room. I shook my head. *These people are crazy. Alright, I think I've overstayed my welcome. Time to get the hell out.* I quietly backed away from the door and turned around to leave.

Curious, dark eyes looked at me from across the hall. The crown prince. Shit. He tilted his head slightly to the right. My heart thumped in my chest. I'd been so caught up in listening to the king that I hadn't noticed him sneak into the hallway. This was bad. One word from him and I'd be back in that cell, and this time it wouldn't be so easy to escape. What now? I thought about the knife gripped tightly in my hand. I was confident that I could kill him with one throw. We were close and there was no wind to factor in. If it had been a guard, I wouldn't have hesitated but this was Prince Edward. I couldn't kill the crown prince! If I did, I'd never be able to move about, let alone work, in the city again. So I just stood there and waited for him to make the first move.

To my complete and utter surprise, he put a finger to his lips and then motioned for me to follow. After a second of stunned bewilderment, I did. If nothing else, I might as well see what else this extraordinarily strange day had in store for me, right?

The black-haired prince led me through a maze of corridors, some dark, some lit by silver candelabras. He didn't speak at all but walked with purpose. I was dying to ask him why he was doing this but I didn't dare say anything in case it would break the spell. It had to be some sort of divine intervention. Why else would a prince, the crown prince of all people, help me, a thief he knew nothing about? Well, regardless, I'm a practical person. I take my miracles where I can find them. So, I shut up and kept walking.

After a while, we arrived at a small, wooden door somewhere on the far side of the castle. Prince Edward opened it to reveal a moonlit garden. Green hedges and colorful flowers arranged in different patterns made up most of it, though there was a taller tree or two in the back, towards the wall. The smell of flowers and grass, warm from the afternoon sun, greeted me as I stepped through the door.

"That tree in back, if you climb it you can get over the wall," the prince spoke for the first time since leaving his father in the study. He raised his arm to point. "Hurry, you don't have much time."

I didn't move. Instead, I kept studying his young face. "Why?" I asked because I knew that he would understand the full question embedded in that one word: *why are you doing this, why are you helping me?*

"I am not my father," he simply stated before turning on his heel and disappearing back into the Silver Keep.

"No, you most certainly are not," I whispered softly to the closing door.

13.

"So, wait, let me get this straight: first you were ambushed by the Assassins' Guild and then by the Silver Cloaks? On the same day?" Bones asked with poorly concealed amusement.

I just groaned and buried my face in my arms.

Bones laughed a long and hearty laugh. "So that's why you came back all covered in bruises and why I haven't seen you in a week?"

It was more of a statement than a question so I only answered with another groan. After I'd scaled the wall in the prince's garden, I'd managed to get back to the Thieves' Guild in more or less one piece. However, I'd been pretty banged up from the beatings and the lashes so I'd spent the next week in bed trying to recover. Today was the first day that my body had felt somewhat normal and my first instinct had, of course, been to go to the Mad Archer for some proper food and drink. Bones had been coming off his shift as Liam and I were heading there so he'd decided to join us. I'd just now finished telling him what had happened. Okay, so it was a modified version of what had happened. I'd left some bits out, like the one about Rain and also that Shade was working for the king. *I* wasn't even sure what to do with that piece of information yet. Since I was fairly certain that Shade wouldn't just have me disappear, because that might start a guild war, the best course of action was to just keep my mouth shut. For now, anyway.

"Wow! That's so cool!" Rogue's excited, boyish voice exclaimed as he seated himself in the fourth chair. "How did you escape?" he continued with wide eyes.

Raising my head from my arms on the table, I squinted at him and was just about to ask why he had once again decided to join us uninvited when Bones intervened.

"I think she was just coming to that part."

"Got myself loose, killed some guards, and snuck out," I said vaguely, because if the real story got out, the prince would be in trouble and I did sort of owe him.

"Cool! Can you teach me?" Rogue asked with eyes that practically sparkled with excitement.

"No."

"Oh." He looked taken aback by my one-syllable refusal and slumped back in his chair. His tousled blond hair made him look even more like a sad, little kid.

Look, I know that everything was new and exciting for him, but I just don't have the patience for things like this. If people want to learn, good for them, but don't come to me for help. I have way more important stuff to do with my time than to teach some rookie how to be a thief.

"So you said that the king talked about executing all his nobles and also beheading his wife?" Liam asked in order to get the conversation going again after the rather awkward silence I had left in my wake.

"What?" Rogue asked in utter confusion.

"Yeah, it's so weird. I think he might have finally lost his mind completely. First he wants to chase some imaginary elves in the forest and now he wants to kill all his nobles and his wife too."

"Actually, I think the first two are related," Bones interrupted.

Liam leaned forward on his elbows. "How so?"

"Okay, look, the king is powerful but he's still just one man. He can't be everywhere and do everything. He needs someone to do it for him and that's where his nobles come in. They supervise the merchants, collect taxes, outfit the army, train the army, house the army, feed the army, and all that, you get it."

"Yeah, he needs people to do day-to-day stuff while he's busy ruling," Rogue chimed in.

Bones nodded. "Exactly. But, word on the street is that some of his nobles are working against him and that's why he wants to have them executed."

"Really?" Rogue asked, surprised. "Do you know who?"

"No idea. But I know why. See, here's the thing, the royal family's power rests on the belief that they're keeping us safe from the elves. Only problem is, no one actually believes that story anymore. That's why the nobles have become bold enough to start actively working against him. That's why the king is going into the forest to fight the elves and that's also why the nobles are trying to stall the battle. They just don't believe in it or the king anymore," Bones finished.

"Hmm."

The table grew quiet as everyone pondered this information. Seeing that our table was also dry, Barrel came by with four new mugs of ale. The party to our right banged their table rhythmically in anticipation of the rolled dice.

"But that still doesn't explain the beheading of the queen?" I remarked.

To my surprise, this time it was Rogue who answered. "He must've been talking about the Elf Queen."

Three pairs of eyes turned to stare at him.

"What?" he asked self-consciously and scratched the back of his head with his hand. "It makes the most sense."

"How do we even know that there is an Elf Queen? It might be an Elf King. Are women even allowed to rule on their own?" Liam asked and looked at me.

"How should I know? I'm not an expert on elven orders of succession," I answered and gestured exasperatedly.

Liam rolled his eyes at me.

"Well, it makes more sense than him killing his own wife, I guess," Bones conceded.

"Hmm," we all nodded in agreement.

We sat there in silence for a while longer, sipping our ale, and looking at the people around us. Occasionally, someone commented on something that happened but we mostly just enjoyed each other's company. The game of dice continued to our right with more banging and cheering.

"Liam?" Rogue suddenly began.

"Hmm?"

"Why do you have a real name?"

Liam slowly put down the mug he'd been holding. The expression on his face displayed both surprise and slight discomfort. When he didn't answer straight away, Rogue continued.

"It's just that, you know, almost everyone else has a made-up name, like Storm and Bones," he said and gestured at us. "I mean the Guild Masters have real names but I figured that's probably because they're powerful enough to choose one for themselves. But it's kind of rare, so why do you have one?" he finished and gave my friend a puzzled stare.

"Are you suggesting that Liam's too weak to have a real name?" I challenged because it annoyed me that he would ask Liam something so personal.

"No, no, I... uhm..." the blond rookie stammered while I continued glaring at him.

"Storm, it's okay," Liam sighed and waved a hand dismissively at me.

I knew that Liam didn't like to talk about this. Demonstrating my highly developed social skills, I had forced him to tell me this story after I'd had to fight off our attackers entirely by myself during our first fight together. He'd been embarrassed, I'd been pissed off, and I had demanded an answer. Afterwards, I had regretted that.

"I used to have a family," he began while staring into his mug.

"Oh."

Liam looked up from under his curly brown bangs and stared straight at me. He held my gaze for another second before shifting it to Rogue. "They died in a fire. I was ten."

"I'm so sorry, I..." Rogue began apprehensively.

"Yeah, me too," Liam cut off before he could finish.

So, the truth but not the whole truth. However, I couldn't understand why he gave me that look before. As if I would tell the others what I knew. If anyone understood the desire to keep past events secret, it was me. Though, I suppose, Liam didn't actually know that yet.

The conversation stagnated a bit after Rogue's rather inconsiderate question but Bones made a valiant effort in bringing the comfortable cheerfulness back. I didn't contribute much to it but it worked anyway. Soon they were back to talking and laughing as usual. Once I'd seen Liam smile and laugh with sincerity again, I emptied my mug and stood up.

"Alright, guys, I'm still not fully recovered from my... adventure, last week," I began, "so, I'm just gonna head back to the guild and get some more sleep. I'll see you around."

"Should I...?" Liam began.

"Nah, it's alright, you stay here. I'm just gonna sleep anyway."

"I hope you get better soon," Rogue said and looked at me with concerned eyes.

I almost felt bad for cutting him off earlier. Almost.

"See you around, Storm," Bones called as I gave the three guys at my table one last wave before disappearing into the crowd and out the door.

14.

I stretched my arms and let out a satisfied groan. "That was a good sleep."

Rolling out of bed, I looked at the little silver clock on my desk. Hmm. So, either I had slept for twelve hours or for twenty-four hours. Either one was within the realm of possibility in my current state. However, after the food and drink yesterday, and with the long uninterrupted sleep today, I felt as though the exhaustion had finally seeped from my bones. My stomach growled. Okay, so probably twenty-four hours. I got dressed and headed over to the Mad Archer.

As soon as I walked in, I signaled to Hilda that I wanted food. At Barrel and Hilda's tavern, warm food was always ready so she had a plate of food for me almost before I'd even sat down at my usual table.

"Thank you, it smells delicious," I said to her and truly meant it.

"Oh, you're very welcome, dear," she replied in her kind voice and put a glass of water on the table. "Now eat up before it gets cold."

I smiled to myself as I dug in. Only Hilda would ever dare call me *dear*. It felt as though I hadn't eaten in days, but I had to remind myself to eat somewhat slowly and savor the taste. Once the plate and the glass were empty, I leaned back in the chair and watched people coming and going. After a while, Barrel emerged from the back room. He looked as if he'd just woken up. He probably had. Barrel and his wife had to work in shifts to keep the tavern open at all times. His eyes scanned the room as he bent to kiss Hilda on the cheek. When they found mine, he said something to Hilda and then went back into the back room. He reappeared a moment later with a white envelope in his hand. The tavern's patrons greeted him on his way over to me.

"Good morning, Barrel," I said. "Is that for me?"

"Hey, Storm. Yeah, it is," he said hesitantly and placed a white envelope, marked only with the words *The Oncoming Storm*, on the table.

"What's wrong?" I asked, suspicion creeping into my mind.

"It was delivered by a man before I went to bed, so maybe six hours ago," he started and then paused. "Storm, he was wearing plain clothes but I could've sworn I recognized him."

"From where?"

"I think it might have been a Silver Cloak."

I looked at him with a slight hint of disbelief in my eyes. "That's odd. They're normally more of an arrest-first-ask-questions-later sort of bunch."

"Mm-hmm," he commented and then his eyes turned concerned. "Are you in trouble?"

"I'm always in trouble," I answered with a mischievous smile, trying to lighten the mood. "Thanks, Barrel."

"Yeah," he said and patted my shoulder once. "Just be careful, you."

When Barrel had left, I carefully opened the envelope and drew out the letter. I unfolded it and almost swallowed my tongue. At the bottom, the royal seal was stamped in red wax. I closed my eyes briefly. *Crap*. This was going to be trouble. Taking a bracing breath, I read the words etched in black ink. Once I'd finished, I shot up from the table and sprinted back towards the Thieves' Guild. Someone would die for this. And I knew exactly who.

Barely ten minutes later, I dashed across the city, armed to the teeth. Once I reached the intended door, I started furiously banging on the black metal. They would let me in or I would break down that door. After some more forceful pounding, a man's voice rang out from inside the door.

"You're in the wrong place, get lost."

"Oh no, I'm exactly where I want to be. You tell Shade that the Oncoming Storm has come to collect a debt, or I will scream to the whole Marble Ring that this is the Assassins' Guild's headquarter."

The voice inside fell silent. I wasn't sure if that meant they'd gone to talk to Shade or that they'd sent assassins out to kill me. I guessed we'd find out. My question was answered moments later when the door swung outward. Taking a deep breath, I stepped into the death guild's den.

As soon as both my feet were inside the door, it was slammed shut. The muzzle of a gun pressed into the back of my head and two swords appeared at my throat.

"You make one wrong move and you're dead," the voice from before announced with menace.

It belonged to a tall man with dark brown hair tied back in a bun. I could see him because he was standing directly in front of me but because the door was now shut, it was too dark to see the other people I knew to be standing around me with weapons.

"I'm going to search you and remove all your weapons. No outsider comes into the Assassins' Guild armed," he continued.

"Go ahead," I said and spread my arms wide.

He started by removing the ten throwing knives at my shoulders. They clanked metallically as they hit the table behind him. After that, he proceeded to remove the two hunting knives strapped to the small of my back, and the two stilettos in my sleeves, as well as the two blades secured on the outside of either thigh. After he had removed my boot knife, he started a more intimate search.

"Hey! Watch those hands," I warned when they strayed a little too far into my private areas.

He looked at me steadily as the two swords pressed harder into my throat. Fine. I rolled my eyes but kept quiet. His intrusive search led to the discovery of yet another knife, one that I had hidden between my breasts. After one final, very intimate, pat down, he seemed satisfied and turned to look over the pile that had formed on the table. He looked back at me with raised eyebrows.

"Eighteen knives. Eighteen. Girl, you brought enough blades to equip a small army."

I gave him an unapologetic shrug in reply. He motioned for the others to lower their weapons.

"The Master will see you upstairs," he continued and pointed to a staircase on my right.

I slid away from the armed welcome wagon and quickly headed for the indicated stairwell. Nineteen. A smug expression settled on my face as I let the cool metal slide into my hand. Nineteen knives. What? Why are you surprised? I'm a thief. And a damn good one too. Sleight of hand is sort of my thing. Once I reached the top of the stairs, I realized why they hadn't specified a room. There was only one door. I let the knife slide back into my sleeve again before uncerimoniously yanking the door open and striding in.

The black-haired Guild Master stood waiting for me in the middle of the room with a mildly curious look on his face.

"Storm, to what do I owe the pleasure?" he asked nonchalantly and spread his arms.

I slammed the door shut and stalked forward until I was close enough that I would've felt his breath if we'd been the same height. I looked him steadily in the eye and then did something that he wouldn't have expected in a million years. Quick as lightning, I produced the knife, grabbed him by the front of his shirt, and yanked him down while bringing the knife up to rest against his throat. A look of shock hit his face like a basher's bat.

"You traitor!" I growled in his face. "You spineless, worthless traitor. You sold me out to the king last week. What, after you ambushed me, you ran straight to the guards to tell them where I'd be and what I'd look like?"

The shock transformed into confusion but I ignored it and pressed on.

"And then you bow and scrape to the bloody king! Torturing me into submission, for the king. I was wrong, you have no honor," I continued and shook my head in disgust. "That, I can take, though. But this, this, I'm gonna kill you for unless you make it right."

"This, this what?"

"Oh don't you dare act all confused! When I didn't break, you ratted out Liam. You told the king that the way to get to me was to get Liam. You son of a bitch. You will save him or I will kill you."

His eyes now portrayed a mix of confusion and anger. Mine roared with all the fury of a thunderstorm. He narrowed his eyes at me.

"One word from me and the whole guild will come charging in here," he warned.

"You'll be dead before you utter one syllable," I spat.

He arched an eyebrow at me. "Did you really think this through? Huh?" he said threateningly and leaned down further into the knife's edge. "Even if you could somehow manage to kill me right here, you wouldn't survive ten minutes. The whole guild would be coming after you, and who would save Liam then?"

I blinked and took a half-step back. Damn. He was right. I couldn't save Liam if I was running from the entire Assassins' Guild at the same time. As I slowly started lowering the knife, he ripped it out of my hand. I took another step back.

"You filthy traitor," I said, shaking my head. "Working for the king, selling out members of your own world to the bloody leader of the Upperworld. And you call yourself an underworlder."

He laughed a harsh-sounding laugh. "Oh, you ignorant girl. I'm not working for the king, I'm trying to bring him down. I thought you, of all people, would've figured that out by now. You knew I was the one who broke into Lord Eberbach's mansion. And right after that, they found incriminating documents in the hidden safe *you* told me about. Documents that I planted to get the king to kill one of his most loyal nobles. How could you not put two and two together?"

Oh. Uhm, okay. So apparently, I had that incident completely backwards.

"But what about last week?" I pressed.

"You mean when I ran from the Silver Cloak the night I was cornered by the Admiral's men because I'd been out planting more false evidence? Evidence that I was still carrying. Or wait, did you mean that time in the Silver Keep when I didn't torture you, informed you of the timeline you had, which by the way, was incredibly long, and then went out to forge even more proof that all of his other loyal lords are working against him?" he said, and looked at me with a face full of annoyance and exasperation.

"Oh."

Man, did I have all of that backwards.

"So, no, I will not jeopardize my entire plan just to save your little friend."

"Why are you even doing this?" I asked, bewildered. "You're already one of the most powerful and feared people in the city. Why do you need to be king as well? Don't you have enough power as it is?"

"There is no such thing as too much power," he said, voice hard and eyes unreadable.

Bastard. Okay, new plan. My eyes turned hard again and the threatening tone was back in my voice.

"Alright. How about this then: if you don't save Liam I will tell the king everything you just told me," I said and lifted my chin defiantly.

I could almost see the lightning bolts flashing in his eyes at that and I realized that I'd been wrong before. In that moment, his eyes looked exactly like those of King Adrian.

He tilted his head to the right. "You would dare to blackmail me, the Master of the Assassins' Guild?" he said in a terrifying voice. "You have forgotten that this is the death guild and I'm its master. I decide who lives and dies in this city." His eyes bored into me. "If you rat me out to the king, I will put a black mark on Liam."

I recoiled at that. Shade took a step forward. I took a step back.

"You have forgotten the most important element of blackmail: *you* have to have the power." He kept advancing while I kept retreating. "Let me show you what real power looks like."

The Master Assassin continued pressing forward. My back hit the closed door behind me. Just as I realized that there was no more space to back away, the knife I'd smuggled in hit the door with a sharp thud. I let out an involuntary gasp. The blade vibrated slightly where it stuck to the door, a mere finger's breadth from my left eye.

"Take the knife," his insane lightning storm voice commanded.

Turning slightly, I managed to pry it loose. I straightened again, knife in hand, and just stared at him. He stared back at me with wild eyes.

"Now, you will obey my every command, or I will put a black mark on Liam."

My eyes widened in fear.

"So, what should I make you do?" he said and cocked his head slightly to the right again. "Should I make you cut your arm? Maybe cut out an eye? Or how about slit your own throat?"

I opened my mouth to protest but then closed it again. I briefly closed my eyes too. My heart thumped in my chest while cold dread spread through my body like poison. Idiot. What had I gotten myself into? I opened my eyes again and waited for whatever would come next.

"Now, *that*'s power," Shade said with finality and held my gaze.

Yeah, alright. Point taken. Blackmailing the leader of the assassins had been a bad move. Not much to do about that now, though, I would just have to see where my bullheadedness would take me this time. I continued staring at him. A couple of moments later, Shade broke my gaze, the lightning storm receded from his eyes, and he looked me up and down appraisingly.

"Coming in here, to the heart of the death guild, pulling a knife, and trying to blackmail the leader," he began, "you're a girl half the size of every man in my guild and yet you have balls bigger than all of them combined." He barked a short laugh and then waved his hand dismissively. "Get out before I change my mind."

So as to not give him time to do just that, I yanked the door open and practically ran down the stairs while sending heartfelt prayers of thanks to Cadentia. I could barely believe my luck. At the front door, I equipped myself with all of my knives again, this time while staring down the barrel of three pistols. Well, a change of scenery is always nice, I suppose.

Only when I was outside, with the black metal door closed behind me, did I finally allow myself a deep breath of relief. What had I been thinking? This time, I didn't give myself a mental slap, I actually slapped my forehead for real. That could've ended really badly. This is why you should never make decisions while angry. I really needed to stop being so stupid. This was getting annoying. And dangerous.

I started out towards the Thieves' Guild again. Well, there was nothing else for it now. My plan, my not-so-well-thought-out plan, as it turned out, had failed. There was only one thing left to do: give in to the king's demands. It was time to go drop off all my knives and go to the Silver Keep to surrender.

15.

Once again, I was being led through the grand halls of the Silver Keep. I was only mildly annoyed by the fact that I was actually there of my own volition this time. Mostly, I was just worried about Liam. If that vulture had harmed a single hair on Liam's curly brown head I would make it my mission in life to destroy him. Actually, I would probably do that anyway.

The broad marble hall gave way to King Adrian's throne room where the king lounged in his black obsidian throne with an insufferably smug look on his face. The manacles on my hands and feet clanked as I trudged towards the foot of the dais. I noticed that there were an awful lot of guards positioned along the walls of the throne room. Well, that certainly complicated my escape plan. In fact, my chances of escaping rapidly went from slim to none. Still, I was quite flattered. After all, he considered me enough of a threat to warrant all this extra security.

When we finally reached the dais, I drew myself up and stared into his cold, black eyes. He stared back. Then, he motioned for the two guards to withdraw. While they retreated and took up positions on opposite sides of the room, I was again reminded of the icy cold that spilled from his eyes like a frozen, black creek.

"I knew you would return," he said, breaking the long silence.

"Yes, well, now that I'm here, you can let Liam go," I replied sourly.

"Oh, no, I want to enjoy this. Last time you were here you told me that you do not beg. For anything." A wicked smile spread across his lips. "Care to reconsider?"

Shit. This was what I'd been afraid of. I'd held on to a desperate hope that he would just tell me what he wanted and let Liam go. Of course it wouldn't be that easy. I had embarrassed him and made him lose face last time when I'd refused to break and then escaped right under his nose. He wanted revenge. Suddenly, I realized the second reason for all the extra security. He wanted to humiliate me in front of his entire personal guard. A sinking feeling spread through my body. Still I said nothing. I just glared at him with defiant eyes. He only looked amused. After he'd let the silence stretch for a while longer, he snapped his fingers.

A small, wooden door to the left of the throne opened and Liam was half-dragged through it. It took all my self-control not to rush over and attack the two stone-faced guards on either side of him. Instead, I studied Liam with quick eyes. He wore the same clothes that I'd last seen him in, except his shoes were gone. His hands were bound behind his back and he was gagged, but he looked unharmed, or at least as far as I could tell. When his kind, blue eyes found mine he looked both relieved and devastated at the same time. I tried to send him courage as he was led to the front of the dais. King Adrian got up from his throne and walked over to where the two guards had forced Liam to his knees. I tried not to let my panic show as the king took out an ornate, silver pistol and put it to the back of Liam's head.

"Kneel," he said, never taking his cold eyes from mine.

I stared daggers at him and if they'd been real, the king would've been dead several times over by now. But they weren't, and I was out of options. *Shit.* I took a deep breath. There was nothing else for it. After one last defiant look, I cast down my eyes, and got down on my knees.

"Beg," he commanded.

My entire soul screamed at me not to do this. I hadn't begged to a member of the Upperworld since I was seven and a couple of guards had caught me stealing food. They'd threatened to hang me and forced me to grovel at their feet. The shame I'd felt at that had been almost unbearable and I'd sworn never to beg to an upperworlder again. Sometimes, I'd had to bow to a leader of the Underworld, like I'd done with Shade when he ambushed me the second time, but that was different. That was showing submission, but with honor. There were no such notions in the Upperworld. Here, begging was just a form of humiliation, plain and simple. I glanced up at Liam and saw him almost imperceptibly shake his head. King Adrian cocked the gun.

"You do not seem to understand the position you are in," he said, his voice full of quiet fury.

"I am shackled, outnumbered and outgunned, kneeling on the floor at your feet, in the middle of your fortress, while you hold a gun to the back of my only friend's head." I blew out an exasperated breath. "I understand perfectly well the situation I'm in, thank you very much. So why don't you just tell me what it is that you want and I will make that happen for you?"

"Beg," he repeated with a voice that could've commanded thunder. "And you better make it good."

Well, so much for false bravado. Swallowing my pride, I bowed down to the floor. I lifted my forehead off the cool marble only far enough that my voice would carry up to the dais. And then I begged.

"Please, sire," I said with all the humility I could muster. "I will do whatever you want, just please don't hurt him. Whatever it is that you want of me, you can have it, as long as you let him live. Please, I am begging you."

I lowered my head all the way to the floor again, feeling like I was about to throw up. I closed my eyes. That had to have been enough. Silently cursing the royal vulture above me, I waited. The seconds stretched on. Finally, he chuckled.

"Look at me," he ordered.

I did. His face bore a malicious, triumphant smile. I wanted to kick his teeth in.

"I like the way you beg," he said and took the gun from Liam's head. "Let's talk business."

16.

"I've got a job for you," the black-eyed king said once the doors to his study were closed.

"So you said," I retorted before an irritated look from the ruler of Keutunan reminded me that this was not the time to be a smartmouth. "I mean, yes, what would you like me to do?" I amended quickly while struggling mightily not to roll my eyes.

Once the king had been satisfied with his little humiliation, he'd signaled to the guards to take Liam away again. While they'd hauled him to his feet, I had discreetly showed him three fingers and then a fist: the Thieves' Guild hand signal for *I have a plan*. I would listen to whatever it was that the king wanted me to do, and then while I pretended to carry it out, I would get the guild to rescue Liam. Piece of cake. I'd had time to see Liam's nod of acknowledgement before he disappeared through the small, wooden door again and it was my turn to be manhandled.

King Adrian had taken the lead while his guards shoved, rather than led, me behind. We'd stopped outside the very doors I had eavesdropped behind only a week ago to wait for the king to go inside. Once he had entered gracefully and positioned himself in the middle of the book-filled room, the guards had unlocked my manacles. I must admit, I was a bit surprised, and tempted, at first. Imagine what I can do without restraints. Then, however, I'd remembered that if I tried anything, Liam would pay the price. As my short-lived excitement had faded into nothingness, the Silver Cloaks had given me a hard shove through the doors and then closed them behind me.

"I want you to kill the Queen."

My mind stopped spinning and my mouth dropped open a little in surprise. Had I understood that correctly?

"Did you hear me?" King Adrian pressed.

"I heard you," I said forcefully before continuing in a more collected voice, "I'm just having trouble understanding what you're actually saying. You want me to kill your wife?"

A baffled look passed over the face of Keutunan's authoritarian ruler. "What? No! Are you crazy?"

Are you? I thought, but wisely enough, decided not to voice out loud. It struck me, though, that the king spoke much more casually when his guards weren't present. I'd first noticed it when I eavesdropped on his conversation with his son last week, and our meeting today confirmed it. Curious. As if his respect from the guards, and probably the nobles as well, depended on his degree of eloquence. To me, that was hilarious. But then again, I didn't know much about politics.

"I don't want you to kill my wife! I want you to kill the Elf Queen."

"Okay..." I began, waiting for him to elaborate.

He just stared at me with raised eyebrows. I know I should've been respectful and compliant, or whatever, but this was just too outlandish to keep my very limited social graces in check.

"Yeah, okay, let me get this straight," I said. "You want me to go into the forest? Me. In the forest. What about the dragons? And the hellhounds?"

"There are no dragons or hellhounds in the forest!" Adrian yelled exasperatedly. "You common folk and your ridiculous superstitions. The only things that live in those woods are the elves."

"Mm-hmm," I replied, not even bothering to keep the sarcasm from my voice.

King Adrian sighed and shook his head. He looked unusually flustered. Even when he'd stormed off the courtyard last week he'd done so regally but right now, he just looked tired and overwhelmed. It made him seem almost human. How odd. Then, just as quickly as it had appeared, his display of human emotions vanished and he turned back to me with threatening eyes.

"You will kill the Elf Queen or I will kill your friend. Take your pick."

"Alright, alright, I get it," I conceded and threw up my hands. "I'll go into the woods to find someone who hasn't been seen for a hundred and fifty years or so, and then kill them. Great. How am I even supposed to accomplish that?"

"I trust you can figure that out on your own. After all, I've been told that you're excellent at killing people," he answered with a malicious smile.

I frowned at him. Right, in the turmoil of Liam's kidnapping I'd forgotten about that. If Shade wasn't the one who'd fed the king information about me, then who was it?

As if reading my mind, the king continued in an amused voice. "Speaking of, there's someone I want you to meet. Frederick, come join us!" he finished by calling loudly.

The side door that I'd heard the prince use last week creaked open. It was dark beyond it so I couldn't yet make out who was lurking there in the shadows. As the figure stepped over the threshold, light from the study's silver chandelier spilled across his face. The shock hit me as if the marble ceiling had fallen down on me.

"No, no... it can't be," I bargained while desperately shaking my head.

"Surprised?" the familiar face challenged with a vicious smile.

"It was you? It was you all along?" I stared back in utter astonishment.

"Oh, Storm, did you really think that you were the only master liar in this city?" Rogue asked with mock pity.

Rogue. The rookie who'd almost wet his pants when I threatened him with a pistol. The clueless kid who'd been excited about everything and wanted to know everything. Wait... wanted to know everything. Oh, crap. How had I not seen that? Actually, I knew exactly why I hadn't seen it coming. It was because of that ridiculous lost puppy look that had constantly been on his face. However, that excited mouth and those innocent eyes beneath tousled blond hair were now replaced by smug arrogance and a malicious smirk. Damn. He was good, I had to give him that.

"It was all a trap then? From the very beginning?"

"Of course." He laughed mockingly. "Did you truly believe that I would let myself be ambushed so easily? Trembling like a coward, ha! As good as you are, you're not nearly as good as you think you are."

I heaved a deep sigh and tilted my head up to stare at the decorated ceiling. My soul felt like a deflated sail. Maybe he was right. What had I actually accomplished lately? I'd been ambushed *three* times, lost a huge heist to someone else, been beaten up, almost gotten myself killed by threatening a Master Assassin, been duped by a royal spy, and worst of all, I had inadvertently put Liam in danger. And I called him a rookie. Hold on. A rookie?

"Oh by the gods," I said in sudden realization, "you didn't actually steal the Midnight Star, did you? You just told the king, and he forced the Admiral to hand it over. Ha! Cheater," I baited with a smirk on my face. My spirits rose and just like that, the sarcastic, scheming smartmouth was back.

"I could have done it if I wanted to!" Rogue defended.

"Mm-hmm," I countered with poorly hidden amusement. "When the Guild Masters find out about this, you're so dead, kid."

"Stop calling me *kid*! I'm eighteen."

"Enough!" King Adrian roared. "Squabbling like children," he admonished and leveled a disapproving stare at Rogue before finally turning to me. "The Guild Masters aren't going to find out."

"That so?" I replied and raised my eyebrows at him. "And why is that?"

"Because I have Liam."

Oh, right. The escape plan. This screwed up everything. If there was a leak in the guild, I couldn't enlist them to save Liam while I pretended to go into the forest.

"So, you see, if you tell your guild about Frederick, Liam dies," King Adrian began and then locked eyes with me, "and if you try to get them to rescue Liam before you've completed your mission, I will know, and he will die."

Alright, now I was worried he might actually be able to read my mind for real. I glanced at Rogue. He'd been quiet ever since being reprimanded by the king but based on the expression on his face, he was dying to rub his power over me in my face. I shot him a scorching scowl.

"Now, this is what's going to happen," the king said. "You will go back to your guild and gather whatever supplies you need and then you will leave. Today. Frederick will go back to the Thieves' Guild as well and make sure you stick to our arrangement. And Liam will stay here."

"Alright," I conceded. "But Liam will be staying in a room and not in that cold, damp, dungeon of yours."

"This isn't a negotiation," the king of Keutunan cut me off. "That boy will stay wherever I say."

"He won't be much of a hostage if he's died of pneumonia," I pressed. "And besides, you've met him, he's not a fighter. He won't try to escape. He will do whatever you say so there's no need for rough treatment."

"Yeah, he's a wimp, that one." King Adrian laughed. "He'll never be a real man."

I wanted to strangle him for saying such a cruel thing about my only friend but I managed to restrain myself. After all, I was the one who had intentionally led him there to make sure that Liam would be treated as fairly as possible.

"Fine," the king said and flicked his wrist dismissively, "the wimp won't die of pneumonia. But until you return with absolute proof that the Elf Queen is dead, your little friend will be locked in a room here in the Keep."

I gave a short nod because I didn't trust my voice. Being polite was too much of a stretch right now. The king held my gaze for a moment longer, as if to make sure I truly understood, before breaking it and turning to his spy.

"Frederick!"

"Yes, Your Majesty?"

"Make sure she gets back to the Thieves' Guild without a fuss," he ordered before some open books on the desk caught his eye. "Oh, and fill her in on what we know about the elves."

"Of course, sire."

"And, Storm?" the king continued in a voice hard as marble. "I will not accept failure. Even if you were to die trying, Liam would not be free. I would keep him here as a prisoner forever. Only the death of the Elf Queen can save him. Understood?"

"Yes."

"Good. Dismissed."

Okay, now what? I glanced from the straight-backed king to his treacherous spy. I wasn't sure what the protocol was here, but I'd never been one for rules anyway, so I simply shrugged and turned to leave. Rogue's hand shot out and grabbed my wrist.

"You will bow before leaving the king's presence," he informed me.

Though I wanted to challenge him, I knew in my heart that it wasn't worth the trouble of getting the king angry again, so I yanked my arm free of the spy's grip and gave as insincere a bow as I could get away with. Turning to leave, I saw Rogue bow deeply. Once my back was turned, I made a mocking face and strode towards the doors.

The Silver Cloaks outside drew their swords when they saw that I was the one to walk through the doors, but when Rogue appeared behind me a moment later and dismissed them, they slid their swords back in their scabbards and retreated to the throne room.

"Let's go," Rogue said once they'd rounded the corner. He raised his hand as if to give the back of my shoulder a shove.

Intercepting his hand midair, I locked his wrist in an iron grip and turned to face him. Once I had him trapped, I summoned the darkness from my soul and met his eyes. He recoiled slightly when he met my gaze.

"If you ever put that hand on me again, I will break every finger on it," I said with deadly fury.

He blinked twice in surprise and opened his mouth, no doubt to remind me that it was well within his power to have Liam beaten if I didn't behave, but before he could do that I released his hand and stalked away. I'd had enough of ridiculous power showdowns for one day, thank you very much! Okay, so maybe the fact that I'd lost every single one of those showdowns did have something to do with it. I blew an exasperated breath. By Nemanan, I swore to balance the scales one day.

We walked through the Silver Keep in complete silence. Only the soft thudding of our feet echoed faintly across the marble halls as we made our way to the front gate. Occasionally, we encountered a couple of patrolling Silver Cloaks but other than that, only the mute faces in the silver-framed oil paintings took note of our passage.

Bright morning sunlight greeted us as we crossed the final threshold and emerged into the courtyard situated between the actual keep and the high defensive walls surrounding it. This part of the king's fortress was called *the kill box*, for obvious reasons. Anyone stupid enough to attack would be trapped here if they ever breached the walls. While the enemy was busy trying to break into the keep, hell would rain down on them from above. With the keep in front and the walls behind, Ghabhalnaz, God of Death, would take them all.

"Northwest," Rogue said once we had cleared the final checkpoint at the Silver Keep and stepped into the Marble Ring. "The king recommends that you leave Keutunan by West Gate and then go north along the tree farms. Once you've passed them, you should head northwest, straight into the forest."

"And the king knows this how?" I questioned and arched an eyebrow in his direction.

"Notes from when his forefather fought the elves."

"Uh-huh. And they couldn't give me a more exact location than *northwest into the forest*? That forest is huge."

"Yep. So you'd better get going."

Bastard. We continued in silence for a while, passing lords and ladies going about their morning business. They all wore beautiful, well-tailored garments in a variety of colors. Even the ladies' decorated umbrellas were of rich hues. We stood out like sore thumbs in our plain, burglar friendly clothes, and were given an abundance of nasty looks. I answered every one of them with a psychotic grin that made them clutch their skirts and hurry past. What? If you're uncomfortable, make them feel uncomfortable. That's how you deal with people who behave like they're socially superior to you.

"They call it *the City of Ash*," Rogue continued.

"The City of Ash, huh? Well, that doesn't sound ominous at all..." I sighed and shook my head.

I glanced back at him expectantly as we reached the outskirts of the Marble Ring. My very limited patience had run dry about half an hour ago, so when he didn't immediately continue, I took matters into my own hands.

"Anything else? Or were a vague direction and a gloomy-sounding name all you had on the elves?" I asked.

"Of course not!" Rogue retorted. "How much do you know about Keutunan's history?"

"Well," I started while running through options in my head. Admitting that I had broken in and read some of the royal historians' books might be bad. However, considering the fact that my life very well could depend on that knowledge, I decided to go with the truth. "I know that Keutunan has always been isolated and that the only other civilization we've found are the elves in the forest."

"Exactly," the spy continued, "and we used to live in peace, you know, trading and stuff. But then, like a century and a half ago, the elves decided that they were the superior race and that they should therefore rule us."

"Yeah, and then King George rallied the nobles and the commoners and marched troops into the forest to fight them, I know. What I don't have, however, is information on the actual elves. Hierarchy, numbers, strengths, weaknesses – that sort of thing."

"According to King George's notes, their numbers are few–"

"Define *few*," I interrupted.

"As far as we can tell, and taking into consideration the time that's passed since it was recorded, maybe a few hundred. King George did slaughter a whole lot of them during the war."

"Hmm."

"Their strengths definitely lie in archery and magic."

"What kind of magic?"

"Fresh fish!" a vendor to my right suddenly called. "Freshly caught this morning and just in from the docks!"

We'd moved into the Merchants' Quarter and the morning market was bustling with people. In the mixed crowd that frequented this daily event, we blended in much better than we had when we walked around the Marble Ring in plain clothes. The melting pot that is the morning market draws people from every step of the social ladder. Dockworkers, watchmakers, and lords too rich to have an actual occupation, mingle in a way that is inconceivable at any other place or time. Well, except for the public hangings. Most people love the public hangings.

"There's no definite knowledge on the kind of magic they use but based on their longevity and their battle skills, we've been able to make some educated guesses."

"Such as?"

"They've got some kind of life spell that they use to steal life force from other creatures. Also, King George's notes suggest that they were notoriously difficult to spot in the woods so probably some kind of cloaking spell too. And apparently their arrows could hit targets that should've been far out of reach and from angles that just shouldn't be possible, so we think they can manipulate objects as well."

"So, I'm supposed to kill an immortal queen that I can't see and who can direct arrows at me from ridiculous distances. Fantastic."

That produced a burst of laughter from Rogue. A moment later, he seemed to catch himself and transformed his merriment into a cough, as if he was above laughing at my sarcastic remarks now that he was the king's spy again.

"The good news is that they do have a weakness: they don't use guns."

"... anything else?" I asked expectantly.

"No, but that's a huge advantage," Rogue answered as if I was mentally challenged.

Right. The only weakness they'd been able to find was that they didn't use guns. What an incredibly helpful shortcoming considering the fact that neither did I. Bloody brilliant.

"Mm-hmm," I muttered.

We continued our trudge in silence until the Mad Archer appeared in the distance. There was still one question I wanted an answer to before we reached the Thieves' Guild and I had to pretend that everything was fine again.

"Rogue?" I began.

"What?"

"Why me? The king has an entire guild of assassins at his command, why can't he just send one of them?"

"It's true that the king has the loyalty of the Assassins' Guild. After all, every Master of the Assassins' Guild has been sworn to serve the king of Keutunan, ever since the founding of that guild. That's why he wanted someone else."

I squinted at him. "I don't follow."

"Our benevolent king has a guild full of lethal and utterly loyal assassins. Why would he want to waste them on this suicide mission? Because you have to know that's what it is, right?"

Yeah. I had come to the same conclusion a while ago too.

"King Adrian has never sent anyone into the forest before because it wasn't until now, when he's about to launch his attack, that he needed the Elf Queen dead. He's not a fool, he knows that since no one has attempted this before, the odds of success are slight. You're a long shot. At best," Rogue said and turned to me with a smug expression on his face.

I wanted to slap that arrogant look right off his sharp cheekbones.

"So," he continued, "the king wanted someone who is good at killing but also replaceable, someone no one will miss." A vicious smile spread across his lips. "Like you. The Beggars' Guild doesn't turn out any fighters, and neither does the Pleasure Guild. The bashers are too brawny and loud for assassination work. Apart from the Assassins' Guild, only the Thieves' Guild has the potential to produce members who are both stealthy and good with weapons."

"And that's why you decided to make the biggest mistake of your very short life and infiltrate us?" I retorted with malice.

"Biggest mistake, huh? We'll see about that," the traitor answered. "Anyway, imagine my surprise when I found the perfect candidate even before I'd begun the infiltration. My careful investigation once inside the guild only confirmed it. There you were: a bad-tempered loner with a talent for killing. My ticket to the king's favor."

I glared at him as we descended the final steps to the Thieves' Guild entrance. He thought I was his ticket to a better life? Oh that ignorant, naïve, little boy. He had no idea who he was dealing with. As I lifted my hand to knock, I swore to the God of Death that I would be his ticket to hell before all this was over.

17.

"When the green-clad gentleman laughs..."
"... the whole manor disappears."

The door to the Thieves' Guild swung open silently to reveal Bones' muscled frame. "Storm. Rogue. Good to see you," he greeted us.

"Hey, Bones!" Rogue exclaimed in an enthusiastic voice.

And the excited puppy was back. It was almost uncanny to see how swiftly he could switch from his arrogant, malicious self to the happy rookie he pretended to be. I nodded briefly at Bones before disappearing down the stairs with Rogue on my heels.

"Remember, I'll be watching," Rogue warned as I turned off towards my room and left him in the deserted hallway.

Slamming the door to my room shut, I threw myself on the bed and let loose a seemingly endless string of profanities. How could I've been so stupid? I'd been worried about the mysterious, black-clad assassin when it was really the cheerful, blond kid I should've been wary of. Shade had fit the part of a spying backstabber perfectly. Rogue most certainly had not, and because I'd fallen for that, here I was, knee-deep in shit from the fallout. This wouldn't even have been an issue if I'd simply steered clear of people in the first place. I was getting soft.

Spitting out one last curse, I pulled myself off the bed and gave my body a good shake.

"Alright, focus," I said to the empty room. "I'm going into the forest for an unknown amount of time. What do I need to bring? Knives. Water. Food. And... uhm..." My very limited knowledge about the tree-covered outdoors stared back at me blankly. "No, yeah, that's all I got."

Seeing as I'd never set foot outside the city walls, I had absolutely no idea what someone might need to survive in a forest but I figured that with those three things, I would make do. I'm typically more of a plotter and a schemer but I'm by no means a stranger to simply winging it. I would be fine. Hopefully.

While climbing the stairs back up to the front door, I had a strange feeling in my stomach. I'd strapped on some of my knives, grabbed a bag, and packed up the rest of them along with lockpicks and some money. Finally, I'd put on my dark gray cloak before going to the Thieves' Court. Once there, I'd left enough money to pay for my and Liam's guild rates for a couple of months on Master Killian's black chair. I had also left a note explaining that we were going on a trip and didn't know when we'd be back. That was the best way to do it because if I'd faced the Guild Masters directly, I would never have been able to lie my way out from underneath Master Caleb's observant eyes. Besides, the money and the note were safe there. No one would dare steal from the Guild Masters' chairs, though Rogue would probably sneak up and read it to make sure I didn't spill the beans. He was stalking me like a shadow.

"You're leaving again?" Bones asked once I reached the top of the stairs.

"Yeah, Liam and I are going on a scouting trip," I lied casually.

"Is that right?" the gatekeeper asked, surprised. "Where to?"

"We're gonna check out some of the villages along the coast."

"What for? We've only found fishing villages there. Do they really have anything worth stealing?"

"Won't know that until we check it out," I replied and shrugged lightly.

"I guess. So, where's Liam?"

I could feel Rogue lurking in the stairwell behind me. This was the opening I'd been waiting for. *Careful now.* Pretending to adjust my backpack, I turned my back squarely to the stairs and brought my hand up to my chest. I met Bones' eyes and then threw a quick glance at my hand before flashing him the Thieves' Guild hand signal for *hidden message*. Thumb-ring finger, thumb-middle finger, fist. His eyes widened slightly.

"He's down by the docks," I said, keeping my voice casual but my eyes fixed intently on the gatekeeper's. "The boat's taking in water. We never should've trusted one of those new, young dock workers with it and now Liam is paying... to fix it," I added after a barely perceptible pause. After that, I broke his gaze and finished off by saying, "So while he does that, I told him I'd go and get all our stuff and then meet him there."

"I see," Bones answered. "Well, I look forward to seeing both you and Liam when you get back then. Be careful."

"Same. Take care of the guild," I said, hoping that he'd understood the message, and started out towards the door.

"Always do," I heard him promise before the door to the Thieves' Guild closed behind me.

Outside, I stopped and looked back at both the guild and the Mad Archer. My whole life, this city had been my home. I had lived, fought, loved, and lost here. Thousands of memories came flooding back until I almost drowned in them. Tipping my head up towards the sky, I closed my eyes against the pain. I wondered if I would ever see it again.

18.

"Man, there sure are a lot of trees here," I said to no one in particular.

In fact, even if I had meant to say it to someone else, there was no one there to hear it. On my way from the Merchants' Quarter to West Gate, I'd stopped to buy some supplies. Along with the knives already packed up in there, dried food, a couple of waterskins, a compass, and some rope now filled my backpack. Finding my way past the tree farms had been easy: I only had to follow the walls going north. Now, however, came the tricky part.

"Alright, northwest," I announced and pointed my arm straight ahead and a little to the left.

Following the direction of my arm, I stared at the mass of trees before me. There wasn't even a semblance of a path as far as the eye could see.

"Would it really kill them to construct a road and maybe put up a sign: *This way to Elf City*?" I muttered. The arrogant face of the warmongering lunatic sitting on the throne in the city behind me suddenly sprang to mind. "Yes, it probably would." Staring at the endless forest in front of me, I adjusted my backpack and shook my head. "I am so screwed."

However, there was no point in delaying the inevitable, so after my ominous proclamation, I simply charged right in. On the bright side, at least it was summer. I could've been trudging through the forest in the cold of winter, the biting wind pulling on my cloak. Instead, rays of sunshine found their way through the canopy above and warmed my skin. The sea breeze that provides cool for Keutunan's warm city summers was having trouble finding its way in there and I soon found myself sweating. While you might need a cloak for the brisk summer mornings by the sea, hiking through the woods at noon did most certainly not require one. Stopping briefly, I removed my dark gray cloak and stuffed it into the backpack. While I was at it, I also took out the compass. There was no way of knowing if I had walked straight northwest up until this point because I had refused to walk with the compass in my hand. What if I had to fight off a hellhound? I needed both my hands. Instead, I trusted my instincts and settled for simply reconfirming my course every once in a while. Hoisting my backpack, I started out again.

As I walked, my boots left footprints in the lush, green grass and moss that covered the ground. I had never seen this much green in my entire life. Not even in the Artisan District, where the dyers and the painters worked, had I ever seen colors this vibrant. The air also had an unfamiliar scent. Taking deep breaths through my nose, I tried to figure out what it was but I couldn't quite place it. As I continued deeper into the woods, the scent grew even richer.

"Well, it's afternoon already and I still haven't been attacked by any hellhounds. Or dragons. So, that's good," I noted to myself as I stopped for a break.

While listening to the birds sing and the crickets play, I leaned against a tree and ate some of the dried food. After a gulp or two of water, I began packing everything up again.

"Hello there," a man's cheerful voice suddenly said to my left.

"Gah!" I yelped in a rather undignified manner and leaped away. "Who are you?" I said warily and waved a hunting knife at him.

Across from me stood a short man with an amused smile on his weather-wrinkled face. I quickly scanned him for weapons. Apart from the sturdy, wooden walking stick he was leaning on, he didn't seem to be carrying any. His clothes of green and brown didn't sport any suspicious bulges and the small, star-shaped, blue flower clutched in his hand could hardly be classified as a weapon.

"Me? Oh I'm just a wanderer," he answered and waved his right hand as if to say that there was no need for knives.

Squinting at him, I lowered the blade but didn't drop it. There was always need for knives.

"Where did you come from?" I asked, befuddled, while turning my head this way and that. "Are you from Keutunan? Well, of course you are. Where else would you be from? There is nowhere else to be from," I continued rambling before stopping myself. "Wait. How did you find me?"

"How do you know that I was the one who found you? Maybe you are the one who found me."

"Huh?"

He just waved a hand in front of his face again and smiled. "How do you like the forest?"

"I wouldn't be here if I had a choice," I said sourly. "It's big, it's green, and it smells strange. Do you smell it too? What even is that smell?"

He chuckled. "It's fresh air."

"Well, I don't like it," I said with a scowl.

His laughter filled the clearing once again. "So, city girl, you are not here because you want to but you are searching for something," he stated. "What is it?"

I hesitated. An odd stranger who suddenly appeared out of thin air didn't exactly inspire trust. I reasoned that he could be working for the king. It might also be the elves. Or the assassins. Damn. How in Nemanan's name had I ended up in the middle of such a complicated power struggle? Regardless, I figured that my situation couldn't possible get any worse by telling him what I was looking for, so I decided to answer honestly.

"I'm looking for the elves. Do you have any idea where to find them?"

"Ah, the elves," he mused. "But of course, the Queen and I go way back."

"You know the Elf Queen?"

"If you continue straight ahead," he said while pointing to the northwest, "you will find a cluster of ash trees. Once you find them, take a right, and then just keep following the ash trees."

"And they will lead me to the elves?"

"Yes."

"Huh." Looking into his eyes, I tried to spot any lies hiding there but I came up empty. Thousands of years' worth of wisdom seemed to swirl around like wisps of clouds in his light green eyes but I could detect no deception. "That sounds simple enough. Thanks."

"There is a storm coming," he said with a face that had suddenly turned grave.

I looked up towards the sky. The canopy was thicker here in the deep parts of the forest and I had trouble making out the color of the sky beyond. "A storm? Are you sure?" I said while straining my neck to see past the leaves.

"Make sure that you are on the right side..."

"The right side of what?" I asked, giving up my futile attempt to study the sky and instead turned to the mysterious stranger.

I recoiled, completely stunned. Whipping my head in every direction, I tried to figure out what had just happened.

"Uhm... hello?" I called tentatively.

The strange little man was gone. I definitely should've been seeing his retreating back if he'd walked away after giving his final advice. No one could walk that far, that fast. I studied the footprints in the grass. Mine were clearly visible but uncertainty filled my chest as I realized that he hadn't left any. I was beginning to question whether our encounter had truly happened when I saw the small, star-shaped, blue flower he'd been holding. It rested neatly in the grass, as if someone had placed it there carefully, with the crown pointing in the same direction that the odd man had done. After one last glance around the clearing, I shrugged.

"Did *so* not see that one coming," I declared and shook my head. "Alright, let's go find some ash trees." I hoisted my backpack again.

Walking in the direction of the flower, I journeyed deeper into the forest. When the light seeping through the canopy dimmed and I still hadn't found any trees covered in ash, I stopped to assess the situation. Maybe I should've asked what an ash tree was. I'd just assumed that it was a tree covered in ash but now that I'd walked for hours without finding a single ash-covered tree, I was beginning to doubt that I'd interpreted it correctly. Maybe an ash tree was a type of tree? I studied the leaf-clad giants around me but they only stared mutely back.

"Oh don't look at me like that!" I yelled in frustration at the silent trees. "I know what a tree looks like, okay? It's brown at the bottom and green at the top. And then there's round green and there's pointy green. How the hell was I supposed to know that there were different kinds of pointy and different kinds of round?"

I picked up a small stone and hurled it at my impassive spectators. It produced a small thwack as it hit the nearest tree trunk but in the fading light, I could barely see it bounce away. I needed to find somewhere to make camp. As the remaining light disappeared from the world and the cold settled in, I realized that I had absolutely no idea how to make a fire. In the city, there was always a light source of some kind: an oil lamp, a torch, moonlight. When the sun had set here in the dense forest, however, it was as dark as the blackest pit of my soul. I didn't make it far before it was so dark that I could no longer see my surroundings. Deciding that here was as good a place as any, I dropped my pack. With my backpack as a pillow and the cloak swept tightly around me, I curled up against a tree. While cursing this tree-infested forest and ridiculous mission one last time, I drifted off to sleep.

19.

My eyes shot open. The pale light of dawn trickled down through the leaves. Twigs snapped behind me as heavy footsteps drew closer. Muffled panting followed it. On instinct, my hands went for my throwing knives but they met empty shoulders before I realized that I'd packed them up and put them in the bag. It was difficult to carry ten throwing knives and a backpack on my shoulders at the same time. Standing up and positioning the backpack against my leg, in case I needed to use it as a shield, I slid out my hunting knives and waited. It was close now. Dry leaves crunched beneath the heavy steps. I readied my knives. Any second now.

A large black muzzle swung around the tree trunk. I let out an involuntary gasp as the creature attached to the muzzle became visible. Only a couple of strides away stood a huge, black bear. My exclamation of surprise made the large animal whip its head around. *Oh no.* The bear reared up and started swatting the ground with its front paws while blowing and snorting. Shit. Now what? Was I supposed to act threatening or non-threatening, attack, distract it or play dead, run or stand my ground? I wished there'd been more time to read up on all this forest stuff. Threatening. I decided to go with threatening.

Making myself as big as possible, I started frantically waving my arms while yelling incoherently. The bear answered by lunging at me. I brought my arms up to protect my face in anticipation of the blow but it stopped just short of me. The black bear continued snorting and swatting the ground. Nope, that was not the right choice. I returned the hunting knives to the small of my back. Since I was fairly certain that I wouldn't get another chance to get it right, I decided to risk it all with my next move. While slowly backing away, I reached into the backpack I was now clutching to my chest and drew out my pack of food.

"Nemanan, if you're listening, I could really use your help," I whispered.

I opened the food pack to make sure that it would spill out and then heaved it to the left of the bear. Once I saw its brown eyes turn to look at the decoy, I decided to demonstrate my skills in tactical retreat and ran like a bat out of hell in the opposite direction.

Only when it was growing increasingly difficult to suck air into my lungs did I stop sprinting. Leaning against a tree with my chest heaving, I sent earnest prayers of thanks to the God of Thieves, or whichever god had listened. That could've ended badly. I slid down the tree, brought my knees up to my chest and rested my head against the trunk. On the plus side, I hadn't been mauled to death by a bear. The downside, however, was that I'd sprinted in an unknown direction for an unknown amount of time and thus had even less of a clue where I was than before. Also, I had no food. I heaved a deep sigh. One problem at a time. After drinking sparsely from one of the waterskins, I headed out to find some food.

While birds chirped their morning greetings at me from the branches above, I analyzed my options. I was confident that I could hit some of the birds with my throwing knives but there was one crucial piece of the puzzle missing in that plan. Catching and eating the bird was simple enough but how in the world did one go about transforming a dead bird into an edible dead bird? I hadn't the faintest idea. All my life, when I'd been hungry, I'd simply stolen or bought food that was already prepared and edible. Was I supposed to skin the bird? Are all parts of a bird edible? Also, how was I even supposed to cook it if I didn't know how to make a fire? I shook my head. This wasn't going to work. In the end, I decided to go with food sources that didn't need preparation: fruit, nuts, and berries.

"One would think there'd be lots of edible plants here, it is a forest after all, but no," I complained to the insects buzzing around me after I'd scoured the woods for hours without finding a single piece of fruit.

My stomach grumbled in protest.

"Yes, I know!" I snapped at my discontent abdominal organ. "I'm trying to find..."

I trailed off as something colorful caught my eye. A thick bush filled with rich purple berries peeked out from behind a tree.

"Oh, fina-fricken-lly," I exclaimed and rushed across the clearing.

My hunger convinced me that these were the most beautiful berries I'd ever seen. They were big and bright and as the midday light glinted off them, I realized that the hues actually ranged from dark red, to purple, to midnight blue. Not even bothering to take off my backpack and sit down for a proper meal, I shoved bunch after bunch of delicious, juicy berries into my mouth. Only after finishing my satisfying splurge did I sit down on the warm grass for a much needed rest.

"Aah, that was good." I yawned and stretched my arms above my head.

I cast a glance at the lifesaving bush behind me. There were still enough berries left on it to last me a couple of days. Alright, that was one problem solved. For now, at least. That only left the issue of being totally lost. The best course of action was of course to look for ash trees but that plan only worked if I actually knew what the damn things looked like. The next best thing was to keep heading northwest. I figured that no matter which direction my hasty tactical retreat had taken me, northwest was still northwest. Before heading off in search of something edible, I'd taken out my compass to make sure I walked in that direction. I would do the same once I'd gathered the rest of the berries but for now, I wanted to enjoy my well-deserved break. Being attacked by a bear and sprinting through the forest did take its toll. I looked at the vista before me. It was beautiful. Tiny sparkles floated around the tree trunks and the grass seemed to glow from within. The forest practically glittered. I squinted at the scene before me while my mind turned suspicious. It wasn't supposed to be shimmering like this.

"You! Are you seeing this?" I asked my companion. "No, of course you're not. You can't see anything from down there."

I picked up my small companion and turned my hand in every direction to make sure that the view was unobstructed. As my friend took in the sights, I smacked my lips and tried to chew the air.

"Hey! The air tastes like sweet rolls. Can you feel it?" I asked and looked down at the silent partner in my hand.

With deeply furrowed brows, I studied my companion for a long moment. A breath of clarity pushed its way to the front of my mind and I let my hand drop.

"And I'm talking to a pine cone..." I sighed in disbelief as I watched it roll from my hand and settle back into the green, glowing grass.

I brought my hand back up to my face and turned it over several times. It was glittering. And purple. I flexed my fingers and then traced the muscles in my arm up towards my shoulder. It was also covered in purple stardust. Looking down at the rest of my body, turning my arms up and down, I saw that it, too, sported that shimmering hue. I held my hand up to the light trickling down from the leaves. It was starting to look translucent. I glanced suspiciously from side to side. Was I beginning to fade away? I stabbed a finger at my palm. No, it was still solid. Good.

"I need t' get outta here," I slurred and pushed to my feet.

Thankfully, I hadn't taken off my backpack when I sat down, because at that moment, I couldn't have figured out how to thread my arms through the straps if my life depended on it. Swaying unsteadily on my feet, I surveyed the sparkles around me through narrowed eyes. The ground to my right looked to be the steadiest and the least sparkly so I concluded that was the way out. I took a step forward. My foot sank through the glowing grass and the world spun upside down repeatedly as I fell down the hole in the forest floor. Once it came to a stop, I found myself lying on my back, staring at shifting swirls of paint strokes above. I lay there in the timeless glen and stared at the beautiful kaleidoscope of colors that had chased the darkness away.

"I'm not really sure what's going on here but I'm pretty sure I can smell the color nine," I mumbled to the unseen sky artist and giggled.

After half a second and a thousand years, I stretched my arm up towards the colorful sea and let my hand glide through it. The paint swirled around my fingers. As I looked at it, the swirls turned into deep ruts and the surface cracked like a dried up painting. It shattered and pieces of broken glass rained down all around me. I scrambled away and started stumbling madly through the glowing forest to escape the falling sky.

The endless forest finally ended with a huge waterfall cascading down a steep rock face. Water pooled into a lake before it. I was about to approach it and drink its crystal clear contents when I saw a majestic, green dragon resting in the water.

"Oh crap," I said and scurried back behind a mighty tree.

"Do you know what happened to the purple berries?" a girl's voice asked.

"No, but have you seen the dragon guarding the waterfall?" I exclaimed, wide-eyed, as I switched from peeking out behind the tree to looking at the source of the voice.

A girl of about eleven years old, with shoulder length brown hair, studied me with intelligent brown eyes. I squinted at her.

"Rain?" I asked, dumbfounded.

"Hi, Storm! It's been a while," she replied and broke into a broad grin.

"You're dead," I stated while continuing to stare at her in disbelief.

"Mmm," she began and tipped her head from side to side, "*dead* is such a limiting word. I like to think of it as not being alive in the traditional sense."

"That's what being dead means."

"Is that right?" She smiled and winked at me.

Rain. She looked just like I remembered her: mischievous, happy, and so full of life. Her looks clashed thoroughly with the irrevocable fact that she was dead. My heart began bleeding through the cracks in the stone wall that I'd erected around it.

"Why are you here, Rain?" I sighed.

"You're losing yourself," she said, her face suddenly serious and her voice stern. "This isn't you. I don't even recognize you anymore."

"Well, a lot of shit happened, remember?" I retorted.

"Shit always happens!" Rain yelled back at me. "It's how you deal with it that defines who you are."

"Easy for you to say: you're dead, you don't have to deal with anything anymore!" I snapped before instantly regretting it.

Unbidden tears streamed down my face as I slumped to the ground. Rain sat down cross-legged in front of me.

"I'm sorry," I said, meeting her eyes.

She shook her head. "It's not your fault."

"Yes, it is. If I hadn't–"

"Listen to me. It is not your fault," she interrupted and wiped the tears from my cheeks. "I am proud of the woman you became. Though, you still have a lot to work on," she finished with a half-smile.

That drew a burst of laughter from me.

"You should get some sleep," Rain said and stood up.

"What about the dragon?" I asked as she started walking away.

She turned around but continued walking. "What dragon?" she answered with a knowing smile and spread her arms.

I turned and looked around the tree trunk. The dragon was gone. "Where did it..." I began before realizing that Rain was gone too. "Wait!" I called and got to my feet. "Don't leave me again..."

Without knowing which direction she'd gone in, I stumbled blindly through the forest. No matter how far I walked, I couldn't locate her again. After a while, my body gave out and I collapsed on the ground, falling into a deep, dreamless sleep.

20.

"Mmm..." I groaned and opened my eyes.

My cheek rested against a patch of damp moss. While blinking repeatedly, I slowly pushed myself into a sitting position. The forest swayed before me and I felt as though someone was pounding on my head with a hammer. After wiping some drool off my chin, I studied my hand. It wasn't purple, or sparkly, anymore.

"What in Nemanan's name happened?" I asked and looked around.

I didn't recognize my surroundings. The thick bush with the purple berries was nowhere to be seen and there were a lot more moss-covered boulders spread across the forest floor than before. The trees looked the same, though. But then again, to me, most trees did. I gave another groan. Moving my head too much made my skull feel like it was splitting open. I pushed the heel of my palms to my temples in an effort to reduce the pain. Once it had lessened a little, I very carefully removed my backpack which, thankfully, had survived my strange adventure.

As I drew out my remaining waterskin, I tried once more to make sense of what had happened. My time perception was completely distorted; I didn't know if it'd been an hour, a day, or a week since I ate those berries. However, based on my level of dehydration, sleep deprivation, and hunger, I was forced to conclude that it was probably somewhere on the higher end of that scale. Closing my eyes against the stabbing light, I guzzled down the rest of the water. Why die of dehydration today when you could do it tomorrow? For a long while, I just sat there on the damp moss, letting the water work its magic.

"Note to self: don't eat the purple berries," I said at last and then began the challenging task of getting myself into an upright position.

It took much longer than usual and the forest seemed to shift unnaturally several times. Once on my feet, I took out the compass and stared at it for several minutes before I actually understood what I was looking at. I didn't look forward to start trekking through the forest again but I didn't have much of a choice: I had no food, no water, and no clue where I was. This was ridiculous. I tipped my head up towards the canopy above.

"I refuse to die here in this stinking, bloody forest!" I screamed at the sky. "Do you hear me? I refuse!"

"You really shouldn't yell so much. It scares way game," an annoyed voice suddenly stated.

I whipped my head down towards the source and took a shocked step back. Five tall elves had materialized in the clearing. I quickly glanced down at my hand to see if it was purple and sparkly. It was not. Oh. Okay, so they did exist. Elves actually existed. Wow. I was forced to concede that the king might not be a complete lunatic, after all.

Looking back up, I studied my surprise visitors. They were stunning. There was simply no other word for it. All of them were tall, slender, and graceful, and despite the fact that only two of them were women, they all had long flowing hair. Each elf also held a beautifully carved bow. My only problem with that was that they were all drawn and pointed at me. Damn. I drew my hunting knives.

"Oh I suggest you put those back," the elf who seemed to be in charge warned.

Scanning the clearing, I analyzed the situation. My throwing knives were still packed away in my backpack and even though I could technically throw the hunting knives, I only had two of those and they were much harder to aim. They outnumbered me and they all had ranged weapons. Also, based on Rogue's information, they were all incredibly skilled in how to use them. I figured I could still try to fight them close range, and on my best day, it might end relatively well. However, in my current state, I was starving, dehydrated, sleep-deprived, and still trying to recover from an accidental acid trip. I would not win.

"Alright," I yielded, slid the knives back in their holsters, and raised my hands.

My plan had been to take out the Elf Queen from afar, without any elves ever seeing me, but since that plan was already ruined I decided that being brought to their city was the next best thing. Even if it was as a prisoner. I had, after all, broken out of prisons before.

"Any other weapons?" he asked.

"Yeah... lots, actually," I answered and shrugged apologetically.

What? He was going to find that out as soon as he searched me anyway. I might as well use this opportunity to build some trust. Trust that I could later abuse. He looked at me through narrowed eyes.

"Why are you here?"

As soon as I had switched tactics from simple assassination to infiltration, I'd decided on a cover story to use. "The king of Keutunan sent me. Or, well, I mean, I don't really work for him, he sort of forced me. But anyway, he wants to restore trading between our cities, so here I am."

"Trading?"

"Yeah. We don't really have any other cities to trade with, you know. And neither do you, I assume."

"Elaran, I think we should take her with us. The Queen will want to hear this for herself," the female elf with dark brown hair to my left chimed in.

"Alright, fine. Keya, you and Faelar search her for weapons. I'll check her backpack. And you two," he said and motioned to the two black-haired elves, "watch her. If she makes a move, shoot her in the leg."

"Are you sure you want to trust the twins with that?" the female elf approaching me said while twisting slightly towards the black-haired elves. She laughed teasingly.

"Oh shut up! How was I supposed to know that there was a hornets' nest right there?" the male half of what I assumed was a pair of siblings replied.

"At least I saw the moose," his sister quipped and glanced at her brother while amusement played at the corner of her lips.

"Focus," the leader, whose name I now knew to be Elaran, said with a sigh.

I studied them all with curious eyes but said nothing as the three elves who'd lowered their bows approached me. When the blond male elf reached for me, I braced myself for an uncomfortable search but before he put his hands on me, the female elf, Keya, stopped him. She shook her head.

"I will do it, Faelar."

He only shrugged in reply and took a step back. Keya approached until she stood directly in front of me. Her dark brown hair was also pulled back in a braid, just like mine, but it was much longer and far glossier. Hers was also esthetically decorated with green leaves.

"May I?" she asked and motioned at my body.

That took me completely by surprise so I only managed a nod in return. As she began searching and removing the knives strapped to various parts of my body, I tried to remember the last time a captor had asked permission before putting their hands on me. I came up blank. What an interesting lot.

"Are you serious?" Elaran suddenly said and looked at me. "You have no food, no flint and steel to make a fire, and two *empty* waterskins. What kind of amateur are you?"

"Do I really look like someone who spends any extraordinary amounts of time trudging through the woods?" I replied from under arched eyebrows.

"No," he scoffed. "Keya, what did you find?"

"Six knives."

"I found another thirteen wrapped up in here," Elaran answered.

"She's like a one-woman army," the male black-haired elf said and chuckled across the clearing.

"Yeah, too bad she can't eat or drink any of those knives," Faelar jeered.

All my captors smiled at that. I let them laugh. We'd see who was laughing in the end.

"Tie her up," Elaran said and threw the rope he'd found in my backpack to Faelar. "And put the rest of the knives in her backpack," he added and looked at Keya.

Faelar pushed his flowing blond hair back behind his pointed ears as he approached me once more. He snapped his fingers and pointed at my wrists. Not much of a talker, that one. I offered up my hands, wrists up, to him without protest. As he yanked the knot tight, the auburn-haired leader strode towards me with a piece of cloth.

"What? No! There really is no need for–" I began but he ignored my protest and tied the blindfold over my eyes. Great.

"Alright, let's move out," he called and, with a firm hand on my shoulder, started steering me through the forest.

I'm not an adept forest hiker even on my best day and at that point, I was thirsty, hungry, tired, hungover, and blindfolded. Suffice it to say that walking was a challenge for me. After tripping for the fifth time over a root, stone, or blade of grass for all I know, and falling on my face, I'd had enough.

"Would you just remove this bloody blindfold!" I yelled, cutting off Elaran's snickering. "I don't know where I am anyway and I can't tell one tree from another."

"It is going to take forever to get back if we have to keep picking her up every few steps," Keya's voice reasoned somewhere to my right.

Elaran sighed behind me. I waited for my sight to be returned but let out a yelp of surprise when I was lifted off my feet instead.

"Hey! What the hell do you think you're doing? I'm not some sack of potatoes you can just throw over your shoulder," I complained but he ignored me and continued walking. "Are you listening? I'll not–"

"I swear," he cut off, "I will tie you to a tree and leave you there for the wolves if you don't pipe down."

Biting back a snarky reply, I fell silent. I wasn't sure if he would actually follow through on his threat but I didn't want to push my luck. This was, by far, the best chance I'd ever have of finding the Elf Queen.

As he walked on, I realized how much more graceful his steps were than mine. If I'd been carrying someone on my shoulder, they would've bounced up and down on this uneven ground. On his shoulder, however, I lay surprisingly still. A gust of wind snatched up his smooth hair and it cascaded around my face on its way back down. It smelled like a warm afternoon in the forest. Despite my ill feelings towards everything tree-covered, I considered it a nice smell. Warm, stable, and yet, mysterious.

"I am going on ahead to alert the Queen," Keya said after we'd walked for what felt like an hour. "I will see you back in Tkeideru."

A barely audible rustle of leaves was the only sound that marked her departure. My other captors continued walking in silence. After a while, the sounds of a city brimming with life floated through the air. Since my time perception was still scrambled, I couldn't tell for certain how long it had taken us to travel from the clearing to the elves' city, which, based on Keya's remark, I assumed must be called Tkeideru. I felt a strange tingle run up and down my arms. The sound grew louder. Though I could still not hear what they were saying, I heard the murmur of people talking in the distance. The metallic clanking of steel being hammered, the twang of bowstrings, and the laughter of children also reached my ears before long.

"Ow!" I huffed as my grumpy bearer dumped me unceremoniously on the ground.

"Get up. You're walking from here," Elaran instructed and yanked the blindfold from my head.

While I blinked against the sudden light, one of the twins helped me to my feet.

"Thanks," I mumbled before turning to look at the infamous City of Ash.

My jaw dropped. Majestic trees as tall as the Silver Keep towered before me. Elegantly decorated wooden dwellings were located up and down the thick tree trunks and flowing staircases connected the different levels. Between the regal trees, a network of narrow, wooden suspension bridges tied the city together. It was spectacular. The most astonishing fact of all, however, was that it didn't look like someone had built it. The decorated dwellings, the spindling staircases, and the smooth suspension bridges all looked to have grown right out of the trees.

"It's gorgeous," I said, mouth still gaping and eyes wide.

"Yes, it rather is, isn't it?" the female half of the twins said and laughed softly.

"Haela, go find Keya and see what the Queen wants to do about this one," the auburn-haired leader said. "Tell her I'm locking her in the holding cell for now. Faelar, Haemir – you're with me," he finished and jerked his head over his shoulder.

"You're the boss," the female twin, Haela, said and gave a playful salute before trotting away.

I watched her back disappear into the crowd. Rogue had said that they numbered a few hundred but based on what I'd been able to see so far, my estimate was closer to a thousand. As I watched Haela's black hair swing across her back, I realized that there was a multitude of colors represented: all the way from silvery white hair, through blond, to flaming red, through brown, and finally to hair black as midnight. To be honest, that surprised me. I'm not sure why but I'd always assumed that all elves would look the same. There were similarities, yes, like the fact that they were all tall, beautiful, and slender. They all also walked with the grace of a cat. But apart from that, they all had an individual look. I turned to stare at my three remaining captors as I noticed another similarity.

"You all have yellow eyes!" I exclaimed. "Yellow!"

"It took you this long to notice that?" Elaran replied while Faelar snickered beside him.

"Well excuse me for being somewhat preoccupied with the arrows you were pointing in my face before," I muttered. "I was also blindfolded, remember?"

"Move," he ordered instead of dignifying my snarky statement with a reply.

With a firm grip on my arm, he led me through the city. Faelar and Haemir followed behind. The elves we passed stopped to stare at me but instead of meeting their gaze, I glanced away self-consciously.

"By Nature's grace, is that a human?"

"What is she doing here?"

I knew how to handle staring humans in Keutunan but these were elves. A week ago, I hadn't even believed they existed and I had still doubted it all the way up until some of them actually showed up and pointed arrows at me. I was so thoroughly out of my depth here in the forest, surrounded by strange people, that my usually rock-solid confidence was wavering. It was time to do something about that.

"Do you really need three men to guard me? A woman? And a tied up woman at that," I said and held up my wrists.

"What does you being a woman have to do with anything?" Elaran said and looked down at me with a puzzled expression.

"Uhm... well..." I began, equally nonplussed, because to me it was obvious: men didn't usually consider women to be much of a threat.

"And besides, I don't know you. You could be incredibly dangerous for all I know," he continued.

"Have you forgotten that you were carrying nineteen knives when we found you?" Haemir chimed in.

"Exactly. So, you will stay tied up and locked up until we can figure out who you really are," Elaran finished with a challenging expression on his face.

I offered a nod in reply to illustrate that I didn't plan on challenging him over that. On the inside, however, I gave an impressed smile. Smart move. I knew it made my job harder but I was still impressed to find a fellow distrusting professional out here in the woods.

"Haemir, find her something to eat and drink," Elaran said.

Oh thank the gods. I was parched and starving but pride had prevented me from asking them for food and drink. Haemir nodded and took off towards some of the ground level dwellings to our left. I followed his retreating back before a sight unlike any other pulled me back. The largest tree I'd ever seen rose up before me; the trunk must've been four times the size of every other tree in the city. Before it met the ground, it spread out like a gigantic umbrella and a multitude of branches, thick and thin, made up a great hall complete with pillars and windows. They were all decorated with leaves and colorful flowers. Not being able to help myself, I stopped and stared in wonder. This had to be the heart of the city.

"Hey, no lollygagging," the grumpy leader said while pulling me away.

However, I thought I saw the ghost of a smile on his lips before the stern mask returned to his face. Maybe there were emotions hiding under all that seriousness after all. As we continued walking further into the city, I added mental notes to the ever growing list in the scheming part of my brain. I had long ago come to the conclusion that every potential weakness is worth exploring because you never know what you might need to do in order to survive.

"Get in," Elaran commanded and pulled open the door to a tiny house on the ground level.

So, we'd finally reached our destination. I looked around as I stepped across the threshold and concluded that the word *house* was a bit too generous. It was more like one room, really. Light spilled in from the only window, which was nothing more than a narrow hole in the ceiling, and illuminated the room. A wooden bed and a bucket was all it contained. However, I gave an appreciative nod as I noticed that there was a mattress and a blanket on the bed. I'd definitely been through worse. The sound of a knife being pulled filled the room. Damn it. Why did I have to jinx it?

"Hands," Elaran said, twitching two fingers at me, ordering me to come closer.

I answered with a suspicious frown. He gave an impatient sigh and shook his head while flicking his eyes towards the ceiling.

"So you don't want that off then?" he challenged and nodded at my wrists.

"Yes..." I admitted.

"Then get over here right now or I'll walk."

After brief consideration, I surmised that if he was going to hurt or kill me, he would probably have done so already. Approaching warily, I held out my hands. He severed the rope with one swift cut. I added *good with knives* to my mental list. While I rubbed my sore wrists, Haemir returned with one of my waterskins and a plate so full of food it almost spilled over the edge. My stomach grumbled loudly. The black-haired twin gave me a small smile as he set down both items on the mattress. My head swam as the heavenly scent of cooked food threatened to overpower my senses.

"Don't make trouble," Elaran warned as he and the others backed out and closed the door. A heavy bolt slammed in place on the other side.

I shook my head wearily. "Make trouble? By all the gods, where in the world would I find the energy to make trouble right now?"

Slumping down on the bed, I attacked the plate of food with all the ferocity of a pack of wolves. The smoky grilled meat, the warm potatoes, and even the strange vegetable that I didn't recognize disappeared faster than a thief before a squad of Silver Cloaks. I gulped down half of the water in the waterskin before collapsing on the bed. Darkness claimed me almost before I'd managed to pull the blanket over my body.

21.

"You sure are a heavy sleeper."
"Gah!" I shrieked and scrambled away.

An elf woman was sitting by the foot of the bed. She was lounging in a chair, studying the nails of her hand, with her feet up on the mattress and her ankles crossed.

"Who are you?" I asked after concluding that I wasn't in any immediate danger.

"The Queen sent me," she said, shifting her eyes from her nails to my face. "Did you know you've slept for two days straight?"

After rubbing the rest of the sleep from my eyes, I frowned at her. Two days? Was that even possible? Images of me hiking, sprinting, and stumbling through the forest, of bears, purple berries, and mazes of trees that all look the same, flashed through my mind. Tipping my head a little to the side, I shrugged slightly and nodded. Alright, fair enough.

"I was tired," I said and spread my arms.

"You think?" She laughed and then practically jumped up from the chair. "Well, are you coming?"

I stared at her. She looked both cheerful and fierce at the same time. Her silvery white hair was pulled back from her face with three short braids: one at the top of her head and the remaining two starting at each temple. The braids ended in a high ponytail that held the rest of her hair together before it cascaded loosely down her back. With a fearless look in her eye and a broad smile on her lips, she motioned at the door.

"Coming where?" I asked, glancing at the entrance.

"To get something to eat," she replied and gave a short shake of her head as if that had been obvious.

"You're letting me out?"

"Yes. What? Are you going to try to escape?"

"Disregarding the fact that I'm here on a mission, I probably would if not for the fact I have absolutely no idea where I am," I answered. "I'm not much of a woodsman."

Sometimes, the truth is the best lie.

She gave me an appraising look while doing a very poor job of hiding her amusement. At last, a burst of laughter that was more of a snort slipped out. "No, I know, Elaran told me. Come on," she called, opened the door, and walked out.

I only hesitated for a moment before shrugging and following this strange elf out the door.

"You're wearing the wrong colors," she said as I caught up with her.

"What do you mean *the wrong colors*?" I asked while we wound our way through the city.

"For being in the woods. It's not the right palette."

Studying the people around us, I pondered her words. It was true. The types of clothes I was wearing were very similar to the ones that the elves wore: close fitting pants, a long-sleeved shirt, and leather boots. Waistcoats of different styles and materials were also a rather common sight, though none of them were as complex as the custom-made, leather waistcoat with knife slots and hidden pockets that I was wearing. However, the color scheme was completely different. Whereas my clothes all ranged from black to different shades of gray, theirs were in hues of green and brown. Interesting. In the same way that I needed the black and gray to become invisible in the city, I guess they needed variations of green and brown to blend in with the forest. I drew up short next to a wood carver's workshop as I realized something else.

"All women are wearing pants," I stated while whipping my head from side to side.

"Of course. It's kind of hard to move about in the forest in skirts and dresses, you know. Don't women in your city wear pants?" she asked and looked me up and down. "You're wearing pants."

"Well, yeah, it's not unusual for women to wear pants if they've got a job that makes wearing a skirt difficult but the most common is skirts or dresses. And for highborn ladies it's mandatory."

My silver-haired companion laughed and shook her head before giving me a small wave to suggest that we should keep moving. I fell in beside her as we moved out again. After sparing a glance at the position of the sun behind the trees, I concluded that it must be late afternoon. In Keutunan, most people would be closing up their shops right now, heading home or to taverns for some food and drink. As we continued further into the city, I noticed that the elves of Tkeideru were doing the same.

"Don't you have a fancy-dressed, wealthy nobility who do nothing all day?" I asked.

"You humans and your obsession with highborn and lowborn," she scoffed. "No, we don't. Unlike you, we don't consider some people to be better than others."

I frowned at her. Yeah, right. The history books had specifically stated that the elves had tried to conquer us for that exact reason: they thought that they were the superior race. I guess equality only applied within the elven race.

"But what about your queen? Isn't she highborn?"

"No, the Queen is the same as everyone else," she stated flatly. "In here." She pulled me by the shirt into what sounded like a tavern.

At first glance, as the door opened, I thought it looked a lot like one too. When she continued pulling me across the threshold I was met by warmth, cheerful voices, and the smell of food. Wooden tables were crammed together in a haphazardly fashion, tapestries depicting animals and forest scenery decorated the walls, and the back wall was made up entirely of a majestic tree trunk. As I studied the occupants of the various chairs, I noticed people laughing, eating and drinking, playing dice, and telling stories. Yep. This was most definitely a tavern. I yanked my sleeve from the silver-haired elf's grip.

"That table in the back," she said and nodded over her shoulder.

There were still several unoccupied tables in the tavern to choose from, but following her gaze, I understood which one she referred to. It was a sturdy table for six positioned by the slightly curved trunk that made up the back wall. As I weaved my way through the maze of tables, I couldn't help noticing the similarities in atmosphere between this tavern and the Mad Archer. Or any tavern in Keutunan, really. I'd imagined the elves kind of like the nobles of my city: fancy, cultured, and measured. But instead of people in elaborate clothes conversing delicately while listening to someone playing the harp, I'd found them laughing and cheering in a boisterous tavern. Strange. I wondered what the Queen was like.

"Food and drink – seven!" I heard my mysterious companion call close to the bar.

"You got it," a blond elf behind it answered.

After a brief analysis, I decided that the middle chair on the far side was the best position since it provided the best view and kept my back protected.

The Queen's envoy reappeared moments after I'd seated myself in it. She dropped into the opposite chair with a broad smile. "Hungry?"

"Yeah," I nodded before glancing up sharply to see my armed welcome wagon making its way towards our table.

"How was the hunt?" the silver-haired elf asked as Elaran lowered himself into the chair on her right and Keya into the one on her left.

"Good. We got a couple of deer and pigeons," Elaran answered while Faelar slid into the chair opposite him.

"There were some rabbits in the snares too," Keya's soft voice added on the other side.

"Hey, you're forgetting the best part! Haemir actually got the moose this time." Haela laughed and dropped down in the remaining chair to my right.

"Are you ever going to let that go?" Haemir sighed as he dragged over a chair from another table.

"Nope," Haela grinned at her brother as he squeezed himself in between her and Keya.

Laughter broke out around the table. I studied them with curious eyes. Real camaraderie is hard to fake and this didn't seem staged. The way they talked and joked suggested that they were most likely close friends who often met here to drink and share stories at the end of the day. A pang of sadness wrenched my heart as I thought about Liam and all the wonderful mornings we'd spent in a similar fashion. I had to find and kill the Queen so that I could get him out. Quickly. I watched the elves at my table talk amongst themselves. This was a perfect time to do some sneak interrogations. They would never know what hit them. I was about to give a small, premature grin when I realized that the table had suddenly gone quiet. All eyes were turned on me.

"So, who are you?" Elaran asked and leveled a challenging stare at me.

"I already told you, I'm here because–" I began.

"I wasn't asking why you're here. I asked who you are," he interrupted.

Punching him in the face would probably be a bad idea. I wanted to, though. I really, really wanted to. But I managed to exercise restraint and only shoot him a venomous stare.

"Storm. My name is Storm. Actually, it's *the Oncoming Storm*, if we're being specific, but most people just call me Storm. Now, I know all of your names," I said and swept my gaze around the table before stopping at the silver-haired elf opposite me, "except for yours."

"Faye," she said, meeting my gaze.

"Faye," I repeated. "Keya, Haemir, Haela, Faelar, Elaran," I continued and looked at each elf in turn.

At the sound of their name they all returned my gaze with a nod of acknowledgement. All except Elaran. He just continued glaring at me. I shook my head slightly at that before a thoughtful look crossed my face.

"You all have such strange names," I mused.

Haela burst out laughing. "*We* have strange names?" She threw her head back, laughter bouncing off the ceiling above. "Honey, we're not the ones named after a weather phenomenon."

The whole table joined the merriment at that. I smacked my lips. They did have a point, I suppose.

"Good to see you laughing, Faelar," the blond elf from the bar said as he approached the table with two large trays.

The blond elf sitting in the chair beside me snapped his mouth shut and drew his eyebrows down. "I wasn't laughing."

"Uh-huh," the barkeeper replied with a smile as he circled the table putting a plate of food and a cup in front of each person. "I grew up looking at that disagreeable stone face of yours, don't you think I can spot the minute it cracks and some cheerfulness slips out? I'm your brother, remember?" he finished and winked at the now thoroughly embarrassed-looking Faelar.

"Being the older sibling is the best, right, Faldir?" Haela said as the blond server put the last plate and cup down in front of Elaran.

"For sure," he beamed and clapped Faelar on the shoulder before disappearing back towards the bar.

I studied the food before me. There were potatoes on the plate, of that much I was sure, and there also seemed to be some kind of meat stew. And I thought I could spot some carrots too.

"What do you mean *older sibling*?" Haemir protested. "We're twins!"

"Yes, but I came out before you. That makes me the older sibling."

The cup was made of thin, delicately carved wood and contained liquid of a light amber color. It smelled sweet.

"A couple of minutes! That barely applies."

I lifted the cup to my lips and was about to sample the strange liquid when I realized that the table had gone quiet and everyone was staring at me again.

"What?" I asked and lowered the cup a little.

"In our culture, when you are drinking with others, it is customary to raise your cups together before your first taste," Keya said and gave me a small smile.

"Yeah, it's kind of rude not to, actually," Haemir continued and shrugged one shoulder.

"Very rude," Elaran filled in.

"Elaran," Keya said and leaned in to look at him, "be nice, she does not know about any of our customs."

He clicked his tongue but didn't press the matter. I glanced from one to the other with my cup hovering midway between the table and my lips, unsure of what to do now. At last, Faye broke into a broad smile and raised her cup. Everyone else followed suit.

"To health, happiness, and good hunting!" she said.

"Good hunting!" they all responded and looked around at each other.

Once I saw them all finally tip their cup towards their lips, I did the same. The liquid tasted as sweet as it had smelled. Just like the ale at the Mad Archer, it had a somewhat fruity flavor but that was where the similarities stopped. Whereas the ale had a distinct bitter taste, this liquid was sweet and flowery. How odd.

I noticed that the elves had started eating and my stomach was grumbling again so I decided to dig in as well.

"Oh by Nemanan, this is good!" I ended up exclaiming somewhat involuntarily as I tasted the meat.

"It's venison. Have you never had venison before?" Haemir said and raised an eyebrow at me.

"No," I said while continuing to attack the stew, "we don't really have any hunters." I came very close to adding *because of you* at the end of that sentence but stopped myself at the last moment.

"So what do you eat?" Faye asked between bites.

"For meat: fish, mostly. But also some cattle, like cows and sheep. Then of course potatoes and vegetables," I said and poked at what I now knew to be a carrot.

"Who's Nemanan?" Haela asked suddenly.

I put down my cup and stared at her before glancing from face to face. Everyone else just looked back at me with the same puzzled expression she wore.

"What do you mean *who's Nemanan?*" I asked, befuddled. "He's one of the gods."

"There's only one god," Elaran said in a firm voice. "Nature."

"Well, yes, there are gods of nature. But then there are also gods of trading, fishing, war, death, and so on."

They all stared blankly at me. I opened my mouth and then closed it again. Getting into a lengthy theological debate concerning whose gods were real probably wasn't worth it. "I guess this is another one of those cultural differences," I said and waved my hand in front of my face by way of saying that I didn't want to argue.

"I'll say," Haemir stated.

"What is this?" I asked in order to change the subject, and pointed at my cup.

Haela burst out laughing again. Not a mean laugh but more of a surprised I-can't-believe-you-asked-that kind of laugh. "It's wine," she answered at last and pushed a loose strand of hair back behind her pointed ear.

"Wine," I repeated as if tasting the word. "Is there alcohol in it?"

"Yeah. It took our ancestors centuries to figure out how to grow grapes in this climate, but luckily for us, they did. So now we have the best kind of alcohol there is."

"Hmm."

As the conversation shifted to which wine was the best, I continued eating in silence. Since some of my dinner companions had already finished eating, Faldir came and cleared some plates and filled everyone's cups with more wine. I needed to start fishing for information on how to find the Queen.

"So, how do you all know each other?" I asked when the wine discussion dried out.

"What do you mean *how do we know each other*? Everyone knows everyone in Tkeideru," Elaran said beneath furrowed brows.

"Oh, okay. Even the Queen? You know the Queen too?"

"Of course we do," Faye said with a smile.

"What's she like?"

The table fell silent as they all looked at each other. At last, Haela broke into one of her customary grins. "She's pretty cool."

"Pretty cool?" Elaran questioned and rolled his eyes at the black-haired twin. "She's smart, fierce, brave, and she always does what's best for her people."

"Agreed," Faelar said.

"But sometimes I think she might be too smart for her own good," Elaran continued and glanced at the rest of the table.

"Ha! True that," Faye said and burst out laughing. "So, what's your king like?"

As Faldir removed the rest of the plates and filled our cups once more, I considered my options. Though I had no love for the king, I didn't want to give away too much information about Keutunan. Until I could figure out what their intentions were, I was going to have to be as vague as possible while still getting the information I needed.

"He's pretty well-read," I began, "but he's also cruel, paranoid, and he loves to show off his power."

"He sounds awful," Keya said with a horrified expression on her face. "Why, by Nature's grace, did you choose him?"

"We didn't," I replied and frowned at her.

Her eyes widened. As I glanced around the table, I realized that they were all staring at me. Again.

"So, who chose him then?" Haemir asked, breaking the silence.

"No one? The gods? I don't know," I said with an impatient shrug. "He's the eldest son of the last king, who was the eldest son of the last king, and so on."

"But what if the eldest son is a moron, someone unfit to rule?"

"Then we're screwed. Story of my life..." I said and shook my head.

"Huh. No wonder your culture is so–" Haemir began before being silenced by a sharp glace from Faye.

I peered at him. *My culture is so what?* During this entire conversation, I'd had the feeling that they were hiding something. They didn't seem to be lying, not outright, anyway. But they were definitely leaving something out. I added that to my mental list of things to find out. However, the priority was the Queen. Time to reel the conversation back to that.

"Well, thankfully, we barely ever see King Adrian. He lives in his castle surrounded by walls and guards and doesn't mix with common people. Is your queen like that too?" I asked in an innocent voice.

"No, she's really not," Faye said and took a big swig of wine before motioning to Faldir to bring more.

"For real? So, she could just come walking in here, in this tavern, and sit down for a drink?"

"Yep."

"Huh. What a strange royal," I said, shaking my head with a genuinely perplexed expression on my face. "She doesn't wear fancy clothes, she doesn't live in a castle, and she spends time with commoners. Does she at least wear a crown?"

"Nope, she doesn't."

"But then how do you all know who the Queen is when she's there?"

"What kind of stupid question is that?" Elaran interrupted. "We all chose her to be our queen. Do you really think there's anyone who wouldn't recognize her when they saw her?"

"I guess," I mumbled and squinted a little.

He was right, that had been a stupid question. It had been uncharacteristically direct, and also badly phrased. I rubbed my temples. My thoughts were unusually slow and scattered. I looked down at the wooden cup. Was I getting drunk?

Admittedly, I had drunk several cups in rapid succession but no, that wasn't possible. I could drink twice this amount of ale at home without the alcohol dulling my mind. Crap. How much alcohol was in this? Panic gripped my heart like a clenched fist. By all the gods, I couldn't get drunk now!

You know those situations where you are covertly trying to get information from someone while they're doing the same and you're both trying not to give up the information the other wants? This whole dinner was like one of those giant interrogations where everyone wants something but no one wants to give anything. That's dangerous, and to survive a situation like that, your mind needs to be sharp as a blade. It was with growing dread that I realized mine was becoming as dull as a butter knife with every passing minute. The elves exchanged glances around the table.

"I'll get her back," Faye said and stood up.

Thank Nemanan. If I was asleep I couldn't accidentally let something important slip. I pushed to my feet as well. The room swayed before me and I had to grab the edge of the table to stay upright. Gods' balls and tits. I hadn't been this drunk since I'd challenged Liam to a drinking contest. It had turned out that boy could drink. Mightily. He'd drunk me right under the table and I'm not someone who gets wasted easily. Well, except when I eat purple hallucinogenic berries from a strange bush, apparently... But no one was there to see that. Shit. I closed my eyes briefly as the room tilted again. A soft arm latched on to mine. Opening my eyes, I saw that it was Faye holding my arm.

"Come on," she said and smiled down at me while leading me away.

"Okay," I mumbled and awkwardly waved goodbye in the direction of the table.

"Not used to wine, huh?" Faye said as we continued walking.

"No... we drink ale. It's kind of like this, but not really. I mean it's the same, but not. It's more sweet... the wine, I mean, not the ale because the ale is not... sweet," I rambled.

Sometime later, I felt a soft pillow against my cheek and a cover being drawn over me. I didn't know where I was or how I'd gotten there and I knew that I should be worried. But the mattress was so soft and I was so tried.

"This was a good talk. Goodnight, Storm," a woman's voice said somewhere in the distance.

A good talk? What had we talked about? Something, something important, tried to push its way through the fog in my mind but it only made it to the edge of the small, illuminated part that was left before sleep claimed me and everything went black.

22.

"Get up!" a man's voice yelled.

Loud banging followed it. Or was it my head that was pounding? While groaning, I pushed myself into a sitting position. My tongue felt like it was stuck to the roof of my mouth. Working it loose, I looked around while also trying to blink sleep from my eyes. Okay. I wasn't in the holding cell that I'd been locked in last time. This was a room. And not just any room, one of those rooms that are built for people to live in, it would seem. Besides the well-stocked bed I was currently occupying, there was also a wooden desk with a chair, some shelves and cupboards, and a nightstand with an unlit candle. A colorful rug covered the floor and a large chest occupied one of the corners. Curious. The door crashed open.

"I said *get up*!" Elaran boomed across the room.

"I am up," I snapped, glowering at him.

"Then why aren't you answering?"

I clicked my tongue and sighed. Always the charmer. He was standing in the light that spilled in from the open door with his arms crossed over his chest. I knew that I'd messed up last night and that I had probably said something I shouldn't have said. Studying his face, I tried to figure out the amount of trouble I was in. That customary, disapproving scowl he usually wore when he looked at me was still there but I couldn't detect any outright hostility. So, no more trouble than usual then. I surmised that if I'd accidentally let slip that I was here to kill the Queen, I would already be dead. Shrugging, I stood up.

"What do you want?" I asked.

"Come on, we have work to do." He turned on his heel and strode out.

Seeing no reason to argue, I followed him out the door. Blinding sunlight met me outside the room, or at least it was blinding to my poor, hungover eyes, so I stopped to let them adjust.

"Whoa!" I exclaimed once I realized where I was.

Rope bridges floated before me like giant vines. Both above and below me, beautifully carved houses clung to their tree trunks. I stepped forward to the edge of the bridge and looked down. Hundreds of people moved about on the different levels and the ones on the ground were no larger than my hand.

"Are you afraid of heights?" Elaran asked behind me.

"Am I afraid of heights? I've spent most of my life running across–" I began before realizing that sharing my expertise on rooftop running might not be such a good idea. "No, I'm not afraid of heights."

"Good," he answered and jerked his head. "Then let's go."

He took off down the narrow suspension bridge and after a short sprint to catch up, I fell in beside him. I desperately wanted to ask him where we were going, because I hate not knowing what's going on, but I didn't want to give him the satisfaction so I kept quiet. Instead, he broke the silence once we had cleared half of the bridges on our way down.

"As long as you're here you will contribute to the city," he said and peered down at me. "So, what are your skills?"

I racked my brain for an appropriate answer. *Uhm... stealing? Probably best to keep that to myself. Let's see what else we've got. Sneaking. Lying. Forging. Assassinating. Yeah, no, those aren't gonna fly either. Crap. I must have something legit...*

"Do you have any actual skills?" Elaran pressed.

"I'm a decent hunter," I surprised myself by saying.

"You – a hunter?" he scoffed. "Besides, I thought you said you humans didn't have any hunters. So tell me, oh decent hunter, what are you good at hunting?"

"Birds...?"

It was true in theory at least. I'd never actually tried, but with my aim, I was confident that I could take down several birds without much trouble.

"Birds. Sure," he sniggered.

I wanted to punch him in the face. "Give me back my knives and I'll prove it," I challenged.

"Remember that promise because I'll hold you to it one day. I bet it's going to be a very amusing day for me," he said and smirked at me. "But for now, I'll hold on to your knives."

Ha, gotcha! Now I knew that he was the one who had my knives. Once I'd figured out who the Queen was, I would just go and steal them back. Sneak interrogations were so much easier when you weren't drunk on ridiculously strong wine.

"I look forward to it," I grinned back.

"Hmmph. Since you don't have any useful skills, you'll accompany me in the forest today," he switched topic and drew his scowl back down. "Don't slow me down."

No useful skills, huh? We'd see about that. When his queen was lying dead on the ground in a pool of her own blood, we'd see who the useless one really was.

※

BIRDS CHIRPED ON THE branches above as sunlight trickled down through the leaves. It must have rained a little during the night because the smell of wet soil hung over the forest. After making a short pit stop to get some food and water, the auburn-haired malcontent and I had left Tkeideru behind and made our way into the forest. Elaran walked with determination so I assumed that we weren't just wandering around aimlessly. We hadn't spoken much since leaving the city and I really needed to continue fishing for information. So far I'd only been able to find out that I wouldn't recognize the Queen if I saw her, since she didn't have any distinguishing clothes or accessories.

"When will I get to see the Queen?" I asked. "I did come here with a mission: to talk about trading. Remember?"

"You will see the Queen when the Queen says so," Elaran informed me.

"What even is her name anyway? Our king is King Adrian but here everyone just keeps saying *the Queen*, without an actual name."

"Do we have more than one queen?" he asked and arched an eyebrow at me.

"No...?" I replied, glancing from side to side.

"Exactly. So why would we need to specify which one? She is simply *The* Queen."

Shrugging in reply, I had to concede that he did have a point. Unfortunately, such logical thinking didn't help my assassination plans. If I knew her real name, I could find people to investigate when I heard them speak that name. Wait. Heard them speak. A sudden realization hit me like a shovel to the back of the head.

"You all speak my language!" I blurted out. "Why do you all speak my language?"

He stopped and stared down at me. "We don't speak *your* language, you speak *our* language," he answered and shook his head slightly. "Our ancestors were here long before your people came and settled on the coast."

"Our ancestors came from somewhere else?" I asked, surprised.

"Yeah. I mean it's been a few thousand years, but yes. After they settled, we began trading but it was difficult because you didn't understand what we were saying. So we started teaching you our language. That eventually spread from the merchants to the rest of the people and then you all started speaking it," he finished and shrugged.

"Huh." I blinked. "Do you know where we came from? Or how we got here?"

"No, it was before my time."

Without another word, Elaran started walking again. For a moment, I just stood there under the rustling leaves and considered what he'd said.

"So there *is* something else out there," I mumbled to myself. "If we came from somewhere else then there has to be other civilizations out there, right? Other cities, maybe even other races. But then, why did we leave in the first place? Maybe we fled some terrible catastrophe that destroyed everything except this part of the world. We might be alone after all." I squinted in thought. "Or maybe not."

Shaking off my musings, I looked around for Elaran. I could narrowly make out his back disappearing through the trees ahead so I ran to catch up with him before he got too far. Getting lost in the forest was not high up on my to-do list for today.

"What are we doing out here, Elaran?" I said and heaved a deep sigh when I caught up with him.

"Hunting."

He had unslung his bow and was now prowling rather than walking.

"But I don't have anything to hunt with," I protested.

"*I* am hunting. *You* are staying out of my way," he clarified and nocked an arrow. "Now be quiet."

I rolled my eyes but did as he commanded. I don't like people telling me what to do but ever since King Adrian had kidnapped Liam, I'd had to learn how to endure it in situations where I normally would've just thrown a knife at the person. While I contemplated how good it would feel to throw something at Elaran, we continued stalking through the forest in complete silence. Occasionally, he would stop and look at something only he could see. His eyes never seemed to stop glancing around in search of prey. After an hour of skulking about without seeing as much as a deer, Elaran shocked me by unleashing a frustrated howl.

"You are too noisy!" he bellowed at me. "You stomp around like a pregnant moose! There's no way I'm going to find any game with all this... noise!" he finished and threw out his arms.

I blinked twice and stared at him in stunned silence. Then his words sank in and a thunderstorm gathered in my eyes.

"Noisy? Noisy?!" I yelled back at him. "I have been called many unflattering things in my life: arrogant, bad-tempered, cruel, and a whole boatload of colorful variations of those adjectives but never noisy. Never."

"Well, you are! You don't know how to move in the forest. I swear you've stepped on every damn dry twig and leaf we've come across, and it *rained* last night! At first I thought you were doing it on purpose but now I realize that you really are just an idiot."

The thunderstorm roared in my eyes, threatening to turn them black, while the darkness boiled in my soul. If I had a knife. Just one. Satisfying images flashed through my head. But the worst part of it all was that it was true; I had no idea how to move quietly in the woods. The art of stalking silently in the city was something I had mastered long ago but the forest floor was completely different. There were too many unknown elements that I didn't understand. I was still pissed off, though.

"At least I know how to braid my hair properly," I retorted. "What, you couldn't find all of your hair? Or you couldn't find the middle of your head?"

Elaran took a small step back and ran his hand over the tight side braid that gathered up all the hair on the left side of his head. He opened his mouth and stared at me with surprised eyes. It had been low blow, and a childish one, I know, but it was also the most embarrassed I'd ever seen him, so I was still satisfied with the result. In fact, at one point I thought he might shoot that nocked arrow at me. His fingers twitched but he fought against it. It seemed to take great effort but at last Elaran managed to put his customary scowl back on his face. He shook his head violently.

"How did I get stuck on this ridiculous babysitting duty," he muttered. "Let's go, we still have work to do."

After a deep sigh he returned the arrow to its quiver and the bow to his back. The previously flustered elf looked at me expectantly and then started out. He did calm down quickly, I had to give him that. When the darkness had subsided and the thunderstorm had receded completely from my eyes as well, I jogged to catch up with him.

"At least you're decent at trading insults," he said and threw a glance at me from the corner of his eye.

"As are you," I replied.

I had to admit, that pregnant moose comment had been a good one. He released an amused breath. It felt as though we'd reached an uneasy truce and I didn't want to ruin it, because it might be my way into the Queen's presence, so I stayed quiet.

"Since we can't do any actual hunting," Elaran began and cleared his throat, "we're just going to check the snares and also see if we can find any berries to pick."

"Okay. What's supposed to get caught in these snares?" I asked.

"Rabbits are the intended target but occasionally the odd fox and squirrel finds its way in there."

"So, what should I do?" I inquired.

"You will scare the animals with your trampling," he said with a barely hidden smile, "so I'll get the snares, you'll look for berries. If you walk in that direction," he lifted his arm to point, "you'll find lots of purple berries–"

"Oh no," I interrupted, taking a step back and shaking my head while images of my own unfortunate berry encounter flashed through my mind. "I'm not falling down that rabbit hole again."

Elaran squinted at me as a bemused expression settled on his face. Then, the fog cleared in his eyes. "Oh by Nature's grace, you ate journeyberries, didn't you? That's why you didn't wake up when we first checked you out."

"I don't know what they're called," I muttered, "but yeah, I may or may not have accidentally eaten some purple, hallucinogenic berries that..." I trailed off. "Wait, what do you mean *checked me out*? Were you watching me?"

"Yeah, we watched you drool into the moss for about an hour before you woke up and started yelling at the trees," he said, a grin playing on his lips.

I groaned and buried my face in my hands. As far as first impressions go, this one definitely ranked in the bottom five.

"Don't worry, these aren't journeyberries, they're blueberries."

"In case you hadn't noticed, I'm not very woodsy," I said drily. "How will I know the difference?"

"Well, journeyberries grow on tall bushes while blueberries grow on low, prostrate and mat-forming shrubs so you..." he trailed off as he realized I was staring at him with eyebrows that almost reached my hairline.

"Yeah, you know, I feel like you're trying to tell me something, but I don't understand what you're saying," I informed him.

"On the ground," he spelled out, "blueberries grow on the ground, okay?"

"Why didn't you just say that from the beginning then?" I asked and gave a small shake of my head.

"Because you..." he huffed before stopping himself. "Just get the damn berries." He threw a leather bag at me.

"I assume you'll come and get me when you're done?" I said.

"Yeah. Try not to get lost."

"I'm already lost," I called over my shoulder as I trotted away in the previously indicated direction.

I heard him heave a deep sigh in reply before I disappeared into the glen and out of earshot.

"DID YOU TRY ANY?" ELARAN asked.

We were jogging back towards Tkeideru. Elaran had a bunch of rabbits slung over his shoulder while I cradled the bag of blueberries in my arms. It had taken much longer than I'd expected to pick enough berries to fill it and my back hurt from walking bent over like an old lady with a hunchback.

"No," I replied and eyed the bag suspiciously.

"You should."

The afternoon sun slanting down through the leaves warmed my back as I reached down into the bag and pulled out a handful of blueberries. Studying the round objects in my hand, I noticed some differences between these and what Elaran had called *journeyberries*. Whereas their color had ranged from dark red, to purple, to midnight blue, these blueberries were overall dark blue. I popped one into my mouth. When I bit down on it the berry broke apart and fresh juice spilled out. It tasted sweet but with a hint of acidity.

"It's good, right?" Elaran said.

"Mm-hmm," I nodded while chewing.

I poured the rest of the berries from my hand into my mouth as the city became visible in the distance. In my opinion, these were actually tastier than the journeyberries, even though they weren't as sweet. Or perhaps because of that. I was just about to ask what they were used for when something drew me up short.

"Did you feel that?" I asked and looked around.

A slight tingle had traveled up and down my arms. It had been there and then gone so quickly that I had almost missed it.

"Feel what?" the auburn-haired archer asked with a dubious look on his face.

"Well, it was like..." I began and then shook my head. "Never mind."

Elaran shrugged and started out again but I stayed in place for another moment. I was sure that I'd felt something. One more mystery to add to the ever growing list of things to find out, I guess.

The citizens of Tkeideru stared a little less today than they'd done the day I arrived. As Elaran and I crossed the city, I only caught the occasional wary look.

"Hey, Talar!" Elaran suddenly called to a passing elf.

"Elaran," he responded and shot a curious glance in my direction.

"Are you heading to the Storage?"

"Yeah, I've got some pigeons to deliver," Talar said and lifted the sack on his shoulder slightly.

"Could you take these with you as well?" Elaran asked, indicating the rabbits and the bag I was carrying.

"Sure," he said with a light shrug.

Talar took the sack from his shoulder and held it open, allowing Elaran to drop the rabbits inside. After swinging the sack back onto his shoulder, Talar turned to look at me. I cast a quick glance at the bag of blueberries before reluctantly handing over my prize. I'd worked hard for those blueberries and it went against my every instinct to just hand them over. Once the transfer was complete, Talar gave Elaran a short nod and took off again. We continued walking across the city. There seemed to be fewer people here than when we'd left. However, the ones who were still here looked like they were in a hurry to get somewhere else. Not the panicked sort of urgency, rather an excited hurry. A sense of cheerful anticipation hung in the air.

"Shouldn't you have gotten paid?" I asked, because despite the joyous atmosphere, I still couldn't let go of my blueberries.

"Paid?" Elaran asked and looked down at me with a befuddled expression.

I squinted at him. "Yeah, you know, you give them something they want and they give you money in return. And then you can use that money to buy something from someone else. Money transactions."

"Money," he scoffed. "I'd almost forgotten about the ridiculous obsession with money that you humans have."

"It's not ridiculous," I retorted. "How else are you supposed to get something you can't make or do yourself?" I eyed him suspiciously. "How do *you* pay for things?"

"We don't. Everyone contributes to the city in their own way. Some hunt, some teach, some make food or bows or knives, some weave, some grow crops. Everyone contributes and everyone shares in the result. It's as simple as that."

No money? What kind of crazy place was this? If there was no competition between businesses, then there'd be no need to keep improving products and services. There'd be no incentive to get better. Or would there? If everyone could just focus on what they were good at, without the risk of not making enough money to live off, maybe that would make the products even better. Huh. I couldn't decide what I thought about it. It was a strange system, for sure.

"It's interesting," was all I admitted to Elaran before changing topic. "Where is everyone?"

"They're probably all at the..." he began and then stopped once he noticed Haela jogging towards us.

She gave an enthusiastic wave and fired off a beaming smile when she saw that we had spotted her. A cloud of dirt lifted from the ground as she skidded to a halt in front of us, ponytail flying over her shoulder.

"Come on, hurry up! You're gonna miss it!" she exclaimed and threw her black hair back over her shoulder.

"Should we really be doing this right now?" Elaran said with a sigh. "With..." he cast a quick glance at me, "everything else that's going on?"

"Of course we should! And the Queen even said that *everything else* can come along and watch too," Haela said and grinned at me.

"She did?"

"Yes. Now get a move on or we'll miss the start!" she said before turning on her heel and trotting back the way she'd come.

While watching her retreating back I couldn't help thinking about Liam. They both had that same cheerfulness and innocent excitement about everything. Gods, I missed him. I had to keep winning their trust if I was ever going to get close to their queen. Elaran was rubbing his temples with a deep frown beside me.

"Reckless and too smart for her own good," he muttered under his breath while shaking his head. "Fine then! Let's go," he said and threw his arms up.

"What's going on?" I asked as we both ran to catch up with Haela.

"You'll see."

I'm neither short nor tall; my legs are of perfectly average length, thank you very much. The same cannot be said for the elves. I sometimes found it difficult to keep up with Liam's long legs but they had nothing on the legs of elves. Considering the fact that I'd spent the better part of the afternoon trying to keep up with Elaran while jogging, I wasn't in the best position to keep pace with a sprinting elf. When we finally caught up with the black-haired twin, I was breathing harder than I would've liked. Both elves glanced at me and then slowed down a little. My cheeks flushed with embarrassment but I was grateful for the slower pace so I didn't protest.

A sea of people appeared in the distance. The excited murmur of the crowd became louder the closer we got to whatever it was that they were here for. I was reminded of the atmosphere in Keutunan during the king's birthday, when the city was full of games, theater performances, and competitions. That same giddy excitement was present here. Once we had weaved through most of the crowd, I finally saw what they were all looking at.

"It's an archery competition," I declared, peering at the round straw targets in the distance.

"Well, yeah," Haela said and turned to Elaran. "You didn't tell her?"

He just shook his head. Haela rolled her eyes and then put a hand on my shoulder. "See over there," she pointed towards the side of the archery range, "Faye is sitting over there, why don't you go join her?"

Following her hand, I could see the silver-haired elf perched on top of a pair of wooden barrels about a quarter of the way down the range.

"Yeah, I see her, but why aren't you coming?"

"We're gonna participate in the contest, silly," she said with a small shake of her head. "Now hurry, it's about to start," she finished, pulling Elaran with her towards the firing area.

I didn't approve of being called *silly* but she did have a point. If I'd actually used my head, I would've been able to figure that out without much trouble. It was this city. This strange society in the middle of the forest, where nothing was as I was used to, it was messing with my head. I had to spend way too much brain capacity just trying to figure out what was going on all the time to be able to use my head in as shrewd a way as I usually did.

"You made it!" Faye called and waved me over.

"Yeah, Elaran seemed reluctant to bring me at first but when Haela told him that the Queen said it was okay, he brought me along."

She chuckled as I climbed up on the barrel next to her. "That's Elaran alright."

"So," I began in as innocent a voice as I could produce, "is the Queen gonna be here too?"

"Yep, she's already here."

"Can I meet her?"

"All in good time," she promised and winked at me.

So, the Queen was somewhere in this crowd. I scanned the people gathered around the range in search of someone who stood out in any way. Someone regal-looking. To my right, the participants were getting ready to shoot. Bows were being strung and feathers were inspected by scrutinizing eyes. I doubted that the Queen would participate in the shooting so I focused my search to the onlookers. Most of them were talking excitedly to each other, gesturing towards the targets or the contestants. It was incredibly difficult to locate the Queen when the parameters of my search were solely *someone regal-looking*. As my gaze swept across the audience on the other side of the range I reconfirmed my initial assessment: all elves were regal-looking to me. There had to be a way to narrow this down. Hold on. I glanced at my barrel companion. Faye had said that she was working for the Queen which made it more likely that the Queen would be somewhere here, close to her.

Surveying the faces closer to us, I tried to spot someone with an air of authority around them. I came up empty. Looking back in Faye's direction, I realized that she'd raised her hand to wave at someone. A blond elf returned the wave gracefully with a kind smile. When I searched her eyes, it was as if centuries of wisdom swirled around in them. This was a woman who'd been through a lot and the compassion in her eyes told me that these experiences had done nothing to dull her concern for others. There was a strong possibility that this might be the Queen. I added a mental note to investigate further.

"They're about to start," Faye announced.

"Where?" I asked.

She gave me a confused frown. "What do you mean *where*? Over there, of course," she said and pointed at the area where all the archers had been getting ready a moment ago.

Turning my head, I looked from the participants getting in line on one end and all the way down to the small, round targets at the far end.

"You can't be serious?" I challenged. "That's way too far to pull off an accurate shot."

Faye grinned. "For humans, maybe. For us, no."

"Yeah, good luck with that," I breathed.

The first archer approached the line made up of two wooden sticks sunk into the ground. He nocked an arrow on his giant, curved bow and drew back. A breath passed. Twang! The sound of the bowstring echoed across the field, followed moments later by a soft thud.

"Did he hit it?" I asked with a hand cupped over my brow. "It sounded like he hit it," I continued, astonished by the sheer distance the arrow seemed to have traveled.

"You didn't see it?" Faye asked with a surprised note in her voice.

"How could I possibly have seen it? It was moving way too fast for the eye to track! Wait," I paused, "are you telling me that you could see it?"

"Yeah, obviously," she responded with a small shake of her head. "But even now, can't you see it sitting there, on the target?"

"No," I replied, straining my eyes to see as far as possible.

"Your eyesight is awful, do you know that?" She laughed in a good-natured manner.

I clicked my tongue. "Or maybe it's you elves who just happen to have ridiculously good eyesight," I muttered under my breath.

Another observation to add to my mental list. The same process was repeated as several more elves stepped up to prove their skills in archery while bowls of food and cups of wine appeared in the gathered crowd. My own stomach rumbled when the delicious smell of stew carried over to where we were sitting on top of the barrels.

"Isn't that...?" I began.

"Haemir," Faye filled in. "Yep."

The male half of the twins stepped up to the line and drew his dark brown bow. After a moment of aiming, he released it. The arrow found its mark with a soft thud.

"He doesn't have Haela's natural talent but he makes up for it with hard work. Lots of hard work," the silver-haired elf beside me said with a wistful smile.

"Hey, you want something to eat? Drink?" Faldir asked as he appeared from a cluster of elves to our right. He was carrying two enormous trays full of bowls and cups.

"Oh you are a life-saver! We'll take two of each," Faye said and motioned at me.

"For you – anything," he replied and winked at her.

I shot the blond tavern keeper a surprised look. Did these two have some kind of history? He passed each of us a bowl of stew and a cup so full of wine that I spilled some of mine on the ground when taking it.

"So, how's my little brother doing?" Faldir asked.

"I think we're about to find out," Faye said and nodded towards the starting line.

She was right. The taciturn elf approached the line, his flowing, blond hair billowing behind him with each step. While he readied his bow, I shoved several spoons of stew into my mouth. What? My stomach was growling. Faye cast me an amused glance but Faldir was leaning his hip against the barrel with his eyes firmly on his brother. A sharp twang filled the air as Faelar's arrow flew towards the mark.

"Not bad," Faldir assessed with an approving nod. "Alright, I should keep moving."

"Thanks for the food," Faye called after him and lifted her bowl in his direction.

The tavern keeper gave her a broad smile before disappearing back into the crowd. My companion and I ate and drank in silence as several more archers stepped up to try their luck. By the time our bowls and cups were empty, the contestants had moved on to target number three.

"Why aren't you participating?" I asked, studying Faye with curious eyes before realizing that I'd never even seen her with a bow. "Do you even know how to shoot?"

"Some are better than others but *all* elves know how to use a bow," she informed me. "And when it comes to me, I don't participate because I don't have anything to prove. Everyone already knows that I'm good," she finished with a triumphant grin.

That drew a burst of laughter from me. Faye whipped her head towards me in astonishment at the rare sound before a satisfied smile settled on her lips.

"Why did you laugh?" she asked.

"It's just, that sounded so much like something I would say."

Surprise registered on her face before she gave me an appraising nod. On the archery range, a black-haired elf moved towards the starting line with a spring in her step. Haela. She drew and fired off her shot in one fluid motion and then swept her arms out and bestowed a graceful bow upon the audience. Faye chuckled and shook her head next to me. Haela's twin brother crossed his arms in the throng behind her. As he looked towards the target his sister had just hit, his face transformed into a disappointed scowl. Sibling rivalry. I'd only had the briefest taste of what that must feel like. With Rain. I looked up as an excited murmur spread through the crowd.

"Remember how I said I was good?" Faye asked.

"Yeah?"

"He might be better," she said and nodded to the auburn-colored side braid approaching the starting line.

Elaran. The way the crowd responded when he took up position made me think that he was famous here in Tkeideru. Everyone in the audience seemed to hold their breath as he drew his massive, black bow. A sharp twang rang out and the accompanying thud was followed by cheering. Elaran nodded to the crowd before stepping back.

"Well, I guess it's easy to hit targets from this ridiculous distance when you can use magic," I muttered.

"Magic?" Faye asked, surprised. "What makes you think we use magic?"

I'd decided to do some more sneak interrogations. If I was to assassinate the Queen, I would need to know about any potential defense systems.

"Well, yeah, that's what you use, isn't it? In Keutunan, we learn that you're powerful magic wielders who can use magic to guide your arrows to targets that shouldn't be possible, and use magic to become invisible in the forest, or even to live forever," I finished in an innocently curious voice.

"No, it's not. In fact, we don't have *any* magic," my fierce-eyed companion said firmly. Maybe a bit too firmly. "Yes, we do live longer than you, much longer, but no one can live forever."

"But what about your archery skills and how you become invisible among the trees?"

"I suppose it would seem like magic to you humans," Faye mused. "But the secret is practice."

"Practice?" I asked, disbelief coloring my voice.

"Yeah, think about it," she began, "we have centuries to hone our skills. Is it really that difficult to believe that hundreds of years of practice leads to exceptional skills in archery and moving unseen through the forest?"

I bit my lip while considering. She did have a point. My own knife skills were excellent, not because I could wield magic, but because I'd practiced with them since I was a child. If I had centuries to practice with my knives, I would probably be able to do things with them that other people thought was magic.

"No, you're right," I admitted.

As Faye nodded in acknowledgement, I noticed that the crowd was breaking up. The ones who weren't retrieving their arrows from the targets all seemed to be heading back to their homes. Haela and Elaran must have been the last two contestants. Looking up at the sky, I noticed that evening was fast approaching. This was the first night in Tkeideru where I wasn't incapacitated by exhaustion or intoxication and I couldn't let this chance slip by. It was skulking time.

23.

Animals of the night made their presence known as I snuck across the fifteenth or so bridge for the night. Crickets sang in the bushes far below and owls hooted in the tree tops while the moon bathed the tree city in silvery light. I had tried, and failed, repeatedly at locating Faye, Elaran, or the blond, wise-looking elf from the archery competition. But the night was still young. Sneaking on the forest bed may have turned out to be impossible for me, but up here on the solid wooden bridges and platforms, I was in my element. I crept towards the next building. Flickering light spilled from the windows. Lying down on my stomach, I crawled the last bit to the opening and then very carefully raised my head to peek into the window. I ducked down, heart pounding in my chest. Shit. That had been close. An elf inside had very narrowly missed seeing my face. And not just any elf. Elaran. I risked another glimpse to establish who else was in the room with him before ducking down again. This was it. My swift examination had revealed that not only Elaran, but both Faye and the wise-looking elf, occupied the room. Scooting over, I drew myself up and rested my back and head against the wooden wall. Hidden in the shadows where the light pooling out from the window couldn't find me, I settled in to listen.

"–do this anymore," Elaran's voice rang out, "I can't keep pretending to be nice to her!"

"You're being nice to her?" Faye laughed.

"Yeah, I pretended to be nice to her for like half the afternoon. I can't do it anymore."

Ouch. So, our uneasy truce hadn't actually been real, he'd only been pretending. Well, considering that I was doing the exact same thing, I couldn't really blame him. I chuckled silently. He had only been able to pull it off for half an afternoon. Not really a deceiving mastermind, that one.

"Then don't."

"I don't understand how you manage it, you and Keya and the twins. And you're not even pretending, you're actually nice. She's a *human*, have you forgotten what they did?"

"Of course I haven't," Faye snapped. "But Storm's grandparents weren't even born when we were at war with the humans. She can't be held responsible for the atrocities her ancestors committed long before she was born."

Interesting. I had always known that Faelar didn't care much for me, he was always sticking by Elaran, but if this conversation was to be believed, then the rest of them were actually genuinely nice to me. That was a surprise.

"What about the archery competition?" the third elf asked.

"I still think it was too risky," Elaran announced.

"No, it wasn't!" Faye retorted. "It was just the right amount of risky."

"What did you find out?" continued the voice I assumed belonged to the blond elf.

"The humans think we have magic, they can't shoot as far as we can, and their eyesight is terrible."

Outside the window, I bristled at the rude remarks. Okay, fine, so they were true. But still. Rude.

"What about their guns?" the suspected queen continued.

"She hasn't said anything about them but based on her reaction at the archery range, I doubt even their guns can shoot that far."

"Interesting."

"But still, we can't risk another bloodbath like last time we fought them," Elaran cautioned.

"I'm aware," Faye snapped. "But what do you expect us to do? Just wait for them to attack us? Storm said as much when we got her drunk. She's here to gather information because their king is mounting an offensive on us!"

I cringed and squeezed my eyes shut. *Crap.* So that was what I had accidentally let slip when she was leading me back. It was such a huge slip-up that I wanted to slap myself. But I suppose it could've been worse. Even though I'd been too drunk to come up with a more harmless lie, I'd still managed to lie about my true intent, despite having a head filled with fog. Exhaling softly, I thought about Guild Master Caleb's words. Lying really did come as easily as breathing to me.

"So, what should we do, then?" the might-be-queen asked.

"Attack them," Faye said. "We learn what we can from Storm and then we throw everything we have at them with a sneak attack on their city, and kill this damn warmongering king of theirs."

That piqued my interest. It produced an interesting opportunity. They wanted King Adrian dead, and so did I, so maybe letting them attack the city was a good thing. Even if I killed the Elf Queen, I highly doubted that our paranoid and power-hungry king would just let me leave with Liam. But if the elves attacked Keutunan and killed King Adrian, my problems would be solved. Images of the Mad Archer engulfed in flames and the bodies of my guild members littering the halls of the Thieves' Guild suddenly flashed unbidden through my mind. What was to stop the elves from laying waste to the whole city after they'd killed the king? Damn. I didn't want that either.

"Are you sure that's such a good idea?" Elaran asked.

"No, I'm not." Faye heaved a deep sigh. "But it's the best I've got. What do you think, Laena?"

"Attacking might be a good option," the queen-suspect, Laena, said, "but it might also be a terrible one. We simply do not have enough information to decide the most logical option, yet."

"So you're saying we should do nothing?" Elaran questioned.

"Oh no, quite the opposite. Last time they marched into the forest, they did so with the intention of slaughtering us all. And make no mistake, that is exactly what they will do this time as well. We want to live in peace, but once again, these humans want to destroy us. We should most definitely do *something* before history repeats itself," Laena clarified with steel in her voice.

Wait. This didn't make any sense. Weren't the elves the ones who'd marched on us? To destroy us? This Laena was making it sound like they had lived peacefully when we just decided to attack them. My mind reeled. Were we the bad guys? There was no one else there so she wasn't just making it up to deceive someone. Or was there? Was it possible that there was someone else in that room, someone I'd missed at first glance? I had to risk another peek.

After detaching my body from the wall, I used my legs to push myself into a standing position. This time, I needed a slightly different angle if I was to spot something I'd missed on my previous inspection. Inside, they were still arguing about the best way to proceed. I closed my eyes briefly and drew a silent breath to steady myself. Trying to melt into the wall as much as possible, I edged my head forward. Excruciating seconds crept by. At last, I tilted my head into the window frame and scanned the room. This was no ordinary room. There was no bed or nightstand, instead, the room was lined with bookshelves containing scrolls as well as books. A large, round table occupied the main portion of the room and on it, I spotted something similar to a map, though it didn't look like any map I'd ever seen. Faye, Elaran, and Laena were gathered around it. Yellow eyes flicked up. *Shit*. I jerked my head back.

"Someone's here," Elaran said, a warning note in his voice.

His hurried footsteps rang out inside as he rounded the table and advanced on the window. *Shit, shit, shit*. There was no way I'd make it off the platform and across the bridge before he arrived at the window and I couldn't stay where I was either. Jumping down was out of the question as I'd never survive the fall. Only one place left to go. Up. Blood pumped in my ears. By leaping in place, I narrowly managed to get my fingertips over the top of the building. My muscles tensed as I pulled myself up and over the edge. Just as I rolled onto my back, the hunting footsteps stopped. The wood creaked below me as if someone was leaning out the window. My heart hammered so loudly in my chest I was afraid he might hear it.

"What is it?" Faye asked inside the room.

"We should leave," Elaran declared.

The soft rustle of paper being rolled up made its way up towards me, followed by the sound of footsteps. The door opened and closed below me. By twisting my head slightly, I could see that the three of them had made it across the platform and were walking towards the bridge on the other side. I lay back down, forcing myself to breathe normally. I could taste the damp fog drawing its blanket over the city. Only once I was certain that their footsteps had disappeared into the night did I lower myself down to the platform again. That had been close. Too close. I scanned the surrounding area to make sure that no one was waiting to ambush me. It was empty. After one last examination, I sprinted across the bridge in the other direction. Elaran was smart. If he suspected that it was me, it wouldn't take him long to figure out that he should go to my room and see if I was there. The wood swayed beneath me as I skidded across yet another platform and raced onto the next bridge. I needed to make it there before him.

My saving grace was that this city, despite having several vertical layers, actually looked a lot like a normal city. I might not be able to tell one tree from another but I'm very skilled at noticing small differences between buildings. None of these wooden dwellings were identical; they all had their own unique features. While searching for the Queen, I'd created a mental map of the buildings, platforms, and bridges I'd visited. Now, I used that to calculate the swiftest way back to my room. My breath grew labored. Last bridge. Dashing across it, I ducked into my room and closed the door soundlessly behind me. There was no way of knowing if I'd made it. It was entirely possible that Elaran had beaten me to it and already discovered that I was missing. This was his city, after all. With my heart still pounding,

I flopped down on the bed and tried to get my heaving chest under control.

"Gods damn it," I whispered under my breath.

I probably shouldn't have risked that second peek. If I'd stayed hidden, I could've continued eavesdropping and learned even more. Well, no point in crying over spilled ale. I had, at least, learned that the elves were using me to gather information. Much like I was using them too, I guess, so no hard feelings there. However, I'd also been made aware of the fact that they thought we were the bad guys. That was very interesting. It's all a matter of perspective, I guess. Back in Keutunan, the king and the nobles all think that we're the bad ones while we in the Thieves' Guild consider them to be on the wrong side of things. However, at this point, it didn't really matter to me if the elves or the humans were the villains in the Great War. All that mattered was Liam. And to save him, I had to kill the Queen.

Faye had told me that she was working for the Queen and based on how the crowd had reacted to Elaran at the archery contest, which I'd just assumed he won, by the way, I figured that he must be some sort of military adviser to her as well. They had both met with the blond elf, Laena, to discuss strategies. It had to be her.

Footsteps outside caused my analyzing mind to stop short. I closed my eyes and adopted a heavier breathing rhythm. The footsteps drew closer. Finally, they stopped outside the door of my room. A soft groan escaped the floorboards as the person I assumed to be Elaran shifted his weight and pushed down the handle. I continued my rhythmic breathing. Since this wasn't exactly the first time I'd fake slept, I was fairly confident in my ability to deceive him but I was still uncharacteristically nervous.

After all, these elves possessed senses far sharper than any human. Seconds turned into minutes. At last, the door closed with a soft click but not even after I'd heard the footsteps recede did I dare abandon my heavy breathing rhythm. Eventually, the fake sleeping became real as I drifted off into the world of dreams.

24.

I landed on the soft grass. White clouds concealed the heavens as I cleared the last bridge and continued moving through the City of Ash. Before leaving the archery competition yesterday, Faye had told me to meet her in front of Faldir's tavern, the War Dancer, at dawn. I wasn't sure what today would bring but I needed to confirm my theory about the Elf Queen. After last night's exploits, Laena was a strong contender for the position. However, I knew that I would only get one chance at this so I couldn't act until I knew without a doubt that she was the Queen. Assassination is, after all, a very precise profession.

The smell of freshly baked bread reached me as I passed the ovens of the first bakery in the part of Tkeideru I'd come to think of as Food Quarter. Almost all taverns, bakeries, butchers, and other food related businesses seemed to be located here. When the War Dancer finally became visible in the distance, I noticed something else that I recognized. Or should I say *someone* else. Elaran. To say that he didn't look happy was the understatement of the decade. Raw anger shot from in his eyes as he stormed towards me with his massive, black bow clenched in one hand. *Crap*. I continued walking towards him. Since I'd managed to get back to my room before he did, he couldn't know for certain that it was me he'd seen skulking about yesterday. However, the look in his eyes as he advanced on me informed me that he wasn't overly concerned with proof at that particular moment.

"You!" he bellowed. "You sneaking, lying, disgrace! We take you in and this is how you repay us?"

"What the hell are you shouting about?" I snapped.

I knew that using my sweet and innocent persona wouldn't work. Not in this situation and certainly not with him. Besides, my patience was wearing thin.

"Oh, playing ignorant, are we?" he scoffed. "Don't bother. I know it was you who spied on us last night."

"I haven't been spying on anyone! I was in my room, sleeping, all night."

"Yeah, I don't know how you managed to disappear from the window and then reappear in your room, but you're not fooling anyone. I know it was you," he said, fingers twitching by the knife on his hip.

A crowd had gathered around us. As they watched the exchange, their eyes on me turned venomous.

"This is ridiculous," I said, "you have no proof. Everything you accuse me of is solely based on the fact that you don't like me. Now get out of my way, I have somewhere to be."

By first taking a step to the side, I tried to walk past the angry archer.

"Like hell!" he said and threw out his bow to block my path. "You *do not* get to walk away from me."

"Get your bloody bow out of my face!" I snapped and yanked it from his grip.

A gasp passed through the gathered crowd as they stared at me in utter shock. Shit. Uncertainty spread through my stomach. Something had just happened. The ghost of a smirk passed over Elaran's face before he snatched the bow back. What the hell had just happened?

"So, you will even go as far as insulting my honor," Elaran said and shook his head. "I really shouldn't be surprised."

"What?" I asked, completely stunned.

"Touching someone else's bow without their permission is a grave insult. Now, honor has to be restored," he said and placed his bow and quiver on the sandy ground beside him.

"You lost honor because I touched your bow? And now you have to restore it by what? Fighting?" I asked mockingly.

"Yes."

He squared his shoulders and took up a fighting stance before me. Oh. He was being serious. The crowd moved back a few paces to give us space.

"For real? How was I supposed to–" I began before stopping myself.

Of course. He knew that I would have no way of knowing that touching someone's bow was a great insult to their honor. That was why he'd orchestrated this whole scene. His bow had been unslung since before we started arguing and I'd only ever seen him with his bow like that when he was hunting. He'd baited me into touching his bow because he wanted a fight and I'd fallen right into it. Bastard.

"Fine. If it's a fight you want, it's a fight you'll get," I said and rolled my shoulders.

My carefully constructed façade was coming apart and the real me was slipping through the cracks. I was done playing nice. These last few weeks, I felt as though I'd done nothing but bow and submit and smile through insults, and I couldn't take it any longer. It was time to let the real me out. With a quick glance,

I analyzed our surroundings. The crowd formed a ring around us. It wasn't very large so I couldn't employ a technique that required much distance. We were standing on a patch of dirt, rather than grass, which was good since I was unaccustomed to fighting on something as soft as grass. I studied Elaran. If I'd thought I was at a physical disadvantage when fighting Shade, I was even worse off against this tall elf. Elaran seemed intent on fighting without weapons but that didn't really help since I wouldn't win a boxing or wrestling match against someone with this kind of physique. I eyed the knife at his belt as a plan formed in my mind.

"So, the fight is done when someone submits?" I asked.

"Or is knocked unconscious," Elaran replied with a grin.

"Noted. Let's get on with it then."

We circled each other. I waited for him to make the first move because I needed to get a sense of his fighting style before I could set my plan in motion. He lunged at me. Ducking under his arm, I moved out of reach. Elaran spun and aimed another fist at my face, but yet again, I evaded it. I'd been in enough scraps with larger opponents to know that if they managed to land a well-placed hit, it was over. We continued our dance for several minutes: Elaran striking out and me twisting away, just out of reach. He was getting frustrated now. Good.

"Coward! Is this what you call fighting?" he yelled at me, his face scrunched up in irritation.

I touched my tongue to my teeth and grinned at him. He growled and swung at me again but he was getting noticeably sloppier now. Dancing away, I winked at him. That seemed to have done the trick. He released a howl and advanced on me in the most careless way yet. Show time. Instead of twisting out from his arm, as I'd done each time before, I ducked inside it. Surprise registered on his face shortly before I drove my knee up hard between his legs and it was replaced by pain. So, apparently, elves did have the same basic anatomy as humans. A gasp escaped his lips and his step faltered. He was off balance. I didn't give him even a second to regain it. Pressing my advantage, I spun down and hooked my foot behind the ankle that wasn't supporting his weight at the moment while also grabbing a handful of dirt from the ground. Continuing that fluid motion, I straightened, yanked his foot towards me, and threw the sand in his eyes. When he was blinded by the dirt and tipping backwards a little as his leg was extended unnaturally, I saw my chance and threw my whole weight behind a shoulder tackle. We both went down. He gasped as his breath was driven from his lungs when he landed on the ground with me on top of him. While he was still preoccupied with cleaning the dirt from his eyes, I snatched the knife from his belt. When he finally opened them again he found me straddling his chest with a blade at his throat.

"There. Is your honor satisfied?" I asked and gave him a wicked smile.

Oh I wish you could've seen the look on his face. It was priceless. At first, his yellow eyes projected utter disbelief which then transformed into humiliation. I savored those moments before it shifted and they were instead filled with pure rage. An arrow appeared between my eyes. I shot the elf attached to it a disinterested look.

"Just say the word, boss, and I'll kill her right here."

I rolled my eyes. Faelar. Ever the watchful protector of Elaran. Keeping a steady hand on the knife, I grinned maliciously, daring him to do it. When he did nothing, I returned my attention to the fuming ranger beneath me.

"Submit," I ordered, drawing out each syllable.

Rage roared in his eyes but I held them without flinching. The veins in his neck bulged. On the ground, he flexed his fingers as if debating whether or not to give Faelar the signal to shoot me. He opened his mouth and then closed it again.

"I yield," he finally pressed out between clenched teeth.

The heavy silence of the crowd hung over the clearing. Nodding slowly, I withdrew the knife and jumped to my feet. As soon as I was gone, Elaran shot to his feet as well. He dusted himself off while Faelar stood guard behind his shoulder, bow still drawn.

"You damn cheater," Elaran said and shook his head in disgust. "You would never have beaten me in a fair fight."

Of course not. That's why I don't fight fair. I knew he could've beaten me to a pulp if I'd fought the way he expected me to fight. And he probably would have. So I did what I always do. I cheated.

"This is me fighting fair," I baited with a malicious grin. "If I'd really wanted to fight dirty, I would've poisoned you before the fight."

"You have no honor," he spat.

"Honor?" I scoffed. "I have my own kind of honor."

Silence settled over the scene again as we continued staring at each other. The next move was up to him. I knew that it would've been more strategic to just take the beating but I was fed up with this whole charade. Being meek and obedient wasn't my thing. Whatever happened next, I would deal with it just like I'd dealt with everything my whole life: with iron determination and an unbreakable will. Scanning the faces around me, I noticed Faye in the crowd. She was leaning against a post with her arms crossed over her chest, studying me with an unreadable expression on her face. I glanced from her to Elaran.

"Alright, show's over, people," she announced and pushed herself off the wooden pole.

And just like that, the silent spell broke and the crowd started talking again while shuffling off in different directions. Elaran whipped his head around to stare at the silver-haired elf but she held up her hand and instead motioned for two other elves to approach. After receiving instructions that I was too far away to hear, they walked towards me.

"They'll accompany you to your room. I'll see you tomorrow," Faye said, looking me straight in the eye.

I shrugged and turned around as the two elves reached me. It was unclear whether they were there to keep me safe from others or keep others safe from me.

"Oh, and Storm?" she continued. "The knife."

Damn. I'd been hoping that they would've forgotten about that. Turning back around, I produced the knife from my sleeve. Elaran glowered at me. I flicked the knife in his direction. The blade vibrated as it stuck to the ground in front of his feet.

"If you ever want me to kick your ass again, you know where to find me," I taunted and mockingly kissed the air.

I had time to see him take a threatening step forward before I turned on my heels and walked back towards my room, flanked by the two guards.

25.

"So, is this the part where you lead me deep into the forest to slit my throat where no one will ever find my corpse?" I asked.

Faye turned to look at me in surprise. She had come to collect me this morning after I'd spent all of yesterday and last night confined to my room with two guards outside. We had met up with Keya and Haela at the edge of town and now all four of us were walking deeper into the forest.

She laughed and shook her head. "No."

"Good to know."

Even I hadn't been entirely certain if I'd meant that question as a joke or not.

"If I wanted to kill you, you'd already be dead," she continued and winked at me with a smile tugging at her lips.

I barked a short laugh as I was reminded that I had told Shade something similar before all this craziness started.

"What we saw yesterday, when you were fighting Elaran, that was the real you, wasn't it?" Faye suddenly asked in a more serious tone.

"Yeah, it was," I simply replied.

After weeks of it, I was tired of pretending to be someone else. Normally, I only had to do that long enough to get myself out of whatever trouble my smart mouth had managed to land me in at the time. I'm a thief – not a con artist. And say what you will about thieving but it's a pretty straightforward line of work. You break in, you steal stuff, you get the hell out. Not much pretending required.

"Oh I wish I could've seen it!" Haela said. "Anyone beating up Elaran is something for the history books, but you doing it? Ha!"

Keya giggled softly. "It most certainly was a spectacular sight."

"You were there as well?" I asked.

She nodded. "Mm-hmm."

"But I don't understand," I began, "I thought you'd all be pissed off."

"You kidding? I mean, yeah, Elaran's one of my best friends but I've been wanting to kick his ass for years, just to show him that I could."

"Haela..." Faye sighed and leveled an exasperated stare at the energetic twin.

She grinned sheepishly. "Sorry."

"We know that he manipulated you into touching his bow to force a fight," Keya explained. "It was only a matter of time, really."

Huh. Hadn't expected that. I mean, not only had I fought one of their friends, I'd beaten him by fighting dishonorably and these elves seemed like a people who took honor very seriously. Good thing they could see past that.

"What even is his problem anyway?" I asked. "He's hated me since the moment he laid eyes on me, and I haven't even done anything." *Yet.*

Haela and Keya both looked to Faye.

"Elaran has... more reason than most to hate humans," the silver-haired elf began. "Do you know about the war?"

"Yeah," I replied, "you started a war to conquer our city and enslave us."

"History is written by the winner, I suppose," she commented grimly. "No, that's not what happened."

"So, what did happen?"

"Your ancestors began to fear us. We have centuries to perfect our skills, and they were afraid that we'd use those skills to do exactly what you said: conquer and enslave you. So they figured that a preemptive strike was the best option."

"We never saw it coming. It was a bloodbath," Keya added.

"We all lost people that day," Faye continued. "But Elaran, he lost his whole family. Both his parents and his two brothers died fighting the humans. He was alone."

"Oh."

"Yeah, so you can understand why he dislikes your people."

I nodded. The pain written in their eyes when they spoke about this told me that it wasn't a fabrication. I'd seen that pain enough times in my own eyes after Rain died to know that it was real. We continued walking in silence.

"Wait, I know this place," I said after a while. "I've been here before."

Ahead of us, a huge waterfall cascaded down a steep rock face, water pooling into a lake before it. Last time I'd seen it, there had been a gigantic, green dragon lounging in the water. Today, the crystal clear lake sparkled in the high noon sun, completely dragon-free, and the only roaring sound came from the water rushing down to the rocks.

"Wow, it looks much more welcoming when there's no dragon in it," I mumbled.

"Huh?" Haela said.

I waved a hand in front of my face. "Nothing."

"Well alright then, let's go!" She smiled and tugged me forward.

"Let's go where?" I frowned at her. "What are we doing here?"

"Swimming, of course!"

One after the other, they started unbuckling belts and pulling shirts over their heads until three piles of clothes had formed by the water line. They dove in, their graceful bodies forming a lithe arc before disappearing beneath the surface. I looked down at my own body. It wasn't that I was self-conscious, it was just that... Alright, fine. I was self-conscious. I'd like to see how confident you'd feel with this perfectly average body compared to the ridiculous elegance of elves. While they were busy getting submerged, I saw my chance to quickly slip out of my own clothes and slide into the water unseen.

"Ahh, this is why I love summer!" Haela announced as she emerged.

She was right, it was wonderful. The water wrapped around me like soft cloth, cooling my body after the long walk, while the sun warmed my face. Beneath the surface, the waves pulled sand over my feet.

"You do know how to swim, right?" Keya asked when she saw me standing in the shallower part of the lake, even though the water was deep enough to cover my collarbones.

"Well, yeah, I grew up next to a harbor so it's kind of a necessary skill. If people are trying to drown you, it makes their job a hell of a lot harder if you know how to swim."

"So, a lot of people been trying to drown you then?" Faye asked, amused.

"You'd be surprised," I answered with a snort.

"Can't imagine why..." she added under her breath.

"Hey!"

All three of them laughed at my mock offense. I swam out to meet them.

"But seriously, what is it that you do, back in your city?" Faye asked in a more serious tone.

"I'm a thief," I replied with an unapologetic shrug.

That honest answer earned me three pairs of raised eyebrows.

"A thief?" Haela asked, squinting at me. "Is that really a legit job?"

A half-smirk settled on my face. "Depends on what you mean by *legit*."

"Would you mind enlightening us?" Faye prodded with mock formality as she swam closer.

Behind me, a pile of rocks formed an oversized staircase to the side of the lake. I swam over and drew myself up on one of the lowers ones where only my head and neck would be visible. It wasn't that I was tired from treading water, mind you, I just... needed to sit down to focus on my story.

"So, in Keutunan you choose your future job when you're a kid," I said. "Every summer, on the Day of Choosing, all eleven-year-olds go with their parents to the guild they want to join and apply."

"Wait, what? Deciding your future when you're only eleven? You're barely even born then," Haela interjected.

The three elves had joined me on the rocks. As opposed to me, they had no qualms about showing off their graceful bodies and were lounging on the higher outcroppings. Water droplets glinted on their perfect skin as they basked in the sun.

"Haela, their lifespan..." Keya began awkwardly and moved her hands to symbolize a shrinking distance.

"Oh, right. Damn, life must be so stressful for you... trying to cram everything into such a ridiculously short amount of time," Haela continued.

Keya coughed pointedly.

"Sorry," the straightforward twin amended sheepishly.

"You were telling us about the eleven-year-olds and their parents?" Keya nudged the conversion back on track.

"Yeah, that's what the kids do who join what I assume you mean by *legit* guilds. You know, carpenters, butchers, and so on. But that only works if you actually have parents," I said grimly.

"Oh."

"Yeah. Those of us who don't, we apply to join an Underworld guild instead, where we become thieves, beggars, whores..."

"Whores?"

"Mm-hmm. Women in our position don't have a lot of options. Though, for me, that wasn't even on the map. Sweaty men groping my body, putting their hands where they don't belong. No, no one touches me unless I want them to," I finished with steel in my voice.

My elven companions seemed to ponder what I'd shared with them. As far as I could tell, none of the Underworld professions existed in Tkeideru. In a society that doesn't believe in money, there is no need for thieves.

Faye laughed and gave me an appreciative nod. "Based on what we saw yesterday, no, I guess no one does touch you unless you want them to."

"Can I ask you something? All of you," I said, serious again.

The silver-haired elf shrugged. "Sure."

"How do you do it?"

"Do what?"

"Well, you know..." I heaved an exasperated sigh. "Okay, look, you should've seen how the crowd responded to you during the archery thing. They look up to you, Haela. And you," I continued and turned to Keya, "people listen to you – even Elaran! And you, I don't even know where to start with you," I said, staring at Faye, "*everyone* listens to you and does what you tell them."

All three of my targets searched my face for the yet unspoken question.

"You're women and yet they all respect you and none of them seem to fear you – how do you do it?" I finished, now thoroughly out of breath.

"From what I understand, women in your city are regarded as... less," Keya began.

I confirmed her assumption with a humorless laugh.

"We don't see it that way here," Faye continued from where the soft-spoken elf had left off. "All people are just people. Your gender doesn't matter; if you are a person worthy of respect, you will receive it."

The answer she gave me was the one I had anticipated but I was still left speechless. I closed my eyes. Imagine not having to make people fear you in order to have a say in what happened to you. Somewhere where I could just be me without having to fight all the time. Without the darkness. Opening my eyes again, I found them all studying me.

"Wouldn't that be something," I said and pushed off from the rock I'd been occupying.

Water lapped softly around me as I swam to the middle of the lake. I turned over and closed the final distance with a backstroke. With arms gently stroking the water at my sides, I floated there, body just below the surface. The afternoon sun warmed my face, as well as our surroundings, releasing calming scents of warm grass and wet rocks. As the water around my ears made me oblivious to everything but the world beneath the surface, my thoughts drifted.

Despite the fact that I was more or less a prisoner, I'd never felt freer. There was nothing to prove, no groping men to defend against, no starvation to battle. I didn't have to dodge any guards for fear of being hanged. There were no lunatic royals or deadly assassins waiting to ambush me and threaten me. I didn't have to constantly intimidate and fight and kill for respect. Here, I could just use my skills to hunt and live in peace. Peace. If I killed the Elf Queen, there would be no peace. The king's army would invade and this wonderful place would be destroyed.

My mind churned. *Maybe I should get involved. I could tell them the truth and then we could fight King Adrian together. Because this is the right side, isn't it? It sure as hell isn't Adrian's side at least. But what would happen to the guild? Maybe Shade's side is the right side? But then what would happen to the elves?*

"Storm?" Keya called above the surface and poked my arm.

Reality snapped back into place as I jerked away, startled by the sudden disruption.

"Sorry, it is just that we need to get up and start drying off."

"Yeah, okay, on it," I said and followed her back towards the shore.

After all my musings, only one thought seemed to echo in my head: *I don't want this place to be destroyed.*

Water sloshed around my legs as I waded to the shore with the three elves in front of me. When I saw them lowering themselves on the sunlit grass, I turned around to avoid having my whole body exposed. A collective gasp rang out behind me.

"What?" I exclaimed as I whipped back around.

Three pairs of yellow eyes examined my body while horrified expressions marred their faces. My cheeks flushed. Seriously? I'm not *that* bad-looking, you know. In a far more jerky fashion than I would've liked, I dropped to the ground and drew my knees up to my chest.

"Your scars..." Keya began before trailing off, her face turning worried.

"Oh. Yeah..." I said, loosening the grip on my knees slightly when I understood the reason for their staring.

"What happened?"

Thin silvery lines covered parts of my arms and legs. Shallow cuts from various fights. They were minor injuries, really, and only visible if you were paying attention. Others were more noticeable. On the left side, a thick, jagged scar ran the length of my ribcage. A parting gift from a Silver Cloak who had tried to arrest me. Or kill me. It had all been a bit unclear in the moment. Right below my collarbone, another rough scar shone, but this one was round. It was a break-in gone wrong that had earned me a crossbow bolt through my body, leaving a mirrored scar on either side. My lower abdomen sported a stab wound sealed by fire from the night I had lost the only family I'd known. The night I had let the darkness in. But what I assumed had drawn the attention of the elves was the latest collection of scars on my back, courtesy of the extortionist king. Whip scars.

"Life," I shrugged.

I could see them exchange glances but I didn't feel like sharing my life story just yet. Instead, I lay down in the warm grass, stretched my arms above my head, and closed my eyes. The sun warmed my skin. I could almost feel the water evaporate from my hair and body. Birds chirped in the nearby trees while my mind drifted. Peaceful. I wanted to stay there all day, maybe even longer than that.

"Uhm, Storm?" Faye asked, breaking the silence and my wandering thoughts. "Why did your king send a thief to find us?"

Excellent question. Sitting up, I pulled a shirt over my now dry shoulders. "Because it's a suicide mission and I'm expendable," I answered honestly and lifted a shoulder in a lopsided shrug. "No one had seen you in hundreds of years or knew how to find you, so why waste a loyal, law-abiding citizen?"

"When we first met you, you said the king forced you," Keya said, an unspoken question hanging in the air.

"Yeah. He took someone I care about."

Liam's smiling face filled my mind. Maybe telling them was the best decision? Gods knew they could fight, and move stealthily. If we teamed up we could save Liam and then kill the king together. Then, my friend would be safe and this magical place wouldn't be destroyed. Yeah. That would be the smartest choice.

Images of Rain flashed through my head. Spirited, cheerful Rain lying in the gutter of a dark alley, pain and shock twisting her features. The metallic smell of blood. Wet, sputtering breaths as she fights the God of Death in a pool of her own blood. My hands are covered in it. No matter what I do, I can't stop the bleeding.

No. I shook off the image. Last time I had gotten involved in other people's problems, my only friend, my only family, had died. I wouldn't make that mistake again. I'd have to kill the Elf Queen and then I'd go and get Liam back. To hell with everyone else.

"So that's why I have to meet your queen and complete my mission," I instead finished off by saying.

"I understand." Faye nodded. "Come on, we should start heading back."

After I had covered up all my scars again, we left this peaceful pocket of the world by the sparkling lake and began our walk back to the City of Ash. My mind was made up concerning what had to be done. My heart, though... not so much. Irritated, I shoved my disagreeing heart back behind the walls where it belonged and slammed the door before following the unsuspecting elves deeper into the forest.

26.

"Oh, no. I've already been through this with Elaran," I said, casting a quick glance at the last elf who'd tricked me into something like this, "I'm not touching that thing."

Shaking my head, I took a small step back. To my left, Haela was giggling and elbowing Elaran to remind him of how that fight had turned out. He answered with a sullen scowl.

"This is different," Faye assured me, "this time I'm giving you permission to hold my bow."

Only moments ago, all seven of us had been occupying that long table in the back of the War Dancer, just as we had done every late afternoon for the last week. Not for the first time, Elaran had complained about how useless I was and this time he'd focused on the fact that I didn't know how to use a bow. Faye's eyes had sparkled mischievously as she'd jumped up and announced that it was time to change that. So, here I was, at the archery range, peering suspiciously at the long white bow being offered to me.

"Alright," I nodded and held out my hand.

My first thought as she dropped the wooden weapon in my hand was that it was surprisingly heavy. As Faye hooked a quiver to my belt, I turned her bow over in my hands. It was gorgeous.

The flowing curves of white wood bore intricately carved patterns of leaves and vines. A weapon of the forest indeed.

"No! No arrow yet," my archery instructor chided when she saw me reach into the quiver. "First, you need to know how to draw it properly."

I squinted at her. It was a bow. You held it with one hand and drew the string with the other. How hard could it be? However, Faye seemed oblivious to my internal sarcastic comments and instead continued the lesson.

"Now, hold it with your left hand and then lift it up. And then you pull the bowstring back with your right."

Like I said...

"Remember to both pull with your right and push with your left. Oh, and pull with your shoulder and back, not your arm."

"Got it."

After one last internal eye roll, I lifted her aesthetically decorated bow and pulled back the bowstring. Nothing happened. Surprised, I blinked at the unmoving contraption. Using even more force, I pulled again. The string drew back a distance that was roughly equal to the length of my finger.

"Just pull it," Faye said.

"Yeah, I got it," I replied, clearing my throat.

My muscles shook as I used every grain of strength in my body to draw the bow, winning another finger's length. Then it stopped. It refused to budge. Everything I had, all of my strength, had been enough to move the bowstring back roughly the length of my hand. Elaran and Faelar snickered beside me. Releasing the string and the insignificant progress I'd made, I let my arm drop.

"Is this a trick?" I said with an exasperated sigh, irritated if it was but also desperately hoping that was the case.

"No," Faye answered. "And you two," she shook her head at the two laughing elves, "shut up."

The snickering quieted. Looking back at my instructor, I raised my eyebrows. "Are you seriously telling me that you can draw this bow?" I asked. "Right now?"

"Yeah."

She took her bow from my outstretched hands and in one fluid motion, lifted it and drew it all the way back. Damn. I mean, I'd known that I was at a physical disadvantage compared to the elves but I hadn't realized just how ridiculously outclassed I was here. As I glanced at the massive, black bow behind Elaran's shoulder, I tried to calculate the amount of force it would take to draw that thing. Cold sweat ran down my spine as I realized how badly our fight could've ended. He could've cracked my skull with one hit – if he'd managed to land one. Good thing I cheated.

"Wow," I concluded as Faye gently returned the bowstring to its original position.

She smiled and shrugged one shoulder in reply. I had truly meant that. My own embarrassment aside, I was incredibly impressed by her strength. Another badass female warrior.

"I'm going to go get a practice bow," Faye announced.

"Practice bow? Like one of those for kids?" Haemir asked, surprised.

The silver-haired elf bestowed a reprimanding scowl upon him, suggesting that she'd wanted to keep that part a secret.

"Yes. One of those. Now, move a little closer to the target while I go get one."

A little closer became *a lot closer* as the six of us crossed the field until we were only twenty strides or so from the targets.

Haemir and Keya occupied themselves with rolling some barrels closer while we waited for Faye to come back. Her return found Keya and the twins perched on top of the makeshift chairs while Elaran leaned his hip against the closest one with Faelar behind his shoulder.

"Here you go," she said and handed me a much shorter, sand-colored bow. "Try drawing this just as I told you."

After lifting the bow, I pulled on the bowstring. To my immense relief, this one actually cooperated and followed my arm back towards my shoulder. Haela gave me a short but excited round of applause while Elaran rolled his yellow eyes.

"Good." Faye smiled. "Now, slowly return the string. Releasing it without an arrow is bad for the bow."

"She looks like she's trying to strangle the bow," Faelar whispered, not so discreetly, in Elaran's ear.

"Wanna see me strangle something?" I challenged, leveling a threatening grin at the usually taciturn Faelar.

It gave me an enormous sense of gratification when I saw him involuntarily flinch. The reaction was gone almost as soon as it'd happened but I had seen it. And he knew it. Faye slapped a hand to her forehead and shook her head.

"He is right, though," she said. "You do squeeze the bow too tightly. It should be resting lightly in your hand."

Now it was Faelar's time to grin. Turning away from his smug smile, I tried drawing the bow again but this time, holding it more lightly.

"Good. Now you're going to try to shoot. So, after you've nocked the arrow, you draw it back to the corner of your mouth. And when you aim, you'll want to follow the length of the arrow and then you release. Gently."

Alright, that sounded easy enough. I drew back, aimed for the middle of the target, and then released the bowstring.

"Ow!" I yelped as a twang sounded across the grass.

The inside of my left forearm stung and I could already see a red mark forming there. I looked for the arrow. It stuck to the grass a moderate distance from the target.

"It's alright," Faye said. "But you yank too much when you release it. You should just gently open your fingers and let it go."

I heaved a sigh. I'd thought that was what I was doing. Looking around, I saw Keya give me an encouraging nod. Elaran's face had gotten stuck somewhere between a grin and a scowl. I rubbed the sore spot on my forearm. Why did all of them need to be here to watch me fail at archery?

"The string hit you on its way back, didn't it?" Faye continued.

"I believe so, yeah," I replied and cleared my throat.

"That's because the angle of your elbow is wrong. Your arm is too straight, which pushes your elbow in towards the bow. You need to have a slight bend in it."

"Okay, no yanking and bend the elbow," I summarized.

"Yep. Alright, try again."

Once more, I drew back and fired an arrow. It missed as well. And so did the next three arrows. They missed by less and less, but still, they missed.

"You still yank too much," Faye declared, shaking her head.

"I literally cannot release it any softer than this," I snapped and threw out my free hand in exasperation.

"Have you considered that maybe she just can't aim?" Elaran said with a wicked grin on his face.

"You know what," I challenged, "why don't you go get my knives and I'll show you just how good my aim is."

The auburn-colored side braid looked to Faye who seemed to ponder this before finally nodding. Elaran raised his eyebrows but then shrugged and took off with Faelar close behind. I knew that showing them my skills with knives was a risk. I'd been debating whether or not to do it for a while now and had finally come to the conclusion that it was worth it. After all, they'd found me in the woods carrying nineteen knives. I had to assume that they'd already figured out I knew how to use them. As I'd been under guard every night since my little scrap with Elaran, it was also my best chance of getting my hands on my knives again.

"Faye, I've been here for over two weeks now. When will I see the Queen?" I asked, bracing myself for another when-the-Queen-says-so answer.

"Tonight," she surprised me by saying.

The three remaining elves whipped their heads around. I guess they were as surprised by this piece of news as I was.

"Oh. Great," I said, still trying to recover from the shock.

"Yep. Keya will come get you later," she continued. "So in the morning, your mission will be complete and you can finally return to your city and get your loved one back."

"Right," I said, forcing a smile.

Shit. That meant I would only have this one chance at killing her. I would've prefer to just find out who she was and then make a solid plan and assassinate her on my terms but it looked like that wasn't going to work. If they were going to escort me back to Keutunan tomorrow, it would have to be tonight. I would have to improvise. Good thing I'd asked for my knives.

As if on cue, Elaran and Faelar came trotting back with my brown backpack. After one last look at Faye, he threw it in my arms. Setting it down on the ground, I dove in, in search of my deadly companions. With my hands shielded from view, my fingers closed around the knife I usually carried hidden between my breasts. After it had disappeared into my sleeve, I drew out the wrap protecting my throwing knives and set it on the ground. Seeing them glint faintly in the late afternoon sun as I rolled it open filled me with a sense of familiarity and comfort. These knives had seen me through more trouble than I could count. It pained me to know that I would have to leave them behind when I fled after the assassination. Smuggling in ten throwing knives to my meeting with the Queen would be impossible. I would have to rely on the one now resting in my right sleeve. But I would use them all now, one last time. In a practiced fashion, I donned all ten of them.

"Watch this," I said with a smirk directed at Elaran.

He answered by motioning with his hand to get a move on. Hmmph. I'd wipe that disinterested look off his face. Moving quickly, I kept flicking knives at the center of the target until all ten of them had left their holster. After a quick glance to confirm that every single one had buried itself in a cluster at the center of the straw target, I gave a theatrical bow. I had time to see Elaran's eyes widen slightly before he looked away with a *tsk*.

"Wow! That's incredible!" Haela called and jumped off the barrel to inspect the knives closer.

"It is. Very impressive," Faye nodded, a mix of surprise and appreciation on her face. "What about distance? Can you still hit it from further away?"

"You kidding?" I grinned back.

"Alright," she rose to the challenge, "let's make a competition out of it. I shoot, you throw, and each time we move back further until someone misses."

"Done."

After I'd collected my knives, we began. One arrow. One knife. Another arrow. Another knife. She had more arrows than I had knives, so occasionally, I had to run back and retrieve them all to start again. My hits were getting less and less accurate while hers stayed firmly in the center. Even before we'd started, I knew I would lose. I mean, come on, I had seen the elves hit targets from distances that just shouldn't be possible during the competition last week. It was only a matter of time before I lost. And just as I'd predicted, eventually the distance became so ridiculous, at least for me, that I missed the target entirely.

"Damn, you *are* good," Faye said and looked at me with true admiration on her face.

"I still lost," I said and scratched the back of my head with my hand.

"Yeah, but this," she said, motioning from me to the knives still sticking out of the target, "not a lot of people can pull this off."

I smiled at her as we started back towards the targets. Keya and the twins called excited compliments as we drew closer. To no one's surprise, the taciturn blond elf said nothing while Elaran stared at me with a calculating expression on his face.

"Oh I wish you'd been born an elf," Faye said wistfully.

"What?" I asked, taken completely off guard.

She grinned at me. "Imagine the fun we would've had."

"Yeah. Yeah, I think so too. You're alright, Faye."

That might not have seemed like much of a compliment but coming from me, it was. Glancing at the silver-haired elf beside me, I continued pulling knives from the target. I was so glad it wasn't her I'd have to kill. She was a lot like me, and she reminded me even more of Rain. In another place and another time, we would've been friends. And now I had to betray her trust and break her heart by killing someone she cared about. This was going to suck.

27.

My heart thumped in my chest. The sun's last rays had left the sky and a blanket of glittering stars now covered the heavens. Only a few hours ago, Elaran had watched me like a hawk as I returned all ten throwing knives to their wrappings. Luckily for me, he'd assumed I would try to keep one of them after the competition and not that I had already swiped a different one before it even started. That blade now rested in my sleeve as Keya led me through the city. After our merry competition, I'd been confined to my room with two guards posted outside. I'd spent that time wisely by going through possible assassination strategies. However, since my knowledge of the location, layout, and potential interference was extremely limited, it was almost impossible to form a working strategy.

"We are almost there now," Keya said and turned to me with a small smile.

I nodded in acknowledgement. She had come to collect me a few hours after we had left the archery range and now she'd led me through the city and into the woods beyond. The crisp night air out here smelled faintly of jasmine.

"Why is the meeting out in the woods, Keya?" I asked, my suspicion growing.

"The Queen wanted to meet you alone. There are some sensitive issues that she needs to discuss with you. Issues that are best discussed away from prying eyes and ears."

Thank you, Cadentia, Goddess of Luck. Not only would the meeting take place in a secluded location, we would also be completely alone. I could barely believe my luck. These were perfect conditions for an assassination.

"We are here. The Queen is through there," Keya lifted a graceful hand to point, "in the clearing."

Following her hand, I saw a cluster of trees that formed a ring around what seemed like an open stretch of grass. Though I couldn't see her, I knew the Queen was in there. I couldn't believe this was it. I'd been trying to get to this point for weeks and now everything had happened so fast. I would find out who the Elf Queen was, meet her, and kill her, all in the span of a single evening. My heart continued thumping.

"Good luck," Keya said.

"Thank you."

And I'm sorry, I wanted to add as I watched her turn around and walk back the way we'd come. No point in delaying the inevitable. Taking a deep breath, I stepped into the circle of trees and my inescapable fate.

A small pond occupied the center of the clearing. In the reflection of the deep blue water, thousands of stars sparkled, making it look like an eye of the gods looking down on the souls below. Before it stood a silhouette. With the moon directly behind her, I could only make out the contours of a female elf with long, flowing hair and the shape of a crown on her head. So, Faye had lied about the crown. I moved closer. The features of this long sought after elven royalty grew clearer with each step.

My rapid heartbeat pulsed through my ears. This was it. One more step, and I would be close enough to see her face.

"No," I breathed in shock and disbelief. "You... no."

"Hello, Storm," a familiar voice greeted me.

She wore a silver-colored tunic, flowing yet without decorations. On her head, a crown made of gleaming, white gemstones rested delicately. In the light of the moon, its mesmerizing glitter rivaled the heavens above. Her clothes and the crown combined with her silver hair made her look like liquid starlight. Faye.

"Is this a trick?" I pressed, whipping my head around in search of the real queen.

She shook her head softly. "No."

I desperately tried to convince myself that she was lying, that this was indeed a trick, but the logical part of my mind was already connecting the dots. The way people had spoken to her. The way people had spoken about the Elf Queen when Faye was around and the way she herself had spoken about the Queen. The way people had obeyed her. It all made sense. I'd been so stuck on how I thought female royalty *should* behave, how human royalty behaved, that I'd completely disregarded this casual, fierce-eyed elf. Looking at her now, though, there was no mistaking the power radiating from her. Icy dread spread through my stomach. I was going to have to kill Faye.

"What about Laena?" I asked in one last desperate attempt to avoid the truth.

"Laena." She laughed softly. "Yeah, I can see why you'd think it was her; she's the wisest person in the whole city. But no, Laena is my advisor."

"Oh," I mumbled in defeat because in my heart, I knew that she was telling me the truth.

The knife weighed heavily in my sleeve as chaos reigned in my head. My mind screamed at me. *One flick of the wrist. That's all it would take. Do it! Throw the knife. Why are you hesitating? Remember what happened last time you hesitated in killing someone? Rain died. She died! Are you going to let that happen to Liam? Do it!*

The image of Rain lying lifeless in a rapidly growing pool of blood transformed and took on the visage of Liam. No. I couldn't let that happen. If I didn't kill her, Liam was going to die. My heart pounded on the stone walls that I had erected around it so many years ago, screaming to be heard. I ignored its muffled cries. My muscles tensed.

Do it! my mind screamed. *If you don't do it, Liam will die.*

The vicious battering continued. Cracks formed in the wall and through those fractures I heard another voice shouting at me. *Stop! Don't!* A cacophony of contradictory orders filled my head as my mind and my heart tried to drown each other out.

If you don't, Liam dies!
If you do, Faye dies!
DO IT!

"SHUT UP!" I yelled with enough force to level cities. "I can't do it!"

Faye was staring at me with raised eyebrows. I blinked at the scene around me as I realized that I'd said that last part out loud. *Screamed* that last part out loud.

"I can't do it," I whispered, pressing a hand to my forehead. Briefly closing my eyes, I took a deep, calming breath before continuing. "I didn't come here to talk about trading. I was sent here to kill you."

The battle in my soul had brought everything to a head, forcing me to choose between my head and my heart. To my complete astonishment, my heart had won out. I didn't even think I had much of a heart left. What would happen now, after I had confessed to such a terrible crime, was anyone's guess. All I knew was that I wouldn't have been able to live with myself if I'd killed Faye. It would've been like the death of Rain all over again. To my surprise, Faye smiled.

"I am so glad you decided to tell me that instead of throwing that knife you've got hidden in your sleeve at me," she said.

"What?" I blinked, taken aback. "You knew?"

"Yeah," she nodded. "But if it makes you feel any better, I didn't figure it all out until this afternoon."

"You knew I was sent here to kill you and you still met me alone, in the middle of the woods? What if I'd decided to go through with it?"

"You would've died before you ever lifted that arm," a threatening voice announced behind me.

On reflex, I jumped out of the way and whirled around. Barely two paces behind, Elaran towered over me with a drawn bow. While Faye motioned for him to lower it, I blew a strand of hair out of my face. Damn elves and their damned sneaking abilities.

"Reckless and too smart for your own good," Elaran muttered to Faye, shaking his head as he returned the arrow to its quiver.

"So, it was a trap?" I asked.

"It was a test," Faye replied. "One you passed."

"Huh."

"I'm glad you did."

"Yeah, me too," I said and let out something between a laugh and a sigh.

If I'd made a different choice, I would've been the one bleeding to death in a pool of my own blood right now. Everything I'd done, everything I'd been through, to get to this point would've been for nothing. Within a second, I would've been dead and Liam would've been lost. And I would never have seen it coming. With a wry smile, I thanked my heart by letting it flutter in my chest with its newfound freedom.

"But why all the theatrics?" I asked, once again concentrating on the elves before me. "We've been spending time together for two weeks, why didn't you just tell me who you were from the beginning?"

"I wanted to know what kind of person you really are. It took a while," she grinned at me, "but I finally got to see it. And I kind of like you," she finished with a laugh.

I stared at her. These elves were so weird. How could she possibly like me? I'm a sarcastic, scheming smartmouth with a terrible temper and a fondness for knives. That combination usually spelled dislike, or even outright fear, not fondness. Maybe Elaran was the only sane one of them all.

"Come on, let's head back," Faye said, interrupting my thoughts. "We have a lot to talk about."

"Yeah. We do," I concurred.

As we started back towards Tkeideru, Elaran slipped up behind me. "Don't think for a second that I trust you now," he growled in my ear. "If I so much as smell betrayal, I'll put an arrow between your eyes."

"Uh-huh. And if *you* as much as think about betraying *me*, I'll slit your throat," I countered with narrowed eyes.

He clicked his tongue dismissively in reply before stalking off towards the city in silence. Yep. He was definitely the only sane one.

※

THE GREAT HALL AT THE heart of the city, the one I had so creatively dubbed *the Heart of the City*, soared above me like a gigantic umbrella. Even though it was nighttime, the flowers and vines decorating the pillars cast it in colorful hues. In all my time here, I'd never been inside this spectacular gathering hall. Lit candles decorated the tables as well as the ceiling. Tilting my head up, I noticed that it was some sort of metal contraption, like a giant chandelier, that held the candles in place. Flowing metal rows curved around one another, spanning the whole ceiling.

"I feel bad for the person who has to light all of these," I muttered under my breath.

Upon our return, we'd been met by a large party of elves. Some I recognized, others I didn't. Faye had spoken to several of them and sent them away on different errands: maps, drinks, and one person to light all of these candles, I suppose.

"We can sit here," the Queen announced and pointed to a round table roughly in the middle of the hall.

Round seemed to be the theme of this gathering place. Not only was the entire place circular, but all the tables were also round. Well, except for the long, rectangular one on the opposite side of the entrance. The high table. So, they still recognized some hierarchical traditions.

As we took our seats, the previously dispatched elves arrived one after the other, arms full of maps, documents, and cups. The last one walked in with the blond, wise-looking elf in tow.

"Ah, Laena!" Faye called and waved her over with a broad smile on her face.

"I am glad to see that it all worked out as you had planned," Laena said, taking her seat.

"Bah," Elaran muttered.

"You decided not to kill our Queen then?" she continued, turning her head to peer at me with those experienced eyes.

"Uhm, yes," I answered.

"Good. It would have been such a mess to clean up."

A surprised laugh escaped my lips. My previous assessment had been true: these people *were* weird. Weird in the best possible way.

"Alright, let's get started then," the Elf Queen proclaimed. "You were sent here to kill me. I need you to elaborate on that."

How exactly does one go about explaining an assassination plot to the actual intended target of said assassination? This was definitely a first for me. I took a couple of large gulps from my cup and then I laid it all out. After starting with a detailed explanation of the political situation in Keutunan, I moved on to the kidnapping and the blackmail and then finished with my opinion on King Adrian's mental health.

"So basically, he's a lunatic who's going to wage a war against us to stay in power?" Faye summarized.

"Yep, I'd say that sums it up pretty neatly."

She heaved a deep sigh. "Spectacular."

"We need to prepare for a fight," Elaran interjected. "If what she says is true, then they could be marching on us any day now."

I rolled my eyes at the *if* part but moved on. "Yes, they could. But when I left, the nobles were still trying to stall the war effort so it's possible that he won't be ready for another month. But, given how many people he executed for disobedience before I left, it's also possible that he's already mobilizing."

"They are not in the forest yet," Laena said. "This is our territory and we know when it is being disturbed."

"You didn't see me coming..." I pointed out.

"No, but you are a fly and thus easily missed. We would have a hard time missing a trampling herd of bulls."

I knew that she was speaking in metaphors but I still frowned at being called a fly. Lifting my frown a little, I glanced at Elaran. Well, it was an upgrade from *pregnant moose*, I suppose.

"We need someone to sneak into the city and find out," Faye said.

All three of them looked expectantly at me.

"Oh why do you even bother saying *someone*?" I remarked. "Who else is it gonna be? Or maybe you have another human hiding under the table?" I made a show of peeking under the wooden tabletop.

"Fine. *You* need to go," Faye rectified.

"Good. That was my plan as well," I said. "Because you need to understand this, I will help you in this fight, but right now, my first priority is getting Liam back."

"We understand," Laena nodded, eyes brimming with compassion.

I returned the nod. Outside the gathering hall, the night was quiet. Even the crickets had gone silent, as if they understood the gravity of the issues being discussed here under the sea of burning candles.

"Alright, here's the plan," the Queen said. "The twins will escort you to your city. They can't go inside, so you'll have to handle Liam's rescue on your own, but they'll wait for you in the woods outside. While you're there, you will figure out the time plan, the number of soldiers, and any other bits of information we might need. Then, the twins will escort you back and you will report this. And then, we can make a solid plan."

"They will escort us *both* back," I clarified.

Faye raised her eyebrows.

"I'm not leaving Liam in the city. Once the king finds out that I've rescued him, he will stop at nothing to track him down again and kill him. Brutally. And trust me, the city ain't that big."

"Understood. They will escort you both back."

"In the meantime, we will get our people ready for war," Elaran said, eyebrows drawn down over serious eyes.

There was one question that had been nagging me ever since I arrived in this strange place. One question I still hadn't gotten a straight answer to. Magic.

"Faye, I've laid all my cards on the table. I need you to do the same. What about magic?"

Both Laena and Elaran turned to look at their queen. I could see the master archer almost imperceptibly shake his head. That as much as confirmed it for me: they did have magic. Now, I only waited to see if the elves would be as truthful with me as I had been with them.

"We have magic," Faye announced, head held high.

Huh. The truth. Maybe we would be able to make this partnership work after all. Elaran let out a noisy sigh and shook his head.

"But it's not what you think," Faye continued. "I meant it when I said that we don't use magic for shooting or sneaking. All use of magic is outlawed, under pain of banishment. The only thing anyone is allowed to use it for is the cloak around our city."

"I knew there was some kind of magic around it!" I exclaimed. "Every time I walked into the city from outside I could feel a slight tingle on my arms."

"Yes. That shield keeps our city invisible and impenetrable to all humans unless they are accompanied by an elf who lets them in."

Ha! It felt good to be right. I took another swig on wine. But wait. That didn't make any sense. If the city was invisible and impenetrable, why would they need to fight in the first place? When I voiced this objection, the table grew quiet.

"It is true that we are blessed with magic," Laena began, "but everything comes with a price. In order to use magic, we have to pay with time."

"Time?" I asked. "What do you mean *pay with time*?"

"Every spell costs us a part of our future. The bigger the spell, the more of our life we have to give away."

"I don't understand..." I said hesitantly.

"I will give you an example. If I wanted to use magic to move that cup closer," Laena said and pointed to Elaran's cup across from her, "I might have to pay with a minute of my life. But if I wanted to heal someone dying in childbirth, I would have to pay with many years of my life."

I stared at her, my mouth slightly agape. Elaran's eyes had taken on a sadness that I hadn't seen before and he looked away when I made eye contact.

"So if you use magic, you die earlier than you were supposed to?" I asked softly.

"Yes."

Wow. I hadn't expected that. At all. A terrible realization suddenly dawned.

"But the shield, the one cloaking your city..." I trailed off.

"Is draining our life every day," Faye filled in, sadness and determination mixed in her voice. "Once we realized that we wouldn't win the bloodbath your ancestors had brought to our forest, we retreated. Too many of us had died in the surprise attacks. We needed to hide in order to give our people time to recover."

"The elves who raised the shield paid the steepest price," Laena continued. "Now, we only need to maintain it and we have spread that out over all citizens. But it is still draining our lives."

Feeling ashamed over my ancestors' actions, I exhaled deeply. Elaran had become unusually quiet during this part of the conversation. I guess now I knew why he hated humans. Why he hated me.

"So, that's why we need to fight," Faye said. "That's why we need to kill this lunatic king of yours. And after he's dead, we can come to an understanding with the new ruler. An understanding where we can live in peace and not have to sacrifice our people's lives to keep the cloaking spell up."

"But why now?" I asked.

There had, after all, been other kings after King George. They could've tried to reach an understanding with any of them. What made this time different?

"Because now, we have someone on the inside," Faye said and bathed me in a sincere smile. "You."

I returned the smile. "Yeah. You're right about that."

Elaran didn't go as far as smiling, he'd made it very clear that he still didn't trust me, but he did give me a satisfied nod at least. Laena patted me gently on the hand.

"We should get going with those plans for mustering our people," Elaran said, breaking the comfortable silence that had settled.

"Yeah, and you should get some sleep, Storm," the Elf Queen said. "At first light, the twins are taking you back to your home."

After bidding them goodnight, I stood up and wandered back to my room. Home. Yes, at long last I would be going home to free Liam. Never had I imagined that I'd be doing so as an ally of the elves instead of their most loathed murderer. Life. Such a strange thing. As I dropped down on the bed, I sent a prayer to Nemanan, asking him for help in figuring out a plan to save Liam. A plan that would, without a doubt, work. The God of Thieves didn't answer. Maybe he also needed some time to think. The last image in my mind before I drifted off to sleep was that of sparkling blue eyes under a mop of curly brown hair. *I'm coming, Liam.*

28.

Salt. Drawing deep breaths, I could almost taste the saltwater on my tongue. I didn't realize how much I'd missed the smell of the sea until now. Brisk winds blew in from the water to cool the city baking in the afternoon sun. I was home. It had only been a few weeks since I'd left, but given everything that had happened since, I felt as though I'd been gone for years.

While the twins and I had crossed the forest, which, by the way, is a lot easier if you actually know where you're going, I'd had time to think. Since I don't trust others to do their job, my initial plan had, of course, involved me rescuing Liam on my own. However, I had quickly realized that the circumstances of his imprisonment hadn't improved. If I hadn't known for certain that I could save him when he was first kidnapped, why would this time be any different? The stakes were too high. If I was spotted while trying to break into the Silver Keep, King Adrian would know that I'd failed my mission and he would execute Liam immediately in retaliation. I couldn't risk it, so that had ruled out a solo rescue attempt.

My second thought had been to recruit some of my guild members but I had quickly discarded that idea as well. Rogue, that treasonous spy, made that impossible. I needed someone who was skilled and whose presence in the Silver Keep wouldn't be questioned, and most importantly, wouldn't be traced back to me if things went sideways. Shortly before reaching the walls of Keutunan, I'd finally settled on a plan that I was confident would work, which was why I presently found myself weaving through the Artisan District.

My knives and cloak lay packed away because they would draw too much attention. I didn't run, or skulk, I walked with determined steps and my head held high. That's the trick to avoiding unwanted attention. If you look like you're trying to hide, people will take notice of you. But if you walk with confidence, as if you belong there, then everyone will assume that you do and take no special interest in you. Hiding in plain sight. I would've preferred to use the Thieves' Highway but I didn't want to run the risk of being spotted by Rogue, or someone else in the Thieves' Guild who might spread the word that I was back. That was why I'd opted for the route through the Artisan District.

The bustling streets filled with painters, carpenters, weavers, and other creative professions soon gave way to the winding alleys of Worker's End. Since most people were still working, the risk of being discovered here was slight. My biggest problem would be crossing into the Marble Ring, where my destination was located.

Thankfully, because I approached it from Worker's End, it proceeded without incident. Now, as I stared up at the stone building in front of me, I questioned my sanity. Had I really thought this through? The tall, one-story structure ahead was, without a doubt, one of the most dangerous places in all of Keutunan. And I had to go inside.

As I scaled the wall towards the topmost window, the one I'd chosen as my entry point, I thanked Nemanan for the complete lack of security. Well, I suppose there was no need for external security in a place like this. No one would be stupid enough to break in. No one but me, that is.

Talking, cheering, and rowdy laughter escaped through the grimy window as I pushed it open. To my delight, I noticed that the ceiling was full of wooden beams. If I was going to do this, I might as well make a grand entrance. After crawling through the window, I tiptoed across the nearest beam until I crouched above what I judged to be the middle of the room. The drinking, eating, and talking continued around the rectangular tables below me. All of its occupants were thoroughly ignorant of the surprise visitor who would soon be dropping down from the ceiling.

"Am I really doing this?" I whispered to myself in disbelief. "This is insane. I'm going to get myself killed! Well, actually, it's not as if I haven't done insanely dangerous and stupid shit before," I reasoned, tipping my head from side to side, before taking a deep, calming breath through my nose. "Here goes nothing."

I jumped down from the beam and landed on the floor in the middle of the Black Hand tavern. The Assassins' Guild's exclusive tavern.

When I had mulled over my plan, I'd come to the conclusion that the only people who fit the criteria of both *skilled* and *wouldn't be out of place in the Silver Keep* were members of the Assassins' Guild. Since Shade had made it abundantly clear that he wouldn't risk his own mission to rescue my friend, I had decided to skip him and instead put in a general request. After all, the whole death guild apparently worked for the royal family so it mattered little which particular assassin I enlisted. They could, presumably, all make an appearance in the Silver Keep without much interference and would therefore be able to rescue Liam. That is, if I managed to recruit one.

Fifty-odd assassins shot to their feet. Knives, swords, and crossbows gleamed from every set of hands. I threw rapid glances around the room while raising my hands to prove that I wasn't there to fight. My looks were met with threatening stares. Well, I hadn't been killed on sight, so there was that.

"I've come to make a request," I announced before a trigger-happy assassin could rectify that.

"A request?" an assassin peering at me from behind a crossbow asked. "Most people just leave a note at a drop point."

"Yeah, suddenly materializing in the middle our tavern is a pretty risky move," another assassin filled in, and spun his knives. "Who the hell are you to pull something like that?"

"Well, I'm–" I began before being interrupted by a man with dark brown hair pulled into a bun.

"This," he said, pointing a curved knife at me, "this is the Oncoming Storm."

A murmur spread through the room. So, my reputation preceded me. At that point, I wasn't sure if that would help or hinder me. Squinting at the man who had identified me, I tried to remember where I'd seen him before. When he flicked his observant eyes at me, realization struck. It was the tall assassin who had searched me when I'd forced my way into their headquarters to blackmail their leader. Another ridiculously risky thing to do. There seemed to be a lot of those going around.

"So, why has the Oncoming Storm decided to sneak in here instead of leaving a note like everyone else?" he asked.

"Well, my request is somewhat unusual," I began, "and time sensitive."

"Let's hear it then."

I slowly lowered my hands, hoping that they would follow suit. The room of deadly killers didn't lower their weapons. Fair enough. Clearing my throat, I elaborated.

"I would like to request a rescue mission."

Scattered laughter broke out across the room. The man bun looked at me with raised eyebrows. "You're aware that we're murderers for hire, right?" he said, trying to suppress a smile. "We're not in the rescuing business – we're in the killing business."

"Yes, I know. But as it turns out, you're also uniquely qualified to save someone from the particular place I had in mind."

"And where would that be?"

"The Silver Keep."

The tall man looked taken aback. All around me, the room had gone dead quiet.

"Look, I know that you're all working for King Adrian but–"

"That's a very dangerous accusation," Man Bun warned.

"Oh for Nemanan's sake! I've forced myself into Assassins' Guild territory, *twice*, without being invited so I really thought we had already established that the shit I do is indeed a bit risky," I snapped.

The room of assassins stared at me, unsure of what to do. I smiled inwardly. Somehow, I don't think they were used to people talking to them like that. Attack is the best defense sometimes.

"Now, as I was saying," I continued and pushed a few strands of hair back behind my ears, "I know you're working for the king but you're also members of the Underworld which means that your allegiances are somewhat... flexible. So, to put things clearly, I would like you to free someone from the Silver Keep and bring them to me."

"And why would we risk that?" the crossbow-brandishing assassin from before asked.

"Because as soon as you've broken my friend out, the king will know that *I* was the one behind it. He will never suspect you."

"What will you give us in return for this odd mission then?" someone shouted from the crowd.

"How much money do you want?" I asked and spread my arms.

"Money," a blond assassin scoffed to my left. "We can get as much money as we want from normal requests. What else are you offering?"

Oh. Shit. I hadn't expected that. What else did I have to offer? I had assumed that they, like everyone else in the Underworld, simply wanted lots of money. Several of the assassins crossed their arms and looked at me expectantly while others were starting to lose interest. Crap. I couldn't lose this opportunity! In every scenario of things that could potentially go wrong with this ridiculously dangerous plan, I'd never even considered that the form of payment would be one of them.

"Everything," I blurted out desperately because I realized that if this failed, I wouldn't be able to both save Liam and the elves. "You can have all of it. All of my money, all my possessions–"

"We've already told you, we're not interested in money," the blond assassin interrupted.

"My services then. In any way you see fit," I finished, staring steadily at the crowd.

Several heads perked up at that. Hmmph. I guess having the Oncoming Storm owing you did the trick. I really hate owing people favors but I was confident that my pride would survive. Unlike the unlucky assassin who would try to collect on that debt. Accidents do happen, after all.

"Enough," an imposing voice commanded.

As one, all occupants of the room shrank back slightly and bowed their heads in deference. My heart sank as I located the source of the interruption. Shade. He turned his black eyes, dripping with authority, on me.

"You – with me," he ordered and jerked his head towards a door next to the bar.

The room sat back down as I followed the black-clad Master Assassin towards the door. Great. This would probably end well. It wasn't like I'd tried to blackmail him at knifepoint and almost gotten myself and Liam killed last time I saw him. What could possibly go wrong?

The door slammed shut behind me. We were in a small, sparsely furnished back room. As the leader of the Assassins' Guild nonchalantly leaned back against the door and crossed his arms I realized that there were no windows. No other points of escape. Fantastic.

"I thought I made it very clear that I would not risk my position to help your friend," he said, fixing me with an iron stare.

"You did. Which is why I didn't come to you this time."

"Need I remind you that this is *my* guild?"

I suppose he did have a point. Shaking my head to signal that he did not, I made one last attempt to sway him.

"Look, I don't do this often..." I began, "but please. Please help me save Liam. I can't go through with the king's mission so this is my only shot at getting him back. I meant what I said out there, you can have whatever you want in return."

His soul-penetrating gaze scrutinized me. I shuffled my feet uncomfortably but didn't look away.

"You found the elves, didn't you?" he said.

He was nothing if not perceptive, I had to give him that. I considered my options. Lying was, of course, one of them but I had the feeling that it would serve my cause better if he actually knew the truth. After all, Shade was also trying to kill the king.

"Yes," I replied.

"Tell me," he commanded. "All of it."

And so I did. Well, I left some bits out. Like the part about the bear and the hallucinogenic berries. But besides that, I gave him a fairly detailed recounting of my adventures in the forest. Shade listened almost without interruption, only stopping me to ask for clarification a few times. Afterwards, he simply continued leaning against the door with a pensive expression on his face. I was just about to ask him what he thought about it when he broke the stretching silence.

"I have a proposition for you," he said and locked eyes with me.

"I'm listening."

"I'll rescue Liam for you and in return, you will set up a meeting with the Elf Queen."

My eyes widened. Why would he want to meet the Elf Queen? Once King Adrian was dead, I had planned on setting up a meeting with Faye and either Shade or Prince Edward, depending on who took the throne, but why would he want to arrange a meeting now? My suspicion flared.

"Why?" I asked, narrowing my eyes at him. "So you can assassinate her?"

Shade looked genuinely taken aback by that. Huh. So, maybe not then. It still didn't make sense.

"No," he said firmly. "So that we can make a joint plan for how to kill King Adrian."

"Or..." I began, "you could just kill him while you're in the castle rescuing Liam?"

"I can't."

I furrowed my brows. "Why not?"

"If it were that easy, don't you think I would've done it already? It has to be handled outside the guild."

"What does that matter?" I asked, throwing out my arms in exasperation. "You're plotting to kill a king, overthrow the monarchy, and steal the throne, but you can't kill him yourself? What, did you suddenly grow a conscience?"

"It's not about that," he replied with an impatient sigh.

"Then what? You're doubting your abilities? Then I'm starting to doubt if you're really the one who should be rescuing Liam because–"

"I'm not taking the throne for myself!" he snapped.

I recoiled slightly in surprise. Shade looked at me with a face full of determination but I could tell that he was weary. Traces of dark purple crescents had formed under his eyes and his face had that same taut look as a piece of cloth drawn too tight. These last few weeks had not treated him kindly, it would seem.

"Then for who?" I asked.

"I've been feeding King Adrian false information," Shade said, ignoring my question, "trying to get him to execute everyone who is loyal to him, leaving only the ones who think it's time for a change, in the hope that they would overthrow him themselves."

"But?"

"But they're too scared. The king has only descended further into madness since last time you saw him and the nobles are too scared to do anything. I've been at my wits' end on how to force the situation to make way for the new king. The *right* king."

Realization struck. "Edward," I breathed.

"Yes. King Adrian is obsessed with the elves because he thinks that they're the source of his weakening power. But the truth is that they're only a part of it. Keutunan has become stagnant. King Adrian wants everything to stay the way it was when his grandfather, and their grandfathers, ruled. We've lived on this godsforsaken stretch of coast for what? A couple of thousand years? And all we have to show for it is one city–"

"It's a pretty huge city," I interrupted with a light shrug.

Shade glowered at me. "Yes. But it's still only one city and some villages. Right now, we simply don't have enough resources to expand further. To survive, to thrive, we need to grow, develop, explore!"

"And Prince Edward understands this?"

"He does. In fact, he's the one who convinced me. The prince has tried to persuade his father as well but the more uncertain King Adrian's rule becomes, the more he wants everything else to stay the same."

I pondered this. Shade could, of course, be lying about all of this but I didn't see why he would need to. The deadly Master Assassin had had no trouble demonstrating his power before, which I knew because I'd been on the receiving end of that more than once. He had enough power to make people do what he wanted. Then there was the whole honor thing. The first time we'd met, I had sensed a kind of honor in him that's rare for people in the Underworld. People in general, really. And besides, what he said about Prince Edward fit with my own views of him. The prince had proven that he was nothing like his father the day he had helped me escape from the Silver Keep. I searched Shade's dark, intelligent eyes. He wasn't lying.

"I see," I said.

"So now you understand why the death of King Adrian can't be traced back to me or anyone else in the guild?"

"Yes. Because everyone close to the king knows that the Assassins' Guild works for the royal family."

"Exactly. So, if the king is assassinated, suspicion will immediately fall on Prince Edward. And his reign cannot be tainted with accusations of patricide."

Well, killing kings is a messy business. This was good for me, though. If I could get the elves and the future king of Keutunan on the same page even before he'd assumed the title it would make everything so much easier. And I would get to kill King Adrian. Or at least be a part of it.

"Alright," I said, straightening. "You will rescue Liam, and I will arrange a meeting between the Elf Queen and Prince Edward."

"Deal."

The black-haired assassin pushed himself off the door and strode forward. Looking me steadily in the eye, he held out his hand. I shook it. There we were, two shady underworlders shaping the future of two great cities. What a pair we made.

29.

I paced back and forth across the wooden floor. Shade had brought me back to the upstairs study in the Assassins' Guild headquarters before he left to rescue my friend. Weeks ago, I had tried to blackmail him into doing just that in this exact room and now we were working together. Who saw that coming?

He'd been gone for over an hour now. I chewed my lower lip as I walked across the room yet again. My rucksack had been unpacked, packed, and then unpacked again as I willed time to move faster. I'd returned all of my knives to their rightful places because once Liam was safe, I had a loose end to tie up. The window behind me overlooked the back of the Assassins' Guild and even though I knew that they'd be coming through the front, I still cast an impatient glance through it for what had to be the twentieth time. Footsteps sounded on the wooden staircase outside the door. Two pairs. I closed my eyes and sent a quick prayer to Nemanan. *Please let it be him, please let it be him.* The door swung open. Before it had even hit the inside wall, I sprang forward.

"I am so sorry I took so long!" I cried, drawing my best friend into a tight hug.

Liam hugged me back fiercely. For a moment, the rest of the world didn't exist. No assassins, no elves, no lunatic royals. No power struggle and no heartache. Only me and him, locked in a long-awaited embrace.

"Are you okay? Let me look at you," I said and drew back enough to scan his appearance.

He looked thinner than last time I'd seen him. His dark brown locks were ruffled and the usual sparkle that always seemed present in his eyes was missing. It was Liam but he looked... muted. With his back to Shade, who still lingered in the doorway, Liam showed me the Thieves' Guild hand signal that was used to ask if a situation or a person could be trusted. Thumb and pinkie out, hand straight and then quickly turned to the right. I nodded in reply. That seemed to do the trick. All the tension in Liam's shoulders melted away, his dark blue eyes lit up, and he drew me into another hug.

"I'm so happy to see you!" he exclaimed.

"Are you okay?" I mumbled in his ear, trying to keep the tears at bay.

"I am now."

Behind Liam, Shade leaned against the door frame with a smile on his face. It seemed to be part empathy, part amusement but I didn't care. Liam was back.

I STARED UP AT THE two buildings, side by side, that I knew better than any other buildings in the whole city. When I'd left, I hadn't known if I would ever see them again. Yet, here I was. The dark brown, wooden tavern that was the Mad Archer and the gray, stone building of the Thieves' Guild towered before me. Home. I started towards the latter. It was time to tie up a loose end. I had left Liam back in the Assassins' Guild because it was better if he wasn't present for this part. The day of reckoning had come for the treasonous spy known as Rogue.

"When the green-clad gentleman laughs..." I said as the hatch in the door slid open.

For a moment, nothing happened. No sound. No movement. Then, the door shot open and I was yanked inside. Crap. Had Rogue taken over the guild? My body came to a halt as strong hands clamped down on my shoulders. I knew those hands.

"Storm!" our muscled gatekeeper, Bones, exclaimed before drawing me into a bear hug.

This was more hugs than I'd been in, in probably like, the last ten years of my life. But, I suppose, days like this didn't happen all that often. I hugged him back.

"Hello, Bones," I said into his chest.

"I've been so worried," he said, releasing me. "You've been gone a long time."

"I have. And when things have calmed down, I promise I'll tell you all about it over some ale. Actually, lots of ale," I added with a smile. "But for now, where is Rogue? He's a–"

"Spy," Bones finished. "Yeah, thanks to your message we've known and we've been able to feed him whatever lies we want the king to hear."

"Thank Nemanan you understood it," I said and heaved a deep sigh. "He was lurking right behind me so I couldn't be any more specific."

"Told you I always take care of the guild," Bones said with a grin.

I returned the smile. "Indeed you do. But now it's time for Rogue to pay. Is he here?"

"He is. Last I heard he was sleeping in his room. But you'd better go see the bosses first."

"Yeah, you're probably right."

I started down the stairs but then stopped and turned around. Our guild was certainly lucky to have such an intelligent gatekeeper but to me, he was more than that. As I looked up at his strong frame and steady eyes, I realized that I considered him a friend.

"It's good to see you again, Bones," I said.

He gave a short but rumbling laugh. "You too, Storm. You too."

Since I was intimately familiar with every nook and cranny in this building, it was fairly easy to maneuver through its twisting halls and all the way to the Guild Masters' rooms without being seen. When knocking on the black door, I used the pattern that signaled an urgent matter. A crack appeared in the door and a blue eye peered down at me.

"Inside," Guild Master Eliot's grating voice rasped.

I slipped in through the narrow opening and closed the door behind me. All three Guild Masters were gathered in the study that served as an antechamber to their three bedrooms. It looked as if they were getting ready to leave, probably to go to the Mad Archer for breakfast. Evening was fast approaching, after all.

"Well, this is a pleasant surprise," Guild Master Caleb said, lifting his eyebrows.

Now that the door was closed behind me, I dropped down on one knee and placed my fist on the floor. "Please forgive my sudden interruption and my straightforwardness but I have a lot to tell you and not much time."

"Ah. Then we shall not waste any," Master Caleb said and motioned for me to rise.

After standing back up, I quickly recounted the reason for my hasty disappearance and Liam's absence. Bones had told me that they already knew the gist of the matter but I wanted them to hear the full story from me because I had a request to make.

"...but as of half an hour ago, Liam's been rescued," I finished.

"I see," Guild Master Killian said. "We would've very much liked to kill Rogue and rescue Liam ourselves, when we first found out, but since you failed to specify how deep this treachery ran, we couldn't risk it."

I winced. Yeah, I hadn't managed to tell them that Rogue was the only one.

"If the guild was compromised," he continued, "we needed to know how far it had spread before we made a move. We never got that far."

My heart sank. The Guild Masters held me responsible for this. They would never agree to my request.

Guild Master Caleb turned his brown eyes on me. "But, thanks to your presence of mind in communicating Rogue's treachery to Bones, we have, at least, been able to use the situation to our advantage and feed him false information. And now you're saying that Liam is safe?"

"Yes. Which is why I would like to formally request your permission to kill Rogue."

My three Guild Masters exchanged looks. I knew they held me responsible and that they preferred to dispense justice on their own, but given that Liam and I were the ones who'd suffered the most, I hoped they would allow me to do it.

"Granted," Guild Master Killian finally said with a nod.

I sighed in relief. "Thank you."

"Back storage. Ten minutes."

I nodded my understanding. At long last, I would have my revenge.

THE BACK STORAGE ROOM was only used to hold food and fire supplies during the winter months, which meant that it was empty now that summer was here. Well, almost empty. Guild Master Killian had lured Rogue into the room and standing on the other side of the thick, stone door, I could picture him in there. Nervously pacing and wondering why the Guild Masters had asked him to meet them down there but also too afraid to leave in case it would upset them. Or give away his cover. I pulled the door open. Stone grated against stone. Rogue turned to look at the sound.

"You?" he said, taking a step back. "What the hell are you doing here?"

While pulling the heavy door closed behind me, I echoed his own words from so many weeks ago. "As good as *you* are, you're not *nearly* as good as you think you are." A feral grin spread across my face as I turned to my prey.

"The Elf Queen is dead then?" Rogue said, eyes darting across the room. "She'd better be or Liam will pay."

"Will he now?" I asked. "You know, I can't believe I ever mistook you for an underworlder. No one from our world would be stupid enough to blackmail me."

"The king–" Rogue began, licking his lips nervously.

"Oh the king can't save you now, traitor." I spat out that last word. "How did you think that infiltrating an Underworld guild would work out for you? Huh? Did you think that you'd just be able to walk out of here, sunshine and rainbows? Let me tell you: there's no sunshine and rainbows in our world."

"If you touch me, Liam will–"

"I've already told you," I cut off, eyes glittering dangerously. "The king can't save you now. Liam is already free."

So far, Rogue had been standing his ground in the middle of the room but at that, he took a step back. A wolfish grin twisted my features as I stood blocking the door. The spy's pale blue eyes continued scanning the space as if a way out would suddenly materialize out of nowhere. While wringing his hands, he wet his lips again.

"Look, we can come to an understanding," he bargained.

I laughed. "An understanding? No, I don't think so. The time for retribution has come."

Fear etched itself in the royal traitor's face for a moment, but then, it was replaced by stubborn defiance. He stood up straight and jutted his chin out. If I didn't hate him so much, I would've been impressed. When he spoke, his voice held a tone of judgment.

"The gods will send you to hell for this," he declared.

A maniacal laugh slipped my lips. "For this?" I laughed again, darkness seeping into my eyes. "Oh, you have *no idea* what I have done." Memories of blood, pain, and horrifying screams flashed through my mind. "My place in hell has been reserved for many years."

I took a step forward and drew the hunting knives from my back. Rogue retreated. The darkness in my soul churned, begging to be let out. My eyes were going black.

"I will see you down there," I said, a grin tinted with madness on my face.

"No... please," Rogue pleaded, retreating further towards the wall.

Another crazed laugh escaped my lips. Rogue had reached the wall in front of me. With his back pressed up against it, he held up his hands. I kept advancing, knives in hand.

"Don't do this," he begged. "Please, you don't have to do this."

"Oh, but I want to."

I summoned the full force of the darkness from the blackest pit of my soul and let it run rampage through my every nerve. A thundering, roaring storm bled from my eyes as I fixed them on the trembling figure in front of me. Bloodcurdling screams filled the empty, gray room and echoed through all the lower levels as hell came to the Thieves' Guild.

✕

"WAS IT BAD?" LIAM ASKED as we jogged along the northernmost tree farm.

"For him, yeah," I said.

After finishing up my bloody business with the king's late spy, I had returned to the Assassins' Guild to collect Liam and to work out the final details of the royal meeting that I would be hosting. As I dodged a stray root on our way back to the twins, I wondered, not for the first time, how in the world I had gotten caught up in the business of monarchs.

"I'm glad he's dead," Liam surprised me by saying.

Glancing at him from the corner of my eye, I noticed the hardened set in his dark blue eyes. I didn't know what had happened to him during his time in captivity; he wouldn't say and I didn't want to press the matter. He'd told me that he was fine, multiple times, so I had no choice but to believe him.

"Though, I still can't believe that you actually trusted other people," Liam continued. "When Shade showed up, I thought for sure that I was going to die. Of all the things I'd expected him to say, *Storm sent me* was not one of them."

"Yeah, well, desperate times, you know."

Liam laughed. "I didn't believe him at first but when he said to tell me that you couldn't charm a starving dog with an armful of food, I knew it was really you."

"I haven't forgotten about that remark," I said and leveled a mock glare at him.

He laughed a rippling laugh. Oh how I had missed that sound. Now that my best friend was back by my side, there was nothing I couldn't handle. Even a royal rendezvous.

"So this is the infamous Liam?" a voice said to our left.

Liam let out a yelp and whirled around. Next to us, Haela and Haemir had materialized among the trees and the ever-cheerful female twin waved at us with a beaming smile. Liam's mouth dropped open as he stared from me to the tall elves.

"You didn't tell me they were gorgeous!" Liam accused.

"Ohh, I like this one already," Haela said, elbowing her brother in the ribs.

I rolled my eyes. Elves. "Liam, this is Haela," I said, pointing at the satisfied-looking elf, "and that's her twin brother Haemir." I moved my hand towards the more embarrassed-looking twin. "Haela, Haemir, meet Liam."

"Nice to meet you."

"Yeah, you too," Liam said before turning to me with a suspicious look on his face. "Infamous?"

I cleared my throat. "I have talked about you... a bit."

"Well... you're kind of also the reason that she almost stabbed our queen," Haemir supplied.

"What?" Liam exclaimed.

"Alright, calm down," I said and looked at the three of them, "I haven't really had the time to catch him up on everything. There will be time for that soon, but right now, I have news."

"Okay, spill," Haela said.

I provided a brief summary of the events that had taken place this afternoon before moving on to the important part: the proposed royal meeting. The twins listened without interruption until I'd finished explaining about the crown prince and the proposition that Shade had brought us.

"And you really think this is a good idea?" Haemir asked.

"Yeah, I do," I said. "Prince Edward is... different. He's nothing like his father. And I think this is the best opportunity for you too, to solve your problem."

"Hmm."

For a minute, the twins pondered this. The sun's last rays had left the sky hours ago, leaving the forest in gloomy darkness. I drew my dark gray cloak closer around me.

"What about location?" Haela asked.

"Apparently, there's a small cabin about ten minutes into the forest that's been empty, well," I glanced around, "since the war."

"We know it," she confirmed.

"Good. Then you can show me and Liam where it is so that we can sleep there tonight and get it ready for the meeting tomorrow night while one, or both, of you head back and tell Faye about this."

"Yeah, that works. Then we can also make sure that there's no ambush waiting for her when she arrives."

I smiled. Haela was cheerful and good-natured but she sure was no fool. Behind all that playfulness was a sharp mind.

"I'll return to Tkeideru and inform the Queen," Haemir said before turning to his sister. "You're staying here?"

She nodded. "Yep."

"Two hours after sunset tomorrow?"

"Two hours after sunset tomorrow," I confirmed.

Haemir nodded once to me and then to Liam. Haela looked slightly anxious. I smiled as she drew her surprised brother into a hug.

"You'll be alright?" she asked.

Her other half laughed. "Shouldn't I be the one asking you that?" He gently detached himself from the embrace. "I'll see you soon."

With one last wave, he trotted off into the dark forest. Night had drained all the color out of the trees, making the woods seem grim and dangerous. I, of all people, knew just how dangerous the forest could be, I would remember that bear encounter to my dying day, but that was not why my mood had taken a dark turn. As Haela led us towards the cabin, I couldn't shake a sense of foreboding. The mysterious man I'd met here last time had told me that there was a storm coming and that I should make sure to be on the right side. I wondered if this might have been the storm he had meant. A lot of people's fates would be decided here tomorrow and if things went wrong, the consequences could be catastrophic. As darkness swallowed us, I couldn't help worrying whether I had, in fact, made the right decision.

30.

"If this is a trap, you will be the first to die."

I rolled my eyes. "If this was a trap, do you think I'd be stupid enough to still be here?"

Elaran glowered at me but eventually gave a curt nod as if to concede that I did have a point. The sound of moving feet came from outside.

Liam, Haela, and I had spent most of the day in the forest. The black-haired elf had thought it was high time that I learned how to move quietly in the forest and I hadn't complained. Sneaking is always a useful ability. Given that it was Liam's first time in the woods he'd struggled a little, but since I'd already practiced a bit, I got the hang of it pretty quickly. Now that I actually knew what to look for and what to avoid, it was almost as easy as sneaking in the city.

Once Haela was satisfied with my progress, we'd gotten to work on the cabin. The worst of the cobwebs were cleaned out, firewood was gathered, and it was made as ready as it could be for royalty. By pushing all other furniture to the sides of the room, we'd managed to create enough space for the table and the four chairs in the center. A fire in the corner and a spare candle on the table now cast the room in a warm glow. Light danced across Faye's determined face as the door was pulled open and two black-haired men stepped through. Silence fell across the room as the two monarchs faced each other.

This was the part that worried me. No female had ever been allowed to rule our city and now the future king of Keutunan was meeting the leader of the elves who, as it happens, was a woman. As much as I knew that Prince Edward was different from his father, he was still a man. If he treated Faye the way that ladies were treated in the court of Keutunan, these negotiations would end very poorly. The trepidation in the air was almost palpable as a heavy silence blanketed the room. Prince Edward took a step forward. Without realizing it, I held my breath. This was it.

"It is an honor to meet you, Queen Faye," the smartly dressed prince said and held out his hand.

Letting out a deep breath, I could barely hide my relief, or surprise. Men of noble birth don't shake the hands of ladies. Handshaking, on that step of the social ladder, is reserved only for people who consider each other equals. What the young prince was doing here today spoke volumes for his character. Faye stepped forward and took his hand.

"Likewise, Prince Edward," she said with a firm handshake. "Shall we?"

The determined queen and the polite prince took up positions on either side of the table. Once they were seated, Shade and Elaran both lowered themselves into the chairs next to their respective monarch. Since space in the one-room cabin was fairly limited, the twins, Liam, and whatever escort I assumed that Shade had brought, waited outside. There were only four chairs which meant that there was no obvious seating arrangement for me. In the end, I found myself perched on the wooden countertop next to one of the table's short sides. It was the ideal place for me, I suppose, since I didn't technically belong to either side of the negotiations. Across the table, two pairs of yellow eyes met two pairs of black eyes.

"I will get straight to the point," the silver-haired queen said. "It has been brought to my attention that your father is planning an attack on my people."

"He is," Prince Edward confirmed.

"We have no interest in a war. On the contrary, we want to restore a peaceful relationship between our two cities. I have been told that you are different from your father."

"I am."

"And yet, what we are here to discuss is patricide," Faye said flatly. "I mean no disrespect, but I have to ask. Why?"

The logs in the fireplace popped as the prince pondered the question. He didn't seem angry. Rather, there was a sadness in his dark eyes as he replied.

"My father used to be a good man but everything changed when my older brother was taken. Or so I have been told. I was only an infant at the time. My brother was kidnapped when he was just a toddler. The day his body was returned to the castle, burnt to a crisp, was the day my mother died. At least her soul."

"I am sorry for your loss," Faye said, eyes filled with sympathy.

"Thank you. With my brother gone and my mother turned into nothing more than a living statue, my father started spiraling into madness. He became obsessed with reasserting his power so that no one would ever dare touch our family again. Now, he is possessive, vindictive, and he never misses a chance to show off his power. This insatiable thirst for it has warped his mind and the challenges that our city is facing are not helping."

"Which challenges?" Faye asked.

"Stagnation. We should be trading, exploring the forest, experimenting with boatbuilding to see if we can make a boat capable of crossing the wild sea. Not wasting precious lives and resources waging a war with the only other civilization we have found," Edward finished and shook his head in disgust.

Shade had already told me some of the prince's plans but hearing it from his own lips made me truly believe it. And I liked what I was hearing because Keutunan *was* stagnating. People were barely making ends meet and no one had money to invest in new inventions. If what he said was true, that would lead to economic renewal, which for me would mean more money to steal. And besides, I had found that I rather liked adventuring outside the city. If we could build boats capable of crossing the large sea to the south, who knows what adventures we might find.

"My father's desperation for power is not getting better, only worse," Prince Edward continued. "He listens to no one, except for the voices in his head, and he makes life-altering decisions on a whim. Which is why we have no other option than to remove him before the damage to my city and my people is irreparable."

The cabin fell silent. Faye and Edward kept steady eye contact while thoughts churned and decisions were made inside the head of every member present. At last, the Queen spoke.

"I understand the desire to protect one's people more than you know." She peered at the young man in front of her. "You are indeed different from any other human leader we have encountered."

Edward laughed. "I will take that as a huge compliment."

With that, the tension in the room evaporated completely. Queen Faye and Prince Edward gave each other an appreciative smile, one leader to another. Neither Shade nor Elaran replicated the gesture but them being, well, them, I had expected nothing less. The mirthful prince leaned towards his assassin but spoke loudly enough for everyone to overhear.

"You were right about being able to trust Storm," he said to Shade before turning to me, another smile tugging at his lips. "There was indeed no trap waiting for us."

I blew a strand of hair out of my face. "How is it that I get roped into hosting a royal parley, that *both of you* wanted me to set up, but both sides still think that *I'm* the one setting them up for an ambush?"

"Yes, how strange indeed," Prince Edward said with eyebrows raised in mock surprise. "It is almost as if you were a shady member of the Underworld with a questionable moral compass."

A burst of laughter slipped from Elaran's lips before he clapped a hand over his mouth. I stared at him in shock. I didn't think I had heard him laugh before. At all. The closest he'd gotten was that condescending snicker he'd so often directed at me. This was laughter. Real, mirthful laughter. He looked about as surprised by it as I did. Well, if the future king of Keutunan could make even Elaran laugh, then there might be hope for us yet. After this little merriment at my expense, the discussion moved from character assessment to practical details. From atop my wooden counter I watched Shade explain why it would be best if King Adrian died in the forest before sharing that he had the power to influence when and how the king would attack.

Elaran listened and then proceeded to fire off countless questions about where and how this war would be fought in order to limit the number of casualties.

"...if I take the bulk of our force to the Dead Woods, then we can surround King Adrian's troops as they march in," Elaran finished.

"Why?" I interrupted.

All four of them turned to stare at me. It was the first time in a while that I had said anything. By the surprised looks on their faces, I assumed they'd forgotten I was there. A frown quickly settled on Elaran's face.

"Stay out of this. You know nothing of battle plans," he said.

Faye sighed and shook her head. "Let her speak. What do you mean by *why*?"

"Why would you fight them on their terms?" I asked. "They come here, into the forest. This is your home ground. Use it. They're good at fighting in the open so don't. Fight sneaky."

"Fighting sneaky–" Elaran began.

"I know you think that I have no honor," I cut off, looking him straight in the eye. "But what does it matter? Dead is dead. They come here to kill your families. Is it honorable to let them? It doesn't matter how you win. Winning is winning. There isn't always a golden third way!" I said, voice raised in exasperation. "Sometimes it's just about killing them before they kill you."

Silence spread across the room. I knew that it wasn't my place to have an opinion on the matters of kings and queens but let's face it, when have I ever known my place? The grumpy ranger stared at me with steady eyes.

"I didn't think I would say this, *ever*, but she's right," Elaran said.

Having him admit that I was right about something was so satisfying that I almost let out a victorious whoop. I settled for a broad grin.

"Yeah, she does have a point," Shade filled in. "The soldiers only obey King Adrian out of fear. As soon as we take him out, they will retreat. If we send a small assassination party to kill the king before the fighting even starts then the loss of life, on both sides, will be practically nonexistent."

"I like it," Faye said.

"I could go alone, but I have a feeling that you want to be there to make sure of the results," the Master Assassin said and looked expectantly at the Elf Queen.

"Correct. And besides, you might be good at assassination but you don't know the forest like we do. The elves and I will go as well."

The auburn-haired archer was about to protest but Faye silenced him with one hand. If I knew anything about her, I knew that there was no way she would sit this one out. To my surprise, she then turned to me.

"How would you like to be a part of an assassination plot that involves killing a ruler other than me?" she asked with an amused smile.

My cheeks flushed. "Uhm, well, I..." I began.

"You do seem to somehow be in the middle of all this, so you might as well come and see it through to the end."

"Alright, yeah. I guess I would like that," I said, thinking about what the lunatic king had put me and Liam through.

"Okay, fine," Shade said and turned his eyes on me. "But apart from you and me, no other humans, because we can't have this traced back to the prince. We will sneak into the king's camp and kill him while you, my prince," he continued and turned to Crown Prince Edward, "will be in the castle, very visible, where no one will question your involvement."

Edward nodded. "Don't make him suffer," he said, looking each of us in the eye. "Despite everything else, he is still my father."

Each member of the royal conspiracy nodded in affirmation as the prince's eyes moved from one to the next. The plan was set. The pieces were about to move. Future history books would never know that it was here in a cramped cabin in the woods that the assassination of a king and the fate of two civilizations were decided. We would take the secret of this assassination to the grave. Unless, of course, the grave found us first.

31.

"Wow! It's even more stunning in daylight!"

Liam stood gawking at the regal trees of Tkeideru. Craning his neck, he tried to look at everything all at once and for every turn of the head, his mouth dropped open a little further.

We had arrived in the elf city late last night when the bright moon and the glittering stars had covered Tkeideru in a blanket of silver. My friend had spent a good hour standing on the bridge outside our room, drinking in the sight, before I could convince him to come inside. And he was right. It was even more beautiful when the sun glinted off the fresh, green leaves in the trees all around us and the colorful flowers dotting the buildings were in full bloom.

"Careful now, or your jaw is gonna fall off from all that gawking," I teased.

"You're one to talk," Haela said and threw a mischievous smile in my direction before turning to Liam, lowering her voice to a conspiratorial whisper. "She was even worse when she first got here."

Liam giggled in reply before wandering off, though only a short distance, to get a better look. In the brief day and a half that he had known these elves, he'd already managed to charm almost all of them. No surprise there. Only Elaran and Faelar still treated him with stiff formality. Though, given enough time, I was pretty sure that Liam would be able to sway even those grumpy elves.

Haemir let out an impatient sigh. "Where are Faye and Keya? We have a lot to prepare if we're going to be ready for the human army. Why tell us to gather in front of the War Dancer if they're not even here?"

"Oh calm down, she said they're on their way," his sister supplied.

"Don't tell me to calm down! The humans will be here in three days. How are we even going to incapacitate an entire army so that we can sneak right into the middle of their camp and kill their leader?"

"Actually, I have an idea about that," I interjected.

The twins perked up at that and moved closer to hear what sort of scheme I had cooked up this time. Elaran only gave me a disinterested stare from across the grass so I turned my back on the dissatisfied ranger and his stone-faced friend.

"Journeyberries," I said.

A grin spread across Haela's stunning features as her eyes lit up. "Ha! That'll do the trick."

"Yeah, based on how well you handled those," Haemir said with a pointed cough, "we could traipse a herd of moose through their camp without anyone being the wiser if they've eaten a handful of journeyberries."

I ignored the playful insult. "Exactly. So if we sneak crushed journeyberries into their food and drink when they make camp, they'll be out hard all night. Then all we have to do is kill the ones guarding the king's tent and we're in."

"That's a pretty solid plan," Haemir said.

"*Pretty solid*? This is gonna be so much fun!" his sister quipped and shot up in an excited jump.

I couldn't help smiling. Leave it to Haela to be excited even after finding out she was going to have to sneak through a heavily guarded human camp. A mission that could very well go sideways. Fast. And result in death. I shook my head slightly. Haela – ever the optimist.

"Whoa! This bow is gorgeous!" Liam's ecstatic voice came from somewhere behind me.

Bow? Wait a minute. I whipped around to see Liam holding Elaran's massive, black bow that had previously been resting against the wall of the War Dancer. The owner of said bow stared at the excited human with a stunned expression on his face. *Shit*. I shook my head violently at Liam. Between Elaran's stunned scowl, my panic, and everyone else's shock, Liam seemed to gather that something was wrong.

"I'm sorry?" he said tentatively and lowered the bow to the ground.

Elaran took a step forward. *Crap*. I launched myself across the grass. Liam's eyes flicked from me to Elaran to the other elves gathered around us. Elaran's yellow eyes bored into the confused human as he continued advancing towards him and the bow. Liam shrank back. I suppose he had avoided enough fights in his life to know what was about to happen. He lifted his hand and retreated another step.

"I'm sorry. I don't want to fight."

I cleared the distance just as Elaran opened his mouth to respond. He closed it again with a confused frown on his face when I skidded to a halt between him and my friend and threw my arms out wide.

"Don't," I said. "He didn't know. It's my fault. I haven't had time to teach him everything yet."

Elaran scowled at me. I held his gazed with steady eyes.

"I take full responsibility," I continued. "So, go ahead and beat me until your honor is satisfied."

"Storm!" Liam protested, horrified, behind me.

"Quiet," I hissed before turning back to the angry elf. "I won't fight back."

I put my arms behind my back and lowered my eyes. The area around us had gone dead quiet. Everyone remembered what had happened last time Elaran and I had fought and how badly he wanted revenge for that. This was his chance. And I doubted that anyone had forgotten the show of force on the archery range. Least of all me. I knew that he possessed ridiculous strength. This was going to hurt.

"Why are you protecting him?" Elaran asked. "Look at me!"

I complied. He always had a certain air of grumpiness around him but he didn't seem angry anymore. Only flustered.

"You have got to be the most disagreeable person I've ever met," he continued, voice raised in agitation. "You're rude, selfish, and when the real you came out during our last fight, I saw someone who would rather die than not fight back. What's more, you know I could break every bone in your body if I land a hit. And yet, you still sacrifice yourself. Why?"

"Because he saved me," I replied, surprising myself with an honest answer.

"He can't even save himself! How could he possibly have saved you?"

I took a deep breath. The silence his question had left in its wake made the air feel heavy. Only a blacksmith's hammer echoed in the distance. I could feel the eyes of Faelar and the twins on me.

"I was young," I began. "Bad shit happened. I let the darkness in, and when you let the darkness in, it never comes out. My soul and my heart turned black. And then along came this annoyingly cheerful kid," I said and threw an arm in Liam's direction, "who was kind and persistent. He lightened parts of my soul again. So, yeah, offering to take a beating for him is the *least* I can do."

Elaran looked at me, eyes slightly narrowed and lips pursed in thought. His face bore the same expression as someone who studies a curious bird. The seconds stretched on. At last, he took a step forward. I braced myself.

"Make sure it doesn't happen again," he said and gave my shoulder a light push before stepping past me to retrieve his bow.

I turned to look at him in stunned silence. Okay. I had so not seen that coming. He'd been wanting to beat me up since the day we met and here he had the perfect chance. And he'd passed it up. By all the gods, what in Nemanan's name had just happened?

"What's going on?" Faye's voice called across the grass.

Elaran and I exchanged a look. "Nothing," he replied.

"Oh by Nature's grace, you're not fighting again, are you?" the Elf Queen asked, throwing suspicious glances at the two of us as she and Keya joined the group.

"Again?" Liam asked quietly in my ear.

"I'll tell you later," I whispered back.

"I think they've just decided not to," Haemir said in response to Faye's question.

"Good. Because we have to come up with a strategy for sneaking into the humans' camp."

Haela's face broke into a grin. "Storm has the perfect plan for that."

"She does? Let's hear it then."

All eyes turned to me. "Journeyberries."

"Ha! I love it!" Faye exclaimed, mirroring Haela's broad grin.

"Okay, can someone please tell me what in Nemanan's name *journeyberries* are?" Liam interrupted.

The elves looked from one to the other before all eyes returned to me again. They broke out laughing. Even I couldn't help cracking an embarrassed smile.

"You should ask Storm," Keya said with a soft smile. "She knows quite a bit about them."

"Oh you're gonna love this," Haela said.

Liam turned to me with curious eyes and a bemused smile. I sighed and shook my head. They were never going to let me forget that, were they?

"Alright, Storm will fill you in on that while we move," the Queen said. "Grab a couple of sacks from the War Dancer's storage and then we'll head out and go get us some journeyberries."

After gearing up, the eight of us took off into the forest. My last encounter with these berries ranked in the top five of the weirdest shit I'd ever been through. I'd never thought I would go out searching for them willingly again. As I thought about the visions I had seen because of them, I almost felt bad for the unsuspecting soldiers. They were in for a night to remember.

32.

"I don't get it," Liam said, turning his head in every direction. "Why is it called *the City of Ash*? There's no ash anywhere."

The afternoon sun warmed our backs as we made our way towards the War Dancer. We had spent these last couple of days getting ready for the attack. Multiple waterskins filled with juice from journeyberries lay waiting for us in the tavern's storage room. Eating a bunch of them whole had left me tripping for days so we had come to the conclusion that pouring some juice into their stew pots and ale barrels would be more than enough to knock them out for an hour or two. After getting our means of incapacitation ready, we had visited the Dead Woods to plan our advance and we were just now returning from a final scout of the area before the army would arrive tomorrow.

"Good point. I don't know," I conceded before raising my voice to call out to Faye who was walking a little ahead with Keya. "Faye! Why is it–"

"We heard you," she interrupted, turning around with a smile on her lips. "Super senses, remember?" She winked and pointed at her ear.

"Oh. Right."

They stopped, allowing us to catch up with them. Keya retied the knot on her leaf-decorated braid while we closed the distance but Faye seemed content to just look at us. Sometimes I really did feel like an animal being studied.

"Well?" I said, raising my eyebrows once we caught up.

"What do you see?" she asked instead.

"What do I see?" I looked around. "People, homes, shops."

"And?"

"And, uhm… grass? And trees."

"Yep," she said before an amused look spread across her face. "What kind of trees?"

"Are you seriously asking me, *me*, what kind of tree it is? It's a *tree*. It's brown at the bottom and green at the top," I said with a frown.

Faye shook her head. "You can't see anything else?"

"It's the same kind of tree," Liam supplied, squinting at the leaf-clad giants around us.

"Exactly! I'm glad someone around here has a head attached to their shoulders," the Queen said, that same amused look still etched on her face.

I rolled my eyes. "Is this going anywhere? We've established that there are trees in the forest. So what?"

"They are ash trees," she spelled out with an exasperated sigh.

"Oh."

"Yeah. Your ancestors used to call our city *the City of Ash Trees* but I guess the tree part got lost somewhere along the centuries."

Liam pinched his lip. "That does make a lot of sense."

"Alright, if you're quite finished with the history lesson, let's go drink!" Haela called, elbowing past us and yanking open the door to the War Dancer.

Haemir gave an apologetic shrug as he passed us and followed his sister inside. Faye laughed and then turned to call over her shoulder.

"Come on, boys!"

Elaran held up a hand to signal that he and Faelar had heard her and were coming as well. The rest of us followed the twins into my second favorite tavern and the food and drink that waited inside.

"Speaking of names," Faye said once we all had taken a seat at the long table in the back. "What's with all these weather phenomenon names?"

"What do you mean?" I asked.

"That assassin guy, wasn't his name Shade? I've been thinking that maybe it's because he works in the shadows but shouldn't his name be *Shadow* then?"

I gave a short laugh. "It's not from that. Shade is short for Deadly Nightshade."

"Ah! That makes so much more sense."

Right then, Faldir's graceful frame weaved through the tables of eagerly waiting patrons. At the sight of the tray filled with wine cups, Haela rubbed her hands in anticipation. The blond tavern keeper gave his brother a short shoulder squeeze as he set down the last wooden cup.

"Venison stew is coming right up," he said. I drew an excited breath. Faldir chuckled, yellow eyes twinkling. "Yeah, I heard it's your favorite," he said and winked at me before retreating to the bar.

Faye lifted her cup and the rest of us followed suit. "To health, happiness, and good hunting!" she said, raising her cup towards the middle of the table.

"Good hunting!" we all responded, raising our cups and looking around at each other.

The pale, yellow liquid disappeared down the throats of all eight companions. I had come to really like the taste of wine in the weeks I'd spent here. Liam had, of course, fallen in love with it after the first sip. That boy loved everything sweet. Moments after our starting salute, Faldir came back with bowls of stew and for a while, silence reigned as everyone savored the food. Scattered conversations in pairs or threes broke out as we devoured the perfectly seasoned venison. Faldir returned several times, clearing plates and filling wine cups.

"Why aren't you called something weird like Cloud or Sun or something?" Haela said, raising her voice to carry across the table.

Liam glanced around, uncertain. "Me?"

"Yeah," she said, wiping her mouth after having drained her cup in one go. "Your name seems very... ordinary. Especially for an... what is it you call yourselves?" She looked to me but just as I opened my mouth to answer, Haela remembered the word. "Underworlder."

Not long ago, Rogue had asked him that same question and gotten a very short reply. I wondered how much Liam would share with these elves. They'd become fast friends over these last few days but I also knew that this story was one not many people had heard. I looked at him from across a table that had gone expectantly silent. He bit his lip with a pensive look on his face.

"I had a family, and they named me Liam," he began. "I had a mom and dad, and a younger sister until the year I turned ten."

Based on the suddenly serious expression on her face, I think maybe Haela had expected a light answer, maybe something funny. She put the cup down and leaned forward on the table.

"What happened?" she asked.

Liam took a deep breath and briefly looked up towards the ceiling before answering. "I was a troublemaker when I was a kid. Always getting into scraps with people over one thing or another. One time, I got into a fight with an older boy who said I wasn't showing him enough respect."

"Were you?"

"No." Liam gave a sad smile. "Manners weren't really my thing, back then. Having been in a lot of fights, I was a pretty good scrapper, though. And I cheated a bit too. But I beat him. That night, he came back with a group of friends and burned my house to the ground."

Haela sat back in surprise. The murmur of the other guests and the clanking of pots from the kitchen wrapped around our pocket of silence.

"I survived because I had snuck out to make some more trouble," Liam continued after another gulp of wine. "My family did not. They all died because of me. Because I picked a fight with the wrong person." He pushed the cup away from himself on the table. "After that, I never fought again."

Silence blanketed the long, rectangular table as everyone took in the somber words of the otherwise cheerful human. I already knew this story, of course, but my heart still ached for him. The loss and guilt must've been crushing. Something I myself was also intimately familiar with.

"I'm sorry," Elaran surprised us both by saying. With eyes full of sincerity, he looked straight at Liam. "I am truly sorry for your loss. To lose your family... there's nothing worse."

I think Liam recognized the sadness he saw in Elaran's eyes because he nodded and then asked, "you too?"

The ranger returned the nod. "Yes. Both of my brothers died fighting in the Great War. And my parents..." he trailed off and looked at Faelar. The blond elf gave a short nod. "And *both* Faelar's parents and mine sacrificed their lives to raise the shield." Elaran sat up straight and held his head high. "I'm proud to be their son." He looked back at Liam, eyes filled with emotion. "But that doesn't mute the sense of loss, unfortunately."

This was the first time I'd heard Elaran talk about anything personal. With him, it was usually always straight to business. Hearing this altered my view of him completely. Suddenly, he wasn't just the grumpy ranger who hated everything. Now, I could actually see a real person behind that disapproving scowl.

"I'm sorry for the part my ancestors played in that," Liam said, holding his gaze.

Elaran blinked twice in surprise. "Oh, uhm..."

"It is not your fault," Keya said, reaching over to squeeze Liam's arm.

He smiled back. A reflective mood had settled over our group. Thoughts of tomorrow swirled in my head. We had made all the necessary preparations to make the mission as smooth as possible but there was still no question about the fact that what we would be doing tomorrow night was extremely dangerous. Any number of things could go wrong. It was a real possibility that not all of us would make it back alive.

"If we die tomorrow–" Haemir began, echoing my thoughts.

"We are not going to die!" Haela interrupted.

"No, I know," her brother said, though his voice betrayed that he wasn't so sure. "But *if* we were to die tomorrow, what would you regret most?"

I let out a soft sigh. *Oh, Haemir. I have too many regrets to count. Where would I even start?* The rest of the table looked at the twin curiously.

"I mean," he continued, "something that you'd want to do or say or, I don't know, eat?"

A wistful smile crossed Haela's lips. "I want to find a dragon."

"They're real?" I exclaimed. I hadn't forgotten that big, green one I'd seen after eating journeyberries but I had marked it down as a hallucination. I had seen Rain too, after all.

"I don't know," she said with a mischievous sparkle in her eye. "But I want to find out." She turned to her brother. "You game?"

"Yeah, I think I'd like that too," Haemir said. "Someone's got to make sure you don't end up in trouble."

Mirth played at the corner of her eyes as she put a hand to her chest in mock offense. "Trouble? Who, me?"

"Alright," the other twin said, "in *too much* trouble then. As long as we train too. I don't want to die before I'm able to beat you in archery."

Haela laughed a wholehearted laugh. "Done."

"I would regret not telling Laena how much I love her," Faye said and flashed an embarrassed smile. "After my parents passed away, she's been like a mother to me. She's my rock, my fixed point in the universe. Even if the whole world as we know it were to collapse, I know she would be there for me. But I haven't really told her how much she means to me. I really should get on that."

That was news to me. I had no idea that Faye felt that way about the wise-looking advisor. The Queen always seemed like such an independent person. Someone who took care of herself. To know that she also depended on people felt oddly reassuring.

"She knows," Keya said with a comforting smile. "I would regret not being able to learn more about our history. My research is far from complete and I am finding out new things all the time. Did you know that we also came here from somewhere else?"

"We did?" Haela asked. "Where? Why?"

"I don't know yet. Which is why I'd hate dying before finding out."

A low chuckle spread across the table. Keya usually spoke in such a formal manner but in that last sentence, the power of her passion for history had manifested in her words. Everyone should have dreams that strong. What did I want to do? For so many years, all I'd ever really wanted was to survive and to keep Liam safe. But these last weeks had changed me, changed me more than such a short amount of time had any right to, and now I wanted more.

"I want to go on an adventure," I said.

Liam turned to look at me in surprise while Faye smiled knowingly.

"I want to see what's on the other side of this forest," I continued. "And what's beyond the wild sea to the south. I want to see new places, discover wonders, and maybe find other civilizations. I want an adventure."

A grin spread across Liam's boyish features. "Me too!"

"What about you, Elaran?" Keya asked.

He pondered the question in silence for a moment. "I want to protect our people. I can't die before we bring down the shield."

Seriousness spread across the table once more. In addition to the possibility of us dying, if we failed tomorrow, there was no telling what would happen to either of our cities. The elves might have to keep the shield up for another century. Another century of their protection draining their life, slowly but surely. And King Adrian might take out his wrath on Keutunan, executing even more people. The stakes were as high as they could get.

"I want to find love," Faelar blurted out.

All seven of us turned to stare at the usually taciturn elf in utter shock. He threw an embarrassed glance at Elaran before offering us a shrug as if to say *what?*

"That's wonderful, Faelar!" Faye said. "Love, any kind of love, be it a sibling," she looked at the twins and then turned to Liam and me, "or a friend, a parent, or a partner, is what life is all about. Isn't it?"

"Hear, hear," we all chimed in as we knocked our cups against the sturdy wooden table.

Faldir came by with yet another decanter of wine. I suspect that he had heard his brother's confession because he threw Faelar an encouraging smile before drifting over to the next table.

"Storm," Haela suddenly said, breaking the silence. "Can I ask you something?"

The seriousness of her voice sent flares of suspicion through my brain. "Ask me what?"

"The other day you said that some shit happened when you were younger and your life got really dark. Well, until he came along," she said and motioned a graceful hand in Liam's direction. "Can I ask what happened?"

I traced the rim of the delicate cup with my finger. Not even Liam knew what had happened that night nine years ago. Liam hadn't even been a part of the Underworld back then. Nine years ago, he'd still been living with his family in Worker's End. I, on the other hand, had been living on the streets. It was early spring and by my best estimate, I was eleven years old that year. It was the year I was going to apply to an Underworld guild. Well, *we* were going to apply. We only had to wait for summer and the Day of Choosing. I exhaled deeply. Did I really want to tell them that story?

"Rain," I said, surprising myself just when I thought I wasn't going to answer. "Her name was Rain. Or at least, it was to me."

My drinking companions all leaned forward a bit in anticipation. Liam looked at me intently. I gave him a sad smile before taking a long drink of wine. Heaving another deep sigh, I gathered all the courage I could muster. Then, I settled in to tell the story that had taken me nine long, guilt-ridden years to share. The story of my greatest regret.

33.

"It all started when I was seven," I began. "I was alone, living on the street and stealing what I could to survive. One night, I roamed the Merchants' Quarter as the rain poured down on my head. I was hungry, exhausted, and soaking wet. My misery grew with each splashing step. And then, suddenly, there she was." I smiled at the memory. "Every sane person in Keutunan had taken shelter against the pelting rain leaving only the truly desperate to trudge through the streets. And then there was this girl, about my age, with short brown hair and eyes that sparkled even in the dark. And what was the crazy person doing?" I shook my head and exhaled a laugh. "She was out there, dancing in the rain. Dancing. In the middle of a bloody deluge. That's why I called her Rain. I knew from the first moment I saw her, that I needed to have this absolute weirdo in my life."

From the corner of my eye, I saw Faldir approach with more wine. I tossed back the last mouthful in my cup before holding it up to be refilled. Laughter and mirthful chatter drifted towards us from the other tables in the tavern but my table was silent. Waiting for me to continue my story. I took another sip of wine from my now full cup before continuing.

"She was an orphan too, so we became each other's family. I shared all my deepest, darkest secrets with her, and she with me. I trusted her with my hopes and my dreams. She was my best friend. My sister. It didn't matter that we weren't related by blood, some connections transcend that. And ours did. I would've died for her – and she for me. We trained together, stole together, survived together. Rain. She was fearless. She was the fighter. I was the sneaker. So she taught me how to throw knives, fight with knives, and I taught her how to steal. And we were good. Really good. We decided that when we turned eleven, or at least, the year we thought we turned eleven, we would apply to join the Assassins' Guild."

"The Assassins' Guild?" Liam interrupted, eyebrows raised in surprise.

"Yeah, like you said weeks ago, it's the highest ranking, most well-paid guild in the Underworld. And we were little girls with big dreams." I smiled. "Of course we wanted to join the death guild. In the spring of that year, we were prowling the streets of the Harbor District looking for drunk workers to pickpocket. Instead, we found something else."

"What was it?" Haemir asked, leaning forward on his arms.

Dark clouds swept across my eyes for a moment. "Two other girls. They were being harassed by four older boys. Rain was gonna keep walking because that isn't exactly an unusual sight in our city but I stopped. I wanted to get involved. So I convinced Rain that we should help them. I've thought back to that night so many times over the years, desperately wishing that I had just kept my mouth shut, minded my own business, and continued walking." I shook my head wearily. "But I didn't. So we got involved. We drew our knives and jumped the guys in the alley.

Only problem was, they had knives too. Not to mention that there were four of them and the girls we were rescuing weren't exactly fighters. They died relatively quickly. Or so I thought, at least."

"What do you mean?" Faye asked.

"One of them apparently survived. Only, I didn't know that at the time. I actually found out about that just this year. Anyway, they were both down, leaving me and Rain against the four guys. Rain held her own, she eventually killed one of the guys, and I, well, I hadn't died at least." A humorless laugh escaped my lips. "I know you'd never think it now, but I was not a fighter back then. I was more of a hide-and-strike kind of person. Like I said, sneaking was my specialty. A moment came when I had the chance to stab one of them because he was looking in another direction. But I hesitated. It was just for a split second, but a hesitation nonetheless. Only too late did I realize the reason for his inattention: it was fixed on Rain. She had moved to my other side during the chaos of the fight and that extra second that I unwittingly gave the boy was enough to ruin everything. His knife slashed across her stomach, splitting open her abdomen. I could only stare in shock as she collapsed on the ground. A moment later, searing pain blossomed in my own body. I remember looking down to see a knife being pulled from my belly and the dark red blood that spilled out. The shock and pain had me crumbling to the ground next to Rain. Running footsteps smattered across the stones as the three remaining boys fled, leaving five bodies behind in the alley."

While once again tracing the rim of the cup with my finger, I closed my eyes. Pain and guilt bled from my heart. The stone walls around it that I had smashed the day I decided not to kill

Faye were still not entirely back in place. I desperately wanted to slam them back up. I didn't want to feel. I hated feeling. But my heart would not so easily give up the freedom it had now tasted. I blew out the breath I'd been holding and opened my eyes again. All seven of my dinner companions were looking at me, mostly with concern in their eyes. I cleared my throat before their compassion could pull me under.

"Rain tried to breathe but only sickening bursts of blood bubbled from her throat. Her usual sparkle was gone and instead, agony and terror marred her face. I pressed my hands against her stomach, trying to stop the bleeding. But it didn't work. There was just too much blood. The alley was filled with it. Hers and mine. I sat there, fighting to stay conscious, watching the life bleed out of her. When the last glimmer of life had slipped from her eyes and the horrible pops of blood bubbles had stopped, I screamed to any god, any... thing, that would listen. I vowed that I would never get involved in other people's problems again, I vowed to never hesitate again, and most importantly I swore on my soul that I would make them suffer. That I would have my revenge. I could feel my heart turning to stone and my soul going black as I pushed out the pain and the concern and instead steeped every fiber of my being in fury and hate. I don't know what answered my rage-filled screams that night but I wrapped myself in the darkness, pulling it around me like a cloak and letting it seep through my skin. I filled every pit of my soul with that black, roaring thunderstorm. That night, amidst the blood and the bodies of strangers and family alike, that was the night I let the darkness in."

The table around me was dead quiet. Several of my companions seemed to be holding their breath. I didn't know if I dared meet their eyes for I wasn't sure if I could handle the horrified expressions that must surely be present there. Bracing myself, I raised my eyes from the cup I'd been staring at. Looks of heartache, curiosity, and pondering met me. But no horrified disgust.

"What did you do then?" Liam breathed.

"The knife had missed my vital organs so I seared the wound with a smoldering blade and then I went hunting. I tracked down the three guys who had run and then I exacted my revenge. I won't go into detail but they suffered." I smiled a wicked smile. "Greatly. And at length. But after that I couldn't join the Assassins' Guild."

"Why not?" Haela asked.

"Well, only members of that guild are allowed to deal out death in such... quantity, and if they ever found out what I'd done, I would be marked for death myself."

"Huh."

"Yeah. But it turned out that they knew anyway but let it slide because of my understandable revenge motive. Anyway, so instead I joined the Thieves' Guild and about a year later, this ridiculously cheerful kid comes along," I said and turned to Liam with a barely concealed smile. "I was pretty shitty to him in the beginning."

"In the beginning?" he teased with mock outrage.

I let out a low chuckle and shook my head. "Alright, for a while. It's just, after what had happened with Rain, I didn't want to care about anyone ever again. And I didn't think I deserved having someone care about me either. But no matter how mean I was, he just wouldn't give up on me; he kept being nice and kind and annoyingly cheerful. And eventually, I came to love him

– despite my best efforts," I added with a self-conscious smile directed at my best friend. "And then some light finally started seeping into my soul again."

Liam smiled back. "I'm glad you told us."

Me too, Liam. Me too. That was a secret I'd been carrying for nine long years. At times, the weight of it had threatened to drown me but I hadn't dared share the burden with anyone else. If I'd seen someone else look at me the way I looked at myself in the mirror, I wouldn't have been able to carry on. Now, thanks to these extraordinary people, the crushing guilt I always carried in my chest was a little lighter.

"You didn't know either?" Faye asked, surprise registering on her face as she turned to Liam.

He shook his head, making brown, curly locks fall into his eyes. "No."

"Hmm," the Queen mused. "You're a woman of many secrets, Storm. Got any others?"

"Oh, one or two," I replied, a grin spreading across my face.

They all laughed at my obvious understatement. After that, the conversion moved on to lighter topics. Wine kept flowing. Jokes, stories, and laughter now drifted from our end of the room across the rest of the tavern as we avoided the uncertainty of tomorrow and enjoyed each other's company today. The merriment continued long into the night but as we all went to bed, I doubted that anyone would forget the deep, soul-searching secrets we had shared with each other that night. The night before the storm.

34.

A light drizzle hung in the air like curtains between the trees. I thanked Wedra, Goddess of Weather, for the rain that evening, for it was a blessing in more ways than one. The wet ground made it easier to sneak into camp undetected, at least for me, because it decreased the risk of accidentally making noise by stepping on a dry leaf. It also made it harder for the sentries to spot us through the sheets of rain.

"They're just about to make camp," Shade whispered to the six of us.

Faye, Elaran, Faelar, the twins, and I had met the Master Assassin at a prearranged location just outside camp only a minute or two ago. We had left Liam, Keya, and the other elves in Tkeideru. At first, my friend had been reluctant to stay behind but some well-thought-out arguments about his inexperience in the woods convinced him of the logic in it. Keya had been much harder to sway and had protested loudly that she would not be left behind on such an important mission. Faye had argued that she was, first and foremost, a scholar with a mind too precious to risk but she would not be persuaded. When she refused to listen, the Queen had ended up pulling rank and ordered her to stay behind. She was a determined one, that Elf Queen.

"Good," Faye said, keeping her voice low. "Everyone clear on the plan?"

"We sneak in, dump the juice, and sneak back out," Haela said.

"We've got the ale barrels," Haemir said, nodding to his sister. "We'll hit all of them before they're unloaded from the cart."

Faye nodded. "The rest of us will drop the journeyberries into the food pots. Make sure you do it before the cooks start distributing the stew."

"Most of the soldiers will be unpacking the supplies, digging latrines, or setting up tents right now. Use the fray of that to become invisible," Shade said and turned a penetrating gaze on all of us. "Don't take too long. The cooks will start food preparation as soon as the supplies are down and camp will be set up faster than you think."

All five elves gave him an acknowledging nod. When his black eyes turned to me, I followed suit. I studied him. Due to the rain, his already tight-fitting clothes were plastered to his skin and tiny droplets were nestled in his hair. His eyebrows were drawn down over serious eyes, turning his face into a grave mask. All of our futures depended on this mission. I wondered how much confidence he really had in it.

"One last thing," he said, that grave look seeping into his tone. "Remember that they have pistols. Pistols are loud. If you're spotted and they shoot, every soldier in this camp will be alerted to your presence, to *our* presence. I don't need to remind you that we are heavily outnumbered and outgunned. If one of them fires off a pistol, it's over. We will *not* make it out alive."

Looks of understanding passed between black, green, and yellow eyes. There would be no second chance. Any mistake would get us all killed.

"So," he continued, "don't get spotted. Or if you are, make sure to kill them first."

"Once you've poisoned your part of the camp, come back here," Faye said. "We'll wait for the juice to take effect and then we'll move on the king's tent together. Any questions?"

We had, of course, heard the plan before so no one voiced any concerns at this last-minute reminder of our assassination plot.

"Alright, then let's scatter," the Queen said with finality.

After one last nod, all seven of us moved out. We had divided the camp into five sections. Each person was responsible for poisoning the pots in their section while the twins located the wagon with ale barrels and poured the juice into all of those at the same time. According to Shade, for an army of this size, there would be two food stations in each of our sections. My part of the camp was to the west. Moving quietly through the woods along the edge of camp, I closed in on my hunting grounds. I had to skirt further out several times to avoid the keen eyes of the sentries but made it to the west part of King Adrian's camp without raising any alarms. Thankfully.

Weaving through thickets and trees, I crept forward. Shade had been right, most men were busy preparing for the night. Some kind of organized chaos took place in the clearing in front of me. I scanned the area. To my left, at the edge of the camp, men with shovels dug into the wet dirt. Towards the middle, tents were erected, and everywhere else, soldiers moved back and forth unloading supplies. A little to my right, I spotted the first food station. Before a makeshift bench stood a heavyset, bald man with a large knife. He was chopping onions on a wooden cutting board and at regular intervals, he used the knife to sweep the pale, yellow pile into a large cast-iron pot to his right. That was it. That was the pot. Only one more to go. I continued my scan.

The cook to my right had moved on to the potatoes while I still hadn't been able to spot the second food station. My pulse quickened. I needed to get going soon or he would be finished, the camp would quiet down and I'd lose my chance of poisoning this pot. *Crap.* Throwing frantic glances around my section, I desperately tried to find the second one I'd missed. Latrines, tents, food station. Food station, tents, latrines. There was no other food station. There was no other. I prayed to Nemanan that I was right and Shade had been wrong about the number. If not, I might have just screwed up our entire plan. Regardless, I had to move now. I exhaled a long, soft breath. Show time.

Hugging the tree line, I snuck closer to the cook. This was the easy part. The hard part would be leaving the cover of the forest and making it all the way to the pot. *Breathe.* I dashed forward. A supply cart broke my rush and served as shelter as I pressed up against it. Two soldiers walked past carrying shovels.

"Join the army, they said. It'll be an easy job, they said. There will never actually be anyone to fight so you'll just get paid to train. Bah! Out here in the bloody forest, shoveling shit and looking for imaginary creatures," one of them muttered.

"Don't forget the rain," the other said.

"Bah! Don't even get me started on the bloody rain..."

Once they were past, I peeked out from behind the wagon. My next stop would be a cluster of barrels. *Breathe.* I sprang forward. Another soldier, this one carrying a bundle of tarp, closed in. *Shit*. I could make it. I had to make it. Launching myself forward and downwards, I glided the last stretch on my knees. A soft thud sounded as my body connected with the barrels. I ducked my head. My pants were covered in wet blotches mixed with mud after my sliding stunt but I had escaped the notice of the soldier. He hurried past, muttering in much the same fashion as the other two.

Throwing a glance over my hiding place, I assessed the situation. It was not that far to the cook, only a few strides. He stood there with his back towards me, completely unawares, chopping some vegetable or other. However, there was no more cover between my current place and my destination. I would have to make it there, pour in the juice, and then make it back without being noticed. That could be tricky.

I cast another glance around the area. Another soldier. I quickly ducked down. *Shit*. My heart pounded as I waited for his footsteps to disappear. Time was running out. It had to be now. My fingers trembled slightly as I unscrewed the waterskin filled with journeyberry juice. While putting a finger over the opening, to avoid it spilling, I drew a shaky breath. *That's it. Breathe.* I raised my head over the barrel. Everything was clear. No soldiers in sight. *And go.*

I sprinted towards the unsuspecting cook and the food he would unwittingly use to poison his own allies. Once I drew near, I only slowed down enough to not come crashing into the cast-iron pot. The chopping sound of metal against wood drifted towards me as I closed the final distance. There was a mountain of carrots on his cutting board. *Crap*. He was going to empty it into the pot any moment now. I threw the waterskin upside-down over the pot, willing the liquid to pour faster. *Come on, gravity! Have you always been this slow?* The cook picked up the last untouched carrot and put it on the wooden board. *Come on!* I practically shook out the last rolls of juice and then, even before all of it had left the container, I raced back towards the barrels. *Don't turn around yet, don't turn around yet.* I skidded to a halt and threw myself around the makeshift barricade.

My heart hammered in my chest. Heaving unsteady breaths, I waited for the alarm to sound. Nothing came. *Breathe.* But I was not in the clear yet. Two pairs of footsteps drew closer and then disappeared to the other side. Time to move. Darting across the grass to the wagon while casting hurried looks around me, I noticed that no one else was approaching. I could make it. With growing confidence and a small song of victory in my heart, I ran all the way to the tree line. I couldn't believe I actually pulled that off.

My back smacked against the tree as I rounded the first one circling the clearing. Blinking slowly, I let out a long sigh. Astonished, brown eyes stared into mine. I recoiled. *Armor. Helmet. Belt. Sword. Pistol. Pistol.* The surprised soldier moved his hand towards his leather belt, fumbling for his firearm. *Shit.* If he were to fire, we'd be finished. Every soldier in this camp would come running. The king would know it was us and take his rage out on the guild and the elves would have to keep the shield up, slowly dying too. But it wouldn't matter to us because we'd already be dead. *Shit.* I couldn't let him fire that gun!

He got it loose just as he opened his mouth to raise the alarm. A soft thud sounded. And no alarm came. Shock spread across his face as the pistol fell from his grip and he instead reached for his throat. The soldier dropped to his knees, desperately clawing at the knife cutting off his vocal cords. And his breathing. I stood there, looking at him. Only wet gurgling escaped until he finally collapsed on the ground and the night was still again. I exhaled deeply. That had been close. Too damn close. And now I had a bloody corpse to hide. Great. Just great.

DRAGGING A BODY THROUGH the woods and then finding a place to hide it without being spotted by the lookouts had taken a lot of time so when I, at last, reached our meeting place, everyone else had already arrived.

"Where have you been?" Elaran hissed at me.

"Hiding a dead body," I said flatly.

"What?!"

"It's fine. I've taken care of it. But I only found one food station. Please tell me you were wrong about the numbers," I said and turned from the pissed-off ranger to the calculating assassin.

"I wasn't," Shade began.

"But then–" I interrupted.

"I wasn't," he said, cutting me off and leveling a hard stare at me. "But, you and Elaran got the sections closest to the latrines so both of you only had one food station. There were three in mine and three in Faelar's as well."

"So we got them all?" I asked.

"If you poisoned the one in your section, then yes."

I nodded. "Yeah."

A twig snapped behind us. Steel flashed in the dim forest as Shade and I whirled around, a knife gripped tightly in each hand. Two tense, black-clad bodies crouched in an attack position in the fading light. I threw a hurried, and somewhat panicked, glance at the elves because none of them had reached for their bows. Instead, Faye crossed her arms.

"I thought I told you to stay in Tkeideru," she remarked with narrowed eyes.

"You did," a soft voice responded.

"And yet, here you are."

Keya's graceful body became visible as she glided through the sheets of rain. Next to her, a shorter form stumbled over a fallen branch, making another twig snap. I heaved a deep sigh and lowered my knives.

"We will not be left behind," Keya said with steady eyes on her queen.

"Exactly," Liam chimed in. "We have as much right as you to be here."

I shook my head before leveling a stare at my best friend. "Gotten stubborn in the weeks we've been apart, have you?"

He only answered with a mischievous grin.

Faye blew out a noisy breath and threw up her arms. "Fine. As long as you're here you might as well help."

A smile spread across Keya's beautiful features before she gave a short nod.

"And now we wait," Shade said, returning his knives to their proper places.

"And now we wait," the Elf Queen echoed.

WE DIDN'T HAVE TO WAIT long. My little corpse adventure had taken longer than I thought and most of the soldiers were already eating by the time I had rejoined our group. Based on my own experience with the colorful berries, it would only take a minute or two from consumption to incapacitation. My experience proved accurate. Barely fifteen minutes later, every man in the camp, save the ones guarding the king's tent, were either running around like headless chickens or lying on the ground drawing invisible symbols in the air and making undignified noises. I cringed at the thought of having done so myself.

"Alright, let's move," Shade said.

Amid the confusion and the hallucinations, we could walk straight into camp without anyone challenging us.

"Get it off me! Get it off me!" someone yelled while racing past us.

"You're the most beautiful goat I've ever seen," a man to our right said while gently stroking a wooden barrel.

I was *so* glad the elves had only seen me when I had passed out afterwards and not while I was hallucinating. Elaran would never have let me live that down.

King Adrian's tent was the large, purple one in the middle of camp. Actually, *tent* wasn't quite the right word. It was more of a pavilion the size of a generous manor. Well, that is, if the manor only had one floor, no windows, and walls made of cloth.

The soldiers guarding the entrance to the king's temporary residence cast uncertain glances at the mayhem spreading around them but since there was no obvious enemy in sight, they seemed reluctant to leave their posts. We skirted around and approached them from the back of the pavilion. Shade turned to me and raised an eyebrow. I nodded in response to his wordless question. Motioning for the others to stay back, we snuck up on either side of the tent and drew a quick blade across the throat of the two guards stationed there. Warm blood spilled down their armor. A thudding of body parts and the clanking of swords and armor rang out as their knees buckled and the ground received them. Stepping over the still warm bodies, Liam and the six elves joined us outside the entrance. This was it. Shade held open the tent flap and motioned for us to step inside. This was the moment we'd kill a king.

35.

"Carl, if that's you I'm going to have your head! I told you I didn't want to be disturbed!" King Adrian's voice boomed as we made our way into the tent.

Books and papers, along with decorated pillows and blankets, lay scattered around the cramped, makeshift antechamber we weaved through before we entered the tent proper. As the last tent flap curtains billowed closed behind our backs, we saw the king standing on the lush carpets in the middle of his royal purple pavilion. I recoiled as I took in the rest of the space.

Leather creaked as muscled bodies straightened and heads turned. The air seemed to rush out of the room, replaced by the ringing of steel. Before the last curtain had settled, the king's entire war council had drawn their swords and leveled them at our astonished group. Scattered among the men, pistols also gleamed from calloused hands. *Shit.* If we were to draw our weapons, they would fire and some – if not all – of us would die even before we got our weapons out. The same would happen if we tried to run. I swallowed and quickly scanned the room, looking for a way out.

How could we have missed this? An entire war council! Shade had said he'd been watching the king's tent from the moment they'd raised it and only the king and a few servants, going in and out, had been inside. The tent had been watched the whole time. *Wait.* Who had watched the tent while we were poisoning the pots?

"What do we have here?" a cold voice asked. A malicious grin spread across King Adrian's mouth as he took in our shocked appearances.

Shade took a step forward and started moving unchallenged through the forest of armed soldiers. "I've brought you the Elf Queen, sire."

My jaw dropped. "What?"

"What did you say?" Elaran bellowed at him.

Shade ignored us and instead positioned himself behind his king's right shoulder. That unreadable look was back in his eyes. "She's the one with the silver hair. The rest are her advisors. And of course you remember the Oncoming Storm and little Liam. I thought you might want them back where they belong."

"Oh, well done, Shade! Well done!" King Adrian exclaimed. He rubbed his hands with a look of giddy excitement on his face. "I knew I could count on you."

Wait. Shade. Shade was the one who'd been watching the king's tent before we'd arrived. He was the one who'd told us that no one but King Adrian was inside. They hadn't gathered while we were poisoning the pots – they'd already been inside! Why hadn't I seen that coming?

"You fucking traitor!" I screamed at the king's assassin while darkness gathered in my eyes. "How could I ever have trusted you – ever believed that you had even a shred of honor!"

Shade didn't answer. He just cocked his head to the right and looked back at me with expressionless eyes.

"You will die," Elaran said, filling the silence that had settled. His voice was cold, devoid of all emotion, like the impassive sea coming to drown friend and foe alike. "You will die a horrible death." He swept hard, yellow eyes across the room. "All of you."

How was he going to accomplish that? How were *we* going to accomplish that? We'd all get shot before we could move one finger. This was all my fault. I had trusted Shade – vouched for him. And now we were all going to die because of me. Because I had put my faith in the wrong person. The darkness flared up inside me. *No*. My hands twitched, getting ready to release my knives. I was going to get them out even if I were to die trying.

King Adrian barked a condescending laugh. "No, they are not. This is what is going to happen. I am going to kill you. And your queen. And all your friends." He tilted his head slightly to the right. "All except that brown-haired one. She looks like she will break easily so I will torture her until she begs me to lead me to your city. And then, I will slaughter every single elf in this godsforsaken forest. Yes. That is what I–"

A wet gurgling interrupted the king's speech. Metal flashed through the air, glinting in the lit candles. One precise slit and a crimson wound opened in the throat of Keutunan's present monarch. Shock spread across his face as he pressed a hand to the gaping wound and fumbled for the desk to steady himself. I stared at the scene in front of me. All around me, astonished eyes did the same. So, I had been right after all. Disbelief shone in King Adrian's black eyes as he turned them to the knife dripping with blood and the person attached to it. Shade stared back with emotionless eyes. The king opened his mouth, to no doubt voice his own shock at his Master Assassin's unexpected betrayal, but only a blood-filled cough escaped his lips.

The soldiers could only stare at their king in mute horror while life quickly bled out of him as the dark stain on his collar grew and his eyes glassed over. His body hit the carpeted floor and from his head rolled a crown of silver. So ended the reign of His Majesty King Adrian Silverthorn, ruler of Keutunan. The king was dead. Long live the king.

36.

"You now have two choices," Shade said, authority dripping from his voice. "You can either die with your king right here or you can drop your weapons and go home to your families."

The soldiers exchanged looks. "We outnumber you, and well..." a soldier at the back pointed out before trailing off and motioning to the raised swords and pistols around the room.

"Yes, you do," Shade said in a calm voice. "But if you try to kill us, some of you will die as well. And I know you have no love for the king. Are you really willing to risk your lives just to avenge him?"

Some of the armed men started lowering their swords. The Master Assassin swept his gaze expectantly over the rest of them. "Choose."

Uncertain glances passed between the soldiers again. The distinct ringing of a sword grating against a scabbard echoed across the room. They all turned towards the sound. A man with a graying beard shrugged as he let his sword drop the last bit into the scabbard. The same sound filled the whole room as the rest of them followed suit.

Huh. That had been easy. Almost too easy. I furrowed my brows, not sure if I should send suspicion or a prayer of thanks to

Cadentia, Goddess of Luck. Across the sea of disarming soldiers, Shade mouthed something at me. I squinted at him, trying to read his lips, as he mouthed it again. *Kill them all.*

I recoiled. What? I must have misread that. They were disarming. Why would we need to kill them? Realization hit me like a punch to the gut. They had seen our faces. All of these soldiers knew that Shade was involved in killing King Adrian. It would only take one person connecting the dots for our entire plan to come crumbling down.

A loud bang echoed through the pavilion.

"Look out!" Liam shouted.

I whipped my head around just in time to see him leaping forward and shoving an unprepared Faye backwards. The Queen fell, her head connecting with the wooden desk behind her, producing a hard crack. Her limp body slumped down to the ground. As we all turned in utter shock to Liam, his body was jerked backwards by a seemingly unseen force and he collapsed to the ground next to the unconscious queen. These bizarre events took place in only a matter of seconds. Stunned seconds. I stared at their bodies in utter bewilderment. A dark stain started spreading across the front of Liam's dark blue shirt. Pain and shock darted around in his eyes.

"They're going to kill us all!" a man shouted. "It's a trap! To arms!"

A ferocious battle cry rang out as the king's war council drew swords and pistols again. Another shot rang out, hitting the bookshelf next to me and sending chips of wood flying. *Shit.* I knew it had been too easy. I was about to whirl around and unleash a flurry of silver blades on the charging soldiers when a wet cough brought me back to the scene in front of me. My mind went blank. Liam.

"Protect the Queen!" I heard Elaran yell somewhere to my right.

I was only vaguely aware of the elves milling around me, drawing bows and forming a protective ring around Faye and Liam. And me. My focus was solely on Liam. His dark blue eyes, filled with agony and confusion. His ragged breath. The blood welling from the hole in his chest. He coughed. A small, red bubble formed at his lips and popped with a dreadful sound.

"Liam, what did you do?" I asked, desperately looking over his body. "You shouldn't even be here! You've been running from fights since the day I met you! Why did you have to get involved in this one?"

Another blood bubble popped as a cough shook his frame. "Some fights you can't run from," he wheezed. "Shouldn't run from." A wet gurgling sound slipped from his lips.

"No, Liam," I pleaded. "Don't die. Don't leave me alone." A choked sob made it past my constricted throat. "You can't leave me. Please don't leave me alone. Not again." Tears flowed freely from my eyes as I tried to will the blood back in his body.

He lifted his hand clumsily, his blood-soaked fingers smearing red lines on my face as he traced them down my already wet cheek. "I'm glad we met." With that, his hand fell back to the ground and his eyes fluttered close, one last smile still etched on his face.

The darkness ripped from my soul. Tendrils of black smoke, snaking and whipping, gathered around me and my eyes turned black as death. A violent thunderstorm roared around me, its lethal force crackling from my skin. Muffled protests fell on deaf ears as I parted the ring of elves and strode forward towards the attacking soldiers. A living thunderstorm come to sweep the filth away. With hunting knives gripped tightly in my hands, I advanced on the king's war council. A tremor passed through my body and the darkness sang the sweet song of death. Hell had come. The blades spun once in my hands. I would massacre them all.

A dance of death set to the eerie music of dying cries moved through the tent. My body twisted through the screams and the carnage as effortlessly as a trained acrobat in the king's court. Halfway through the pavilion, the company of soldiers broke before the living embodiment of death and fled the tent through slits in the cloth. Shredding the fabric, I followed the bolting men like a wraith. Trees crowded my vision as I closed in on my prey. Knives flashed and sprays of blood painted the forest red. Hoarse shrieks followed it. Time held no meaning. Space held no meaning. Only the dance. The dance of death.

The black fog slowly lifted from my brain. I looked around. The forest bed around me was covered in small, star-shaped, blue flowers. And bodies. Lots of bodies. I held up my hands, turning them over in front of me. They were red. All the way up to my elbows. And so were the knives in them. I looked down my body and saw that my clothes were of a darker color than usual. Blood dripped from my chin when I tilted it downwards. I tried wiping my chin with the back of my hand but it only smeared more blood on it. Blood. My mind was painstakingly slow but then a breath of clarity pushed to the front. Liam.

I stumbled forward, following the trail of bodies. Where was he? All the trees looked the same. Where was I? I shook my head. *Follow the bodies.* As I lifted my foot to take another step forward, my knees buckled. I hit the ground hard. Rolling over, I stared up at the dark sky visible through the canopy. Liam was dead. He'd died. My best friend in the whole world, my family, was gone. Because I'd hesitated. Again. Why had I hesitated? Why had we been there? We should not even have been there! I'd picked the wrong side. This had been the bloody wrong side! I should never have gotten involved. All the adrenaline from the fight was gone and energy drained out of me like a leaking boat. Wanting the blessing of oblivion, I didn't fight tiredness. As I passed into unconsciousness, I begged the gods to never have to wake up again.

37.

I did. Unfortunately. Blinking slowly, I tried to make sense of my surroundings. There were no trees so I wasn't in the forest anymore. It looked like furniture. I blinked again. The room around me came into focus, bringing realization that I was in my room back in Tkeideru. With the comprehension of my location came the memories of last night. Of Liam. Dying. The pain brought the feeling of an invisible hand squeezing my heart. Hot tears rolled down my cheeks leaving salty trails. With growing lucidity, another realization dawned. Dread and shame spread through my chest. I had left him to die alone. I hadn't even been there when he drew his last breath. The darkness had exploded at the thought of losing him and I'd left on a murder spree even before he was gone. I hadn't seen his soul off properly. He'd died alone because I couldn't control the darkness. Liam had died alone because of me. He had died alone.

"You're awake," Elaran declared as the door crashed open. "You need to come with me."

After my recollection of what I had done last night, I didn't want to go anywhere or do anything else, ever again, but Elaran didn't give me time to protest. He yanked me up by the arm and led me out of the room. While we walked down the wooden bridges, I noticed that I wasn't wearing my blood-soaked clothes anymore. In fact, I wasn't covered in blood at all anymore. Someone must have cleaned me off and dressed me in these clothes but I didn't much care. I felt numb. A hollow feeling spread through my body as we made it down to the ground. The elves of Tkeideru were looking at me but I only stared back with blank eyes. Why should I care anymore? I had nothing left.

Elaran pushed open a wooden door to a cabin I had never thought about before and gently guided me into it. My vacant eyes passed over the room. It was large and rectangular, with rows of beds. Light spilled in from the open windows and the air brought in the sweet scent of flowers and warm grass. All beds were empty save two. One in the back and one at the front. My eyes fixed on the figure sitting up in the closest one. I recoiled.

Surprised dark blue eyes stared into mine. "Hello, Storm."

"Liam!" I exclaimed and rushed over to him. Still in disbelief, I drew him into my shaking arms and hugged him tightly. His warm body squeezed me back. It was him. It really was him. "How is this possible?" I asked, tears of profound relief leaking from my eyes.

He gently pushed me back and looked into my emerald eyes. "I don't know either. I remember your tear-streaked face and then everything was going dark and cold. But then I felt this sparkling sensation and I could see fireworks. You know, like the ones on the king's birthday. And then I woke up. Here." He looked around with a befuddled look on his face. I opened my mouth to respond but was cut short when two rangers appeared in front of us.

"The Queen is up," one of them said to Elaran, "you need to come with us."

Elaran nodded in reply and followed him out the door.

"You should come too," the other one said and motioned to us before exiting the room as well.

It took a second for Liam to detangle himself from the sheets but once he had, we both scrambled out the door after Elaran and the other rangers.

We followed them to the Heart of the City, the giant hall with the flowered-covered tree pillars. Inside, Faye was seated in the high-backed chair on the raised dais that usually housed the high table. Now, only the ornate chair occupied the space. The hall was packed with elves, sitting at the round tables or standing along the rim. I spotted Keya, Laena, the twins, and Faelar to the side of the room and made my way towards them with Liam in tow. The Elf Queen wore her silver tunic, and the glittering, gem-covered crown rested lightly in her silver hair. Elaran dropped to a knee before her.

"You used magic," the Queen announced with a stately voice that carried across the room. "You sacrificed *years* of your life to save the human boy. Do you deny this?"

"No," Elaran replied.

My eyes widened in shock as my mind tried to process this. Liam had slumped down in a chair, eyes drooping. He barely seemed conscious of what was going on or what Elaran had done to save him. Being a hair's breadth from death and being brought back must've taken its toll. Elaran had used magic to heal Liam? That meant he'd given up years of his own life! But he hated humans. Why would he have done something like that? And besides, hadn't Faye said that the only magic they were allowed to use was to keep the shield up? As if she had heard my confused thoughts, the Elf Queen continued.

"You did so knowing that all use of magic, besides maintaining the cloak, is outlawed and punishable by banishment?"

I took a step forward but Haela's hand on my shoulder stopped me in my tracks. Faye couldn't banish Elaran! Not for saving Liam! I opened my mouth to say as much but Haela only shook her head.

"Yes," Elaran said.

"Why?" Faye asked.

"The human boy gave his life for you. That is a debt I could never repay. I could *not* let him die. And besides... I kind of like him."

I did a double take. Wow. He certainly had come a long way from hating every human on sight. Saving Liam from the brink of death really did show how much he'd grown. I guess people do change.

"I see. Despite these noble intentions, the law is clear. The punishment for using magic, for wasting elf life, is banishment."

I opened my mouth to protest again but Haela tightened her grip on my shoulder and sent another warning headshake in my direction.

The Queen pushed back the chair and stood up, silver hair cascading down her back. She raised her chin and swept her gaze across the crowd. "I am the ruler, the law and the justice, of Tkeideru. Therefore, I hereby declare that it is no longer a crime to use elven magic to save the life of someone worthy." Her eyes found Elaran's. "Effective as of yesterday."

A cheer broke out and filled the room, floor to ceiling. The auburn-haired ranger looked as confused as I had ever seen him.

As Faye gracefully dropped down from the dais, Haela turned to me with a knowing grin.

"You could've just told me," I grumbled.

The mischievous twin only answered with a wink.

"Rise," Faye said, standing in front of her ever loyal ranger. Once he had, she put a hand to his cheek and bathed him in a smile that could melt the hardest of ice. "I am so proud of you."

Another cheer raised the roof of the decorated gathering hall. I couldn't keep a broad grin from spreading across my face. In the last few weeks, I had gotten lost in the woods, been chased by a bear, and hallucinated about dragons. I'd befriended elves and assassins, and gotten into enough trouble to last me a lifetime. I'd hosted a royal rendezvous and helped broker peace between two cities. I had killed a king. I'd watched my best friend die only to find out he didn't. And I'd watched an elf who hated humans care enough for one to sacrifice part of his life for him. I'd had an exciting life. No question about that. And I couldn't wait to see what else life would have in store for a sarcastic thief with a fondness for knives and talent for trouble.

38.

"...May Ghrese, Goddess of Harvest, bless his reign with bountiful crops and may..." the High Priest droned on below me.

The wooden beam I currently occupied creaked slightly as I shifted my weight to see better. Lords and ladies in colorful clothes crowded the throne room while the guards watched the proceedings from the edge of the throng. Their silver-colored cloaks gleamed in the sunlight spilling in from the tall windows. None of them noticed the thief perched on a beam, high up in the dusky ceiling.

"You're not welcome below either?" I asked the shadows.

"It's better if I make myself scarce for this part," the shadows replied.

I cast a glance over my shoulder as Shade crept up beside me.

"You heard me coming?" he asked, eyes still on the scene below.

"I've been ambushed by you once, never again."

"Twice."

"Huh?"

"You've been ambushed by me *twice*," he said with a lopsided smile and eyes that glittered mischievously.

I graced his statement with a *tsk* and an eye roll. "You had me a bit worried there," I said, thinking about his performance in the late King Adrian's tent.

"A bit?" He chuckled. "You should've seen your face. I thought your jaw was going to fall off."

I let out an indignant huff but I couldn't stop the corner of my mouth from quirking upwards in a smile.

"I heard Liam's alright," Shade said without taking his eyes off the coronation proceedings below.

Hmmph. Nothing happened in this city without him knowing about it, it would seem.

"He is," I said and thought back to our failed attempt at covert communication. "We really should have some universal hand signals, you know, for the whole Underworld and not just inside specific guilds."

The Master of the Assassins' Guild glanced at me from the corner of his eye before giving me a short nod. "I'll see what I can do."

Below us, the High Priest lifted a silver-colored crown, adorned with green gems, from a plush, purple pillow. With his decorated robes swishing around his legs he first held up the crown to the gathered crowd and then he moved towards the figure standing straight-backed in the middle of the dais.

"In the eyes of Gods and Men, I crown thee, King Edward Silverthorn, ruler of Keutunan." The High Priest gently placed the gleaming crown on Edward's head. "May your reign be long and your days blessed." Stepping to the side of the new king, he faced the crowd and took a deep breath. "Long live the king!" he called.

"Long live the king!" the crowd cheered. "Long live the king!"

"Long live the king," Shade and I echoed in the shadows.

Prince Edward, no *King* Edward, nodded to the crowd and then surprised me by tilting his head up and offering a quick nod to the ceiling. Ha! He knew.

"The treaty between Keutunan and Tkeideru stands, then?" I asked.

Shade nodded. "It does. I have a feeling that this is the start of a long and fruitful friendship."

"Yeah. I think so too."

I watched Keutunan's new king make his way through the crowd while lords and ladies called out blessings. Genuine blessings. We had a good king, the elves were safe, and the Thieves' Guild was back to normal. Dared I hope that, maybe, life would only get better from here?

THE MIDDAY SUN BATHED West Gate in a warm glow. Behind us, the city was bustling with people getting ready for the coronation celebration that would fill the city this evening. All citizens were eager to raise a glass for the new king. In front of us, the grass offered a quieter scene.

"Can we make our first stop Tkeideru?" Liam asked. "I really want to challenge Elaran to a drinking contest."

I chuckled at the thought of a drunk Elaran. "Most definitely."

The wind blew softly, carrying intoxicating scents with it. I took a deep breath through my nose. Here on the edge of both worlds, I could smell both the city and the woods. Who would have thought that I would come to appreciate both? Even the fresh air.

"Ready for an adventure?" I asked and looked up at my cheerful friend.

His eyes sparkled as he grinned at me. "I thought you'd never ask."

After one last look back at my home, I hoisted my pack and stepped across the threshold. As my foot touched the grass outside the city walls, giddy excitement filled my body. No one knew what would happen now, where we would go or what wonders we would find. The thrill of the unknown was calling. I was *so* ready for another adventure.

Acknowledgements

Rome wasn't built in a day, and neither was this book. In fact, the creation of *A Storm of Silver and Ash* spans many years. During most of those, I was just creating stories in my head to help me sleep, but a year ago, I started taking those stories and putting them into writing. The road has been long, wonderful, complex, and at times, very difficult. I could not have completed this book without the help of some extraordinary people.

First and foremost, I would like to thank my family: my mom, my dad, and my brother. Mom, thank you for always being there for me – not only for the creation of this book, but for everything in life. You are my safe haven, my rock, and I could not have done any of this without you. Dad, thank you for always believing that I'm destined for great things. Your support for me and this book, even though it's neither your preferred genre nor language, means the world to me. Mark, thank you for being the best brother anyone could ask for. Your steadiness and calm, as well as your enthusiasm for this book, has gotten me through many moments of doubt.

I would also like to thank my partner, Yujin. You have sat opposite me at the dinner table, I don't know how many times, and listened to me ramble on for hours about one thing or another concerning book writing or publishing. Thank you for taking such an interest in my passion and for your continuous support – it means so much to me.

Another group of people who have been instrumental in the creation of this book is my wonderful team of beta readers: Deshaun Hershel, Jennifer Bourgeois, Jennifer Nicholls, Kaitlyn Jensen, and Luna Lucia Lawson. Thank you for the time and effort you have put into reading the book and providing helpful suggestions, comments, and encouragement. The book is truly better for your feedback.

After reading through my book five hundred and seventy-eleven times, I thought I had caught all the grammar mistakes, typos, and missing words lurking in there. I had most certainly not. But someone else has: my amazing copy editor and proofreader Julia Gibbs. Julia, thank you for all the hard work you have put into making my manuscript shine. Your language expertise and attention to detail is outstanding and I couldn't have published this book without you.

You know that old saying "don't judge a book by its cover"? It's not really true, is it? We do very much judge a book by its cover. Therefore, I wanted one that would truly stand out and I was very fortunate to find someone who could make that happen. The gorgeous cover of this book was created by the incredible Dane Low at ebooklaunch.com. Dane, thank you for creating a cover that really captures the book and for putting up with all my nitpicking. I couldn't have wished for a better cover artist.

Support can come from many places and one place where I have found an abundance of it is in the Writing Community on Twitter. It is a place where we both support each other during hard times but also celebrate each other's victories. Therefore, I would like to thank all the wonderful friends I have made there. My friends, thank you for sharing in laughter, tears, successes, and failures, and for joining me on this extraordinary writing journey. Your support means everything.

Last but not least, I would like to thank you, the reader. Thank you so much for giving my book a chance. I know that there are more books out there than anyone could ever read in one lifetime, so I truly appreciate that you took the time to read mine. If you have any questions or comments about the book, I would love to hear from you. You can find all the different ways of contacting me on my website, www.marionblackwood.com. There you can also sign up for my newsletter to receive updates about coming novels. Lastly, I just have one final request before you go back to the real world. If you liked this book, please consider leaving a review – it would really help me tremendously. I hope you enjoyed the adventure!

Printed in Great Britain
by Amazon